BRYANT & MAY
England's Finest

www.penguin.co.uk

BRYANT & MAY
England's Finest

———

More Lost Cases from the
Peculiar Crimes Unit

CHRISTOPHER FOWLER

doubleday

TRANSWORLD PUBLISHERS
61–63 Uxbridge Road, London W5 5SA
www.penguin.co.uk

Transworld is part of the Penguin Random House group of companies
whose addresses can be found at global.penguinrandomhouse.com

Penguin
Random House
UK

First published in Great Britain in 2019 by Doubleday
an imprint of Transworld Publishers

A CIP catalogue record for this book
is available from the British Library.

ISBN 9780857525697

Typeset in 11/13.5pt Sabon by Jouve (UK), Milton Keynes
Printed and bound in Great Britain by Clays Ltd, Elcograf S.p.A.

Penguin Random House is committed to a sustainable
future for our business, our readers and our planet. This book
is made from Forest Stewardship Council® certified paper.

MIX
Paper from
responsible sources
FSC® C018179

1 3 5 7 9 10 8 6 4 2

For Mandy Little

Go where we may – rest where we will,
Eternal London haunts us still.

Thomas Moore

CONTENTS

CONTENTS

A BRIEF HISTORY OF
THE PECULIAR CRIMES UNIT

Britain has a long history of 'backroom boffins', men and women who came up with original ideas out of necessity. Napoleon's nation of shopkeepers became a nation of entrepreneurs partly because there was no funding to be found, and because the twentieth-century wars demanded ingenuity.

Founded by Winston Churchill in 1939, the PCU was one of a number of new divisions designed to combat less tangible threats to the British way of life in wartime. In this hour of desperation, when most able-bodied men had been taken into the armed forces, seven experimental agencies were proposed by the government.

The first was the Central Therapy Unit, set up to help the bereaved and the newly homeless cope with the psychological stresses of bombardment. The unit closed after just eleven months because bombed-out residents continued turning to their neighbours for support rather than visiting qualified government specialists.

A propaganda unit called the Central Information Service (later to become the COI) was set up to provide positive, uplifting news items to national newspapers in order to combat hearsay and harmful disinformation spread about British overseas forces, and to fill the void left by the blanket news blackouts. It was based in Hercules Road, SE1, and was finally closed in 2011 due to government budget cuts.

A third unit based at the War Office employed a number of writers and artists, including novelists Ian Fleming and Dennis Wheatley, to project the possible outcome of a prolonged war with Germany, and to develop stratagems for deceiving the enemy. The most famous wartime deception created by this unit was Operation Mincemeat, in which the corpse of a dead Welsh tramp was disguised as a drowned Royal Marine officer, planted with false plans, and left for the Germans to find.

A subsidiary unit used members of the Royal Academy to develop new camouflage techniques for the British Navy after Churchill realized that the horizontal stripes painted on to warships made them more visible, not less. RA artists explained that the eye plays tricks, and that jagged verticals would be better for disguising fleets.

The most successful of the seven experimental units launched by Churchill in wartime was the cypher-breaking division based at Bletchley, where Alan Turing and his team cracked the Enigma Code, and in doing so laid the foundations for modern computer technology.

The Peculiar Crimes Unit is the only division that still survives. Its revised initiative was aimed at easing the burden on London's overstretched Metropolitan Police Force. All of the units trained people of exceptional talent, employing most of them directly from school, some as young as fourteen. The PCU was created to tackle high-profile cases which had the capacity to compound social problems in urban areas, primarily in London. The affix 'peculiar' was originally meant in the sense of 'particular'. The government's plan was that the new unit should handle those investigations deemed uniquely sensitive and a high risk to public morale. To head this division, several young and inexperienced students were recruited from across the capital.

The crimes that fell within the unit's remit were often of a politically sensitive nature, or were ones that could potentially cause social panics and public malaise. Its staff members were outsiders, radicals, academics and free-thinkers answerable only to the War Office, and later the Home Office. They had no social skills and no resources, but were free to solve problems in any manner that would work, no matter how unorthodox.

Which was how my father blew up our kitchen table.

He and his pals had developed an explosive paint that became unstable after it dried, and someone at the unit had painted all the letters of the headline on his *Evening News*, so that when he threw it on to the table it exploded.

Needless to say, my long-suffering mother found our family life rather stressful.

The PCU remained in operation throughout the war and has continued in one form or another ever since that time. In the past two decades, reorganization of the national policing network has aimed at reducing the influence of individual units, and creating standardized practices operating from guidelines laid down for a national crime database, subject to performance league tables. Bryant and May made it known that they were not fans of this target-related system.

The PCU unofficially aided a number of high-ranking politicians in the past, and as a consequence has remained exempt from these measures. However, a series of high-profile embarrassments placed the unit on a blacklist of *Organizations of Potential Detriment*, which means that the unit is under surveillance by the Home Office and will be closed down if it fails to perform.

BRYANT & MAY: *DRAMATIS PERSONAE*

Raymond Land, Acting Temporary Unit Chief

The unit chief kept his 'Temporary' title for years because he dreamed of escaping the PCU, but never quite managed to get away. Eventually he simply gave up and gave in. An obsessive, meticulous member of the General and Administrative Division, he graduated in Criminal Biology, but often missed the point of his investigations and was subsequently downgraded. This has detrimentally affected his pension. It's said that Raymond 'could identify a tree from its bark samples without comprehending the layout of the forest'. He has the complaining gene, doesn't understand his detectives (or why his wife Leanne left him) and yet occasionally shows some spine and comes through for his staff.

Arthur Bryant, Detective Chief Inspector

How old is Arthur? He'll never tell, but then there's not much about him that's in any way reliable, least of all his memoirs. Elderly, bald, always cold, scarf-wrapped, a wearer of shapeless brown cardigans and overlarge Harris Tweed coats, Bryant is an enigma; a natural ignorer of rules, he's well read, rude, bad-tempered, conveniently deaf and a smoker of disgusting pipe tobacco (and cannabis for his arthritis, so he says). He's also a truly terrifying driver. He wears a hearing aid, has false teeth, uses a walking stick, and has to take a lot of pills. Once married (his wife fell from a bridge), he worked at various police stations and units around London, including Bow Street, Savile Row and North London Serious Crimes Division. He shares a flat with long-suffering Alma Sorrowbridge, his Antiguan landlady.

John May, Detective Chief Inspector

Born in Vauxhall, John is taller, fitter, more charming and personable than his partner. He's technology-friendly, three years younger than Bryant, and drives a silver BMW. A melancholic craver of company, he leaves the TV on all the time when alone. He walks to Waterloo Bridge most nights with Bryant for 'thinking time'. A bit of a vain ladies' man, he lives in a modernist, barely decorated flat in Shad Thames. He's divorced, his daughter Elizabeth died in tragic circumstances and his estranged son Alex lives in Canada.

Janice Longbright, Operations Director

Janice is a career copper; her mother Gladys worked for the unit. She models herself on 1950s and 1960s film stars, and long ago adopted a perversely glamorous appearance to counteract her lack of confidence. She's smart and a lot tougher these days, but hates to show her true feelings. Dedicated to Arthur and John, she always puts work before her personal affairs. She lives a solitary life in her flat in Highgate, and keeps a house brick in her handbag for dealing with unwanted attention.

Dan Banbury, Crime Scene Manager/InfoTech

The unit's crime scene manager and IT expert is almost normal compared to his colleagues. He's a sturdy, decent sort, married with a son, although he gets a little over-enthusiastic when it comes to discussing crime scenes and can bore for England on the subject of inefficient internet service providers and broadband speeds. Bryant exasperates him more than he can say.

Jack Renfield, Operations Director

This sturdy former Albany Street desk sergeant is a brisket-faced by-the-book sort of chap who used to be unpleasant and dismissive of the PCU. Blunt but honest, he tends to think with his fists, and had an ill-fated relationship with Janice Longbright. He blotted his copybook so badly in *The Lonely Hour* that he will never be the same.

Meera Mangeshkar, Detective Sergeant

The stroppy, argumentative, Kawasaki-driving DS comes from a poor South London Indian family, but beneath her cynical shell she has a decent heart. After years of resisting Colin Bimsley, her co-worker, she is showing signs of giving in, not in an inappropriately creepy succumbing-to-a-stalker way but because he's shown real loyalty and kindness to her.

Colin Bimsley, Detective Sergeant

The fit, fair-haired, clumsy cop is hopelessly in love with Meera, and suffers from Diminished Spatial Awareness, which can make him a liability on rooftops. His father was also a former PCU member. Colin trained at Repton Amateur Boxing Club for three years, and has an old-fashioned London temper useful for dealing with villains.

Giles Kershaw, Forensic Pathology

The Forensics/Social Sciences Liaison Officer is naturally curious, winning, well-spoken, Eton and Oxford educated. Promoted to the position of Chief Coroner at the St Pancras Mortuary, he has relatives in high places who can occasionally help the unit out of tight spots.

Crippen, staff cat

Everyone thought he was male until he had kittens. Named after the first murderer to be caught by telegraph, she sadly used up the last of her nine lives in a recent adventure.

The Two Daves

A pair of Turkish builders who came to make the Peculiar Crimes Unit at King's Cross habitable and stayed on as the 120-year-old building started falling to bits. They occasionally interfere in cases, much to Raymond Land's annoyance.

Maggie Armitage

Good-natured Maggie runs the Coven of St James the Elder in Kentish Town, North London. The Grand Order Grade IV White Witch is permanently broke but lives to help others in need of her dubious services. She's part of a network of oddballs, eccentrics and outsiders who help out the unit from time to time.

Surrounding these main characters are what could loosely be described as Arthur Bryant's 'alternatives', consisting mainly of fringe activists, shamans, spiritualists, astronomers, astrologers, witches both black and white, artists of every hue from watercolour to con, banned scientists, barred medics, socially inept academics, Bedlamites, barkers, dowsers, duckers, divers and drunks, many of them happy to help the unit for the price of a beer or a bed for the night.

PRIVATE & CONFIDENTIAL MEMO
FROM: RAYMOND LAND, PECULIAR CRIMES UNIT
TO: ALL READERS

Hullo there. As the chief of a London police unit that's so often in the press these days (usually for the worst possible reasons) I've been asked by Arthur Bryant if I would pen a foreword for this, his second volume of missing cases. They were missing because he left the files on the floor where the two Daves had decided to stand their mini cement mixer, and it was only my quick thinking that saved the day, but Mr Bryant won't tell you that because I never get credit for anything around here unless it goes wrong.

I consider myself a reasonable man. I always give my foreign coins to the homeless. I'll put a lost glove on the railings. I pick up litter. I listen carefully to my bosses before ignoring them. When my wife Leanne asked for a divorce I gave up with good grace, although I did pop something through her flamenco instructor's letterbox. I agreed to her terms. I even threw in the Bang & Olufsen (it didn't work but she could have got it fixed). But when Mr Bryant informed me that he was having another set of our investigations transcribed for the amusement of people who read popular fiction I took umbrage. We are a serious police unit, not a branch of WH Smith. People come to us for help, not a copy of *Barely Legal* and a Galaxy.

It wouldn't be so bad if Mr Bryant just stuck to the facts, but he always embellishes. What starts out as a straight-forward smash and grab usually ends up as some kind of baroque fairy tale. I suppose there's not much mileage in simply describing a spotty nonce in Tommy Hilfiger set-ting fire to an ATM, but that's real life for you: it's boring. Furthermore, Mr Bryant casts himself in a good light and makes me look more stupid than I am. I only wish I had his partner's patience. John May just sits there and smiles indulgently. I must find out what medication he's on.

These days most of our work is sitting behind desks studying statistics. I prefer to deal with facts and figures. There's nothing to break the monotony except Dan launch-ing into one of his periodic rants about broadband speed, Janice coming round with chocolate digestives and one of the Daves going through a mains cable. Jack Ryan wouldn't last five minutes.

That's not the way old Bryant tells it, though. According to him it's all last-minute escapes and surprise culprits. He describes his job the way he thinks it should be, or perhaps the way it is in his mind. He's been ill lately and it's not always possible to tell if he's in King's Cross or Narnia. His thought processes are peculiar. I once got up the nerve to ask him how old he was, and he said, 'I'm all the ages I've ever been, so you could say I'm twenty, just several times over.'

He has a very flexible attitude towards time. He remembers things as if they were yesterday. Unfortunately, he doesn't remember yesterday. Don't get me wrong, he knows a hawk from a handshake when he wants to, but there's a whole team helping him, it's not a one-man show. I tell him there's no 'i' in 'unit'; we all deserve a fair share of the blame.

Bryant wouldn't be told, though, and hired some mad academic to write up twelve more cases that must have occurred in an alternative space/time continuum for all I recognize them. Of course, I know what's happened. The success of the first collection has turned his head. He thought it would only sell about six copies but by my reckoning he shifted at least ten. I said to him: 'There's no need to embellish, just put them down as they actually happened so people can see how pointless our lives are.'

Anyway, here's the result. Being an officer of the law answerable only to Her Majesty's Government I could never advocate breaking the law, but I wouldn't pay full price for this volume if you know what I mean.

A NOTE FROM MR BRYANT'S BIOGRAPHER

Authenticity, that's the key word. When I was writing my biography of Lord Nelson I spent the entire time at my desk dressed as Lady Hamilton. It's important to capture the authenticity of the subject. Unfortunately, I had apparently walked out of the theatrical costumiers without paying again and was forced to earn some fast money to avoid social embarrassment, so I accepted the task of transcribing Mr Arthur Bryant's memories of the cases he and his partner John May had tackled in their long careers.

This presented me with a challenge, as Mr Bryant seems quite capable of remembering things that happened before he was born, or to other people. Verification was made tricky by the fact that many of the places he mentioned did not exist, and some of the people he recalled meeting had died a hundred years earlier, or were fictional. It wasn't until I looked through the books on his shelves that I realized he'd somehow muddled what he'd read with what had actually happened at the unit. Oscar Wilde said that memory is the diary we all carry about with us, but I fear Mr Bryant's diary has a few pages missing.

With this in mind I have had to 'decode' his version of events by visiting his old friends in Scotland Yard and the Metropolitan Police. Unfortunately what they had to say about him was libellous, so I had to make some bits up using old copies of the *Police Gazette* I had 'liberated' from the London Library. I hope my accounts of the following cases catch some of the flavour of life at the Peculiar Crimes Unit, if not the veracity.

I am given to understand that the unit's first biographer was herself murdered, and that the second, an unpopular mid-list author by the name of Fowler, proved most unsatisfactory, so I am aware of the pitfalls that lie ahead. Mr Bryant has appointed me under a state rehabilitation programme, and I hope to prove worthy of his trust. I also hope I get paid sometime soon. I sent Mr Bryant the bill but he's forgotten what he did with it.

Cynthia Birdhanger, King's Cross, London

BRYANT & MAY AND
THE SEVENTH REINDEER

Oluwa stood in the Ship pub in Wardour Street, Soho, watching the other Nigerian, fascinated.

The boy was about the same age as him, but couldn't have been more different. His body shape was extraordinary; he had to be over seven feet tall and was extremely thin, a Giacometti figure with lengthy arms and thighs and a small, round, shaved head. He wore a shiny grey suit jacket, too-short jeans with ironed-in creases and snakeskin boots. He smiled and laughed a lot, but when he moved his limbs he almost ceased to be human. He was a wave in the air.

Everyone who wanted to work in films went to the Ship. It was a known hangout for producers, directors and casting agents. Oluwa had written a script, but in the meantime he was trying to find work as an extra. He'd been planning to talk to the other Nigerian for a couple of weeks now. Both their families must have got out of Lagos when it disintegrated. He wondered how this towering, skeletal student had ended up here. It was 1978, and countrymen were rare on the London streets.

Oluwa had never been much of a conversationalist but curiosity drove him to ask the lad about his background. The student introduced himself politely and formally. His name was Bolaji, and he was the son of the Director General of the Nigerian Broadcasting Service.

'It sounds better than it was.' Bolaji laughed. 'My father says the British used it to blast public areas with BBC propaganda. That was before the civil war. Our family moved to Ethiopia and I came to London. I'm studying graphic design. How about you?'

Oluwa explained that he too had come to build a new life here, and was hawking around a script for a science fiction film he had written, but so far he'd had no luck and was fast running out of money. He had foolishly thought that producers were the gatekeepers to fortunes. He didn't mean to sound quite so desperate.

Bolaji bought them beers. He seemed flush with cash and was good company. After this meeting they made it a habit to meet at the end of each week in the same spot, to discuss the progress of their respective careers.

Then, on a rainy Friday night a month later, when the little man with the ridiculous cigar came into the pub and looked around, catching sight of the pair of them, everything changed. Oluwa had the distinct feeling that the customers were being weighed up by the man at the door. Moments later he joined them at the bar. Hands were shaken, drinks were purchased and cigar smoke wreathed the pair of them like a constricting snake.

The man was a casting agent with a fat wallet, and quite clearly legitimate, judging by the estimable names he dropped. But he wasn't interested in them both, only in

Bolaji. He couldn't take his eyes off him. 'How tall are you?' he asked. 'Seven feet?'

'Seven two,' Bolaji replied, grinning. 'Everyone in my family is tall.'

'I'm nearly six foot four,' said Oluwa, drawing himself up to his full height and wishing he had worn boots with a taller heel. The agent was clearly looking for a specific body type. Oluwa felt himself being gently but firmly closed out of their conversation. He left the pair in deep discussion and went home feeling vaguely aggrieved.

That summer, Bolaji disappeared for six weeks. When he returned he was in even higher spirits than usual. 'Where the hell have you been?' asked Oluwa, back at the bar and poorer than ever. When Bolaji excitedly explained what had happened, Oluwa felt a bitter jealousy claw at his bones. He was pleased about his friend's good fortune, but devastated by his own corresponding lack of success.

Oluwa thought that as the years passed he would feel differently. He believed it was only a matter of time before his big break also arrived. Surely one success would be followed by another. But nothing ever seemed to go right for him after that. London had opportunities to offer to the hungry and eager, but not, it seemed, to him.

'It's a day of peace,' said Alma Sorrowbridge, glancing out of the window at the falling snow. 'Relax, have a glass of sherry, eat some mince pies and watch Bruce Forsyth.'

'As it seems the entire country has been doing since the old king died,' complained Bryant, pulling his ratty maroon dressing gown around him and sinking further into his armchair. 'It's not like this on the continent. They don't spend the day wearing paper hats and moaning about pine needles. All the cafés are open, everyone's laughing and drinking champagne. I'm stuck indoors stuffing myself with nuts and being made to watch *Strictly Come Dancing* because you like the frocks. I hate Christmas. Your turkey was so dry it made my fork squeak. And look what Janice sent me.' He held up her annual Christmas card, which depicted Santa Claus on his sleigh, racing through a starry sky above a manger scene, the three wise men and their camels all covered in rainbow glitter. 'She makes them herself. I made the mistake of rubbing my eyes after I opened it and now I look like a drag queen.'

'My friends from the church will be over later,' said Alma, unwrapping another Terry's Chocolate Orange.

'Oh, wonderful. A bunch of old dears shovelling in Christmas cake and caterwauling their way through "Silent Night", followed by farmyard impressions and Auntie Doris's lecture on Pelmanism. No thank you. I bet John's not stuck at home; he'll be at a glamorous party somewhere full of starlets.'

'Why don't you call him?' Alma suggested.

'What, and make him think I'm bored? He wouldn't want to see me,' sniffed Bryant, 'not when he can be out having fun. What would I say – come over and have some of Alma's famous elasticated turkey gravy while we watch the Queen's Speech for the third time?'

'Very well,' said Alma, heading for the kitchen. Her lodger was an unpleasant old man at the best of times but he was always at his worst over Christmas. She closed the kitchen door and picked up the phone.

John May sat in his bare white apartment in Shad Thames and looked out at the deserted river. He had hoped that his son might call from Canada, but the phone had remained silent. There were two Christmas cards on his mantel-piece, and one of those was from BMW reminding him about his MOT. He was wearing his best suit, polished shoes and a tie. He had never truly known how to relax by himself. *This is what happens when you get older*, he thought gloomily, *your friends all die or move somewhere horrible. Arthur's probably snuggled down beside a roaring fire, Alma cooking, the Christmas tree twinkling.*

When the phone rang he assumed it was a wrong number.

'If that's carol singers throw a bucket of water over them,' called Bryant as Alma went to answer the door.

'Surprise,' said John May. 'Happy Christmas.' He held out a brown cardboard box. 'I didn't have time to wrap it.'

'Well, isn't this nice, you just turning up like this,' said Alma, hopelessly unable to feign surprise.

'She called you, didn't she?' Bryant accepted the box as May seated himself beside the fire. 'She'll wheel in half a ton of Christmas cake now. What's this?'

'The private notes on the Dagenham trunk murder,' said May with pride. 'It was never solved.'

'As it happens, I've got something for you,' said Bryant, reaching under his armchair. 'The witness reports for the Shepherd's Bush blowtorch killings. Clear a space on the table.' He rubbed his hands together with ill-disguised glee. 'I feel a mince pie coming on.'

They settled in and had just finished laying out the evidence in both investigations on the dining-room table when the phone rang again.

'It's a Sergeant Dickie Hathaway from Covent Garden

Police Station,' said Alma. 'I reminded him that it's the Lord's day but he insists on speaking to you.'

'Mr Bryant, I remember you from way back in the Bow Street days and realized I still had your number. I'm only contacting you because I couldn't get hold of anyone else,' said Hathaway.

'How nice of you to eventually work your way down to me,' replied Bryant coldly.

'I do hope I'm not disturbing you.'

'You are.' Bryant unwrapped a chocolate-covered brazil nut. 'This had better be good.'

'A vicious attack, right in the middle of Covent Garden Market,' said Hathaway. 'I can't make head or tail of it, and I can't get hold of anyone to help me. They're all off until Boxing Day. She's famous, for God's sake; it'll get out and everyone will come to us demanding to know what happened. But the station is closed and everyone's gone away for the holidays.'

Bryant could hardly turn the opportunity down. Going through cold cases at home was one thing, but proper crimes were becoming rarer and rarer in a city that was slowly being smothered with fish-eye lenses. Lately they had started to sprout on stalks from every building or sat on the tops of poles in squares, keeping a mindful eye on London in ways that Orwell could never have imagined. It was 2005, and over the coming years the nature of policing would change until there was a camera for every thirty people in the country. On one hand it was a good thing. The Peculiar Crimes Unit would no longer need to maintain a network of not entirely reliable informers. But from a purely selfish point of view it spoiled the fine art of detection.

'We can be there in fifteen minutes,' Bryant promised, trying not to sound too eager.

May's BMW zipped down a deserted Gower Street towards Shaftesbury Avenue. Almost every set of traffic lights was on green. There were hardly any cars in the cross streets. All the pubs were shut; a sign that London had truly closed down for the day. 'No congestion charge on Christmas Day,' said May.

'Oh, that's just a money-making wheeze,' said Bryant airily. 'We don't have to pay it anyway, we're rozzers.'

'No, you're supposed to pay it, then get it signed off and claim it back.'

'I cut out the red tape by simply not paying in the first place. I'm saving the taxpayer money.' Bryant found a tube of Polo Mints and opened them. 'The poor chap sounded desperate. Do you remember old Hathaway? His wife always sang at dinner parties, utterly charming woman. I wonder why we all hated her. Turn left here.'

'You mean right.'

'Yes, your other left.' Bryant had always been hopeless with directions. His brief stint running a cub Scouts' wilderness group had ended in traumatic scenes after he walked his troop into an abattoir.

'I'll have to go around. Covent Garden is pedestrianized,' May warned as they entered King Street.

'Oh, rubbish, no one will mind. Here.' Bryant tried to take the wheel.

'Can you please not do that?' May brought the BMW to a halt on the cobbled walkway that ran past the covered market. 'He's over there.'

The market was festooned with giant green and silver sprigs of mistletoe, but the stalls were all shut and concealed under red and white striped awnings. The portly sergeant was standing in front of a grey nylon tent that had been placed over a section of pavement in the north-east corner of the market square, beside its new pillared walkway. He shook their hands in gratitude.

'Mr Bryant, Mr May, thank you for coming down here. She's been taken to University College Hospital and has gone straight into surgery. She's under sedation but expected to make a full recovery. I thought you needed to see the crime scene.'

'Who was attacked?' asked May.

'An opera singer by the name of Anna Perigorde. Does that ring a bell?'

'No,' said Bryant. 'We're detectives, we don't know anything about opera singers.' Although he did, of course.

'Apparently she's very well known,' said Hathaway. 'She was on her way home from a rehearsal of . . . Hang on.' He fished a bit of paper from his pocket. 'It was full of divers.'

'You mean divas.'

'No, divers. That's it, *The Pearl Fishers*. A big lass. I suppose it's all lungs.'

Bryant peered into the tent and studied the spot where the opera singer had fallen. 'I see what you mean,' he said. 'That's a fair-sized patch of dry ground. Whoever's playing Nadir would have had to brace himself when she fell into his arms.' He thought for a moment. 'Bizet.'

Hathaway looked around. 'You don't expect it to be on Christmas Day.'

'No, you clod. The composer. He wrote *Carmen*.'

'Oh, I've seen that. A load of birds rolling cigarettes on their thighs and bullfighters and that.'

'Toreadors,' said Bryant absently. 'What happened?'

'It looks as if something came up from behind and, well, sort of clawed at her. It's all very strange.'

'What do you mean, *clawed*?'

'She had these nasty-looking bruises and cuts across her right shoulder, and fell there, concussing herself on the cobbles.'

'There's no blood.' Bryant stepped out, turned on his heel and looked back. 'She came out of the rehearsal rooms over there, yes? What time?'

'Just after five.' The sergeant checked his watch. 'A little over forty minutes ago. She attended a meeting with the wardrobe mistress, popped out for some air and was attacked.'

'A meeting on Christmas Day?' said May. 'Isn't that odd?'

'No, they have a performance tomorrow afternoon,' Hathaway explained. 'There's all sorts working today. Opera singers. Binmen.'

'Why would she need some air?' asked May.

'Apparently she always does because the air conditioning gives her a dry throat.'

'Was she still in costume?'

'Yes, a sort of gauzy white gown and lots of necklaces. The EMT say she was more frightened than anything, babbling about some kind of beast.'

Bryant leaned back and examined the edge of the walkway. 'She must have been caught on a dozen cameras.'

'I imagine so,' said Hathaway, 'but I can't get access to any of them. No one's answering phones, it's—'

'Christmas, we know,' said Bryant impatiently. 'What was taken from her?'

'That's the thing – nothing. She still had her purse and handbag.'

'Yet he must have gone through her pockets,' said Bryant, pointing to something glinting on the ground nearby.

'There's about five pounds in loose change on the pavement. Anyone else around?'

'What do you mean?' asked Hathaway.

'What do you think I mean? The square couldn't have been completely deserted.'

'Not at the time when she came out of the rehearsal rooms, no. There were a couple of coachloads of tourists wandering about, photographing old stuff. By the time I arrived they'd gone.'

'Did you talk to anyone? Call a forensic team, check for reports of disturbance? Good God, man, what have you been doing for the last forty minutes?'

'I've been stood here trying to find someone, then waiting for you,' the sergeant said hotly, pointing at the ground. 'I couldn't leave this spot until you got here.'

The new demarcations around the West End had all but wiped out local police stations. Too much time had been wasted by casual callers complaining about Leicester Square's pickpockets and Covent Garden's food outlets, so the stations were being closed. It meant that when a serious assault occurred on Central London's quietest day of the year, finding anyone to cover it was well-nigh impossible.

'Is this what it's come down to?' Bryant fumed to his partner. 'An attack in the centre of London and all we get is a local sergeant? Times have changed. We used to get a bigger turnout for a cat stuck up a tree.'

'Well, I'm sorry, I couldn't leave,' said Hathaway. 'I took a picture of the snow.'

Bryant looked about. 'What snow?' he said. 'I don't see any.'

'We had a flurry here earlier. It had already started to settle when I arrived. That's why I told you it was so strange. Here.' He dug out a tiny pocket camera and searched through his photographs. 'I borrowed this from a French tourist. He needs it back for Stratford.'

'Why, what's there?'

'Shakespeare.'

'Oh, I thought you meant Stratford East. There's no rush, seeing as he's French.'

Hathaway held up the camera. 'I managed to get half a dozen shots off before the snow melted away. First, here's the victim *in situ*. Then – well, see for yourself.'

Bryant wiped his trifocals and pressed his nose to the camera's screen. He gave as much of a low whistle as he could manage through false teeth, then showed the shots to his partner. 'What on earth are those?' he asked.

May took the camera and enlarged one of the pictures. It clearly showed two sets of footprints beside the body. The first, high heels with a broad sole, clearly belonged to the victim. The other consisted of four huge claws, and something that dragged behind them.

'It looks like a giant cat of some kind,' said May. 'Except that it must have reared up on its hind legs.'

'Whose hind legs are shaped like that? Have we got something on the loose around here?' asked Bryant.

'There's a circus on the other side of the market,' said Hathaway. 'But they're not allowed to have any acts with animals.'

'You saw these tracks, yes? Where did they go?'

The sergeant pointed up to the corner of the buildings behind them. 'The snow was coming in through that gap over there so it only settled in one part of the square.' He indicated the wedge-shaped section of wet ground where the snow had fallen. 'I couldn't see anything beyond that corner.'

'Who called it in?'

'One of the coach drivers saw her lying there. Whatever had attacked her had already gone.'

'Well, this is one for my memoirs,' said Bryant. 'Let's see what else we can find.'

John May watched his partner working with interest. Bryant was outside the tent, then lifting its edges with the end of his walking stick, then dropping low to follow a cable that led to part of the seasonal display.

'Now what's he doing?' asked Hathaway.

May gave the faintest of shrugs. 'I'm sure he'll tell us when he's ready.'

Bryant climbed to his feet, his knees cracking like someone stamping on bags of crisps, and returned to the sergeant with an accusing look on his face.

'This cold weather plays silly buggers with my joints,' he said. 'Right, where's Dunder?'

'Who?' Hathaway asked.

'The seventh reindeer.'

'What are you talking about?' asked May.

Bryant raised his stick and pointed around the edge of the square. 'Look, Dasher, Dancer, Prancer, Vixen, Comet, Cupid, no Dunder, then Blixem.' Set on the ground at ten-yard intervals were a series of prancing reindeer, each of them about three feet high, plastic and silver-wire frames wrapped with twinkling lights. Except that on this side of the square the lights were all out and one reindeer, the seventh, was missing. Its cable went as far as the edge of the crime scene tent and reappeared on the other side.

'Dunder and Blixem are Dutch for thunder and lightning,' said Bryant, lifting the side of the tent. 'From the 1823 poem. Blixem was changed to rhyme with "Vixen", the fourth reindeer, but nobody knows why "Dunder" ended up as "Donner". You never know where you are with flying fauna. Please note that there's no Rudolph. Anna Perigorde must have been attacked right beside the seventh reindeer. Thunder's gone.'

'That's odd,' said Hathaway. 'It was here before.'

'Then the attacker took it away with him. Why? Was he behaving like a wild animal carrying off prey? Perhaps she was too heavy to lift so he settled for something smaller.'

'Do you have any idea how ridiculous that sounds?' asked May.

'Of course I do,' said Bryant indignantly. 'I specialize in the ridiculous.'

'Maybe it's just coincidence that there was one missing at this spot.'

'No.' Bryant was adamant. 'Look at the edges of the cables. They've been freshly cut with electrical pliers. There's no water underneath her or on these cuts.'

May knew that his partner had the eyesight of a deep-sea anglerfish and wondered if he might be bluffing, but when he knelt to check the wires he could see that Bryant was right.

'So we don't know whether our suspect is human or animal,' he said, 'but we do know he also attacked a reindeer and carried it off. At least he should stand out on the streets. As the tubes aren't running today and there are hardly any taxis about, he should be easy to spot.'

'You don't seem at all surprised by this,' said the sergeant. 'It's not an everyday occurrence, an opera singer in full regalia assaulted by a giant panther in Covent Garden.'

'You didn't see it, though, did you?' Bryant pointed out. 'You're drawing a conclusion from the evidence that cannot possibly be right. Mind you, it's funny the things you see in London on some days. Do you remember that bloke who was attacked with a penguin, John?' He turned to the sergeant. 'The flightless bird, not the chocolate bar. All we could book his assailant for was cruelty to animals.'

'Even so,' said May, 'we'd better check with the circus, just in case.'

The circus, unfortunately, was shut, but its leaflets proudly proclaimed a total absence of livestock. 'It's not a proper circus if a man in a top hat can't fend off a knackered-looking lion with a dining chair,' Bryant complained in a tone designed to provoke. 'All you're left with is clowns and people swinging from ropes.'

They headed up to University College Hospital, where Anna Perigorde was emerging from sedation. A dark-eyed young man sat beside the bed holding her hand. 'I'm Galvin Perigorde, her son,' he said, shaking their hands with grave respect.

'No husband?' asked Bryant brusquely.

'My mother is divorced.'

'We don't speak to him,' said Anna, looking up at them pitifully. Her right shoulder was heavily bandaged. Lying in a hospital gown without make-up, she had none of the fiery grandeur of her photographs.

'Please don't move,' said her son. 'Your head—'

'Is your husband in the country?' Bryant asked.

'Yes, in Hampstead with his slut of a new wife.' She winced as she attempted to pull herself upright. It was hard to tell if she was in pain or overacting. From her facial expressions she might have been Aida being buried alive.

'Can you tell us what happened?' May enquired gently.

'I'd been to have my costume altered for tomorrow,' Anna explained. 'The stage door opens on to the corner of the square. There was no one around. I stepped outside and walked around the block to get some air.'

'Is that something you often do?'

'Yes. This is my ninth season at the House. It's what we do.'

'You mean we Italians – you are Italian, yes?'

'Of course. I took my husband's name.'

'My mother enjoys – recognition,' said Galvin, not without implying criticism.

'Is this going to take very long?' cried La Perigorde. 'Haven't I suffered enough?'

'Did you have any cash on you?' Bryant asked. 'I mean small change?'

'No, of course not, I am world famous!' The singer grimaced in disgust. 'I only had the credit cards in my purse. I'd just got back to the stage door when this hideous thing came up behind me. It was immensely tall. It tried to punch me on the side of the head and gripped my arm. I saw great black claws close over my shoulder and tried to scream, but he put something over my mouth. I could smell something disgusting, like burned car tyres. Then I fell. We struggled. The creature had a very long whip-like tail. There was something underneath me—'

'The reindeer,' Bryant suggested.

'Yes, that was it, but then I banged my head on the cobblestones. I don't remember anything else.'

'You saw nothing more of this monster?'

'No, I just told you, didn't I? I had the impression of a great black shape, that's all. I was terrified.'

'Do you think he was waiting for you?'

'Well, *obviously* he was.' She shot the detectives a withering look. 'Isn't there anyone more competent I can talk to? You have to find him. Tell your superiors, I want everybody on this. This *monstrosity* does not want me to take my place on the stage tomorrow.'

Bryant appeared not to be listening. 'Is this the outfit you were wearing?' He picked up the diaphanous white gown that had been draped across a chair.

'Yes. The creature tore it,' lamented La Perigorde. 'It's quite unwearable now.'

'You're sure this is all of it?'

'Leave it alone. It's worth more than your annual salary.'

'Sorry.' Bryant set the gown and its necklaces back down. 'Do they think you'll be well enough to go on with the show?'

'It is an opera, not a show. And it depends on whether you catch this ghastly thing before the curtain goes up,' said the diva, deviously.

'I don't know,' said May, shucking off his shoes. 'It's a bit *Phantom of the Opera*, isn't it? The mysterious creature that forbids the singer to perform?' As the offices of the Peculiar Crimes Unit were shut for today they had headed back to Bryant's home and seated themselves in front of the gas fire. 'I don't know where we're supposed to start with this investigation. You hear about the members of opera and ballet companies doing terrible things to one another to sabotage their performances. We'll have to interview everyone starting with the understudies, and anyone else who's been up for the part. There could be all kinds of subtle long-running feuds at the heart of this.'

'Oh, I don't think that will be necessary,' said Bryant, feeling for his Lorenzo Spitfire and a box of matches. 'I've got a fairly good idea who we're looking for.'

'You do? I wish you'd enlighten me.'

'You've seen the same evidence,' said Bryant. 'You heard what I asked her. You could draw your own conclusions.'

'But you and I think differently,' said May. 'You take a sort of lateral approach. Your mind has a crab-like gait.'

'That doesn't sound very attractive. Have you ever been to the opera in Italy?'

'Yes, to the Arena di Verona. An extraordinary experience. The cast parade around the town square afterwards and allow themselves to be greeted by their admirers.'

'Then our thought processes aren't so very far apart after all. You recall I asked her if she was Italian?'

'Yes, but I don't see how that connects to stealing a reindeer.'

'Because you're looking at it the wrong way. It's not the fact that it was a reindeer at all. You didn't try to lift one of them up, did you? They're very light. Tell me, what can you be sure of so far?'

'Sure of?' May accepted a mandarin orange and unpeeled it thoughtfully. 'That the attacker was human because there could be no such monster on the loose.'

Bryant grinned. 'Half right but never mind, keep going.'

'And that the purpose of the attack was to prevent her from performing.'

Bryant looked disappointed. 'No, I think not. You're over-complicating something that's really very simple. Anna Perigorde was assaulted in the heat of the moment, out of spite and jealousy, nothing more.'

'How can you be so sure of that?'

'Because I put the key points of interest together, marking them in my mind like crosses on a grid, then draw the shortest possible lines between them before stepping back to examine the finished drawing. It's like looking at the night sky and delineating the constellations.'

'That's as close as you've ever got to describing your thought processes,' May admitted.

'Except that I don't do it every time,' said Bryant. 'Sometimes my brain is simply flattened by an avalanche of mad rubbish.'

'Damn, I thought I'd nailed you for once. So what were these key points?'

Bryant gave a weary sigh, as if being forced to explain to a child. 'The fiver's worth of small change that didn't belong to La Perigorde. The smell of car tyres. The necklace on the *Pearl Fishers* costume. And the *location*, for heaven's sake.'

'Here, are you going to keep going out and coming in again?' Alma asked from the doorway. 'Because you're treading pine needles all over my carpets.'

'Madam, you are trespassing in my chamber of repose,' warned Bryant.

'This is not your chamber, it's the sitting room and I've got guests arriving for our carol service in a minute, so perhaps you could take your bedsocks off the teapot and retire to your own room for a while.'

Bryant beckoned to his partner. 'Lord help us, they'll be bashing through the entire Judaeo-Christian litany of guilt and redemption for the next couple of hours. Come on, there must be a pub open somewhere.'

'So despite having a strong idea of who we're looking for, you don't plan on taking action tonight,' said May.

'I can't,' Bryant replied, wrapping himself in several yards of moulting green scarfage. 'The "monster" can't be caught this evening. He's shed his skin. We'll get him tomorrow morning.'

*

They did, too, once more driving to the scene of the assault and parking on the cobbles, disrupting the smooth running of the square's restaurants, where waiters were trying to set out tables.

'Come on, back up James Street towards the tube,' said Bryant, waving his walking stick wildly and clearing a path through some startled tourists. 'He'll be here.'

'How can you be so sure?' May asked.

'Because the Underground is running today,' Bryant replied. 'He had to be desperate to turn up yesterday. This' – here his stick nearly thickened the ear of an elderly Canadian – 'is the main thoroughfare linking the tube system to the market. The only people you'll find here are tourists and those who prey on them.'

Boxing Day had nothing to do with sport, although many fixtures took place on that afternoon. It had been named after the time when servants and tradesmen traditionally received Christmas boxes from their masters, employers and customers. And it was always a busy day in the centre of London, because it was the day when all the store sales started.

'So where's your suspect?' May asked, searching the crowds.

'Over there, next to the talking dog,' said Bryant.

May followed his raised stick and saw a man with a painted dog's face and fluffy ears, his head poking out of a kennel with false forearms attached. ''Allo, darlin', wanna come over and play with my bone?' he called after a pretty girl, following it with a series of woofs. The acrobats, artists and street mimes were out in force today, lining the whole west side of the street from the tube to the market.

May's eyes widened. Next to the talking dog was an

alien. To be specific, it was *the* Alien, the one from the movies, or at least, a man in a costume that mimicked it perfectly. The great black head and ribbed body were balanced by a long spiny tail. He stood motionless on clawed feet, occasionally lunging after screaming children.

'That's our man,' said Bryant. 'Do you want to do the honours, or shall I?'

'I don't mind, so long as you're sure and he comes along quietly,' said May warily. 'I don't think I can get handcuffs on him.'

Oluwa sat in the interview room at the PCU without his head. It had been set aside by the window. In testimony to its lost power, Crippen, the unit's cat, had climbed inside it and fallen asleep.

'We arrived from Nigeria at the same time,' Oluwa said sadly, staring into the mug of coffee May had provided for him. He had the graceful full-toned speaking voice of a trained RADA actor. 'Bolaji was even taller and thinner than me, and he got the job that turned him into a legend. They asked him to be inside the creature. He was the alien in *Alien*. Of course nobody saw his face, but he became famous. Friends with the greatest movie stars, invited all over the world, and me, I was nothing. They say he died of sickle cell anaemia. By that time I'd run out of options. I knew how the design of the alien suit allowed it to function because Bolaji talked about it and sketched it for me dozens of times. Finally I built one for myself out of rubber. You can't just go and stand on James Street, you have to be licensed by the council, so that's what I did: I got my licence. And that's what all my dreams amounted to, a man in a suit busking for coins, year after year. I was trapped. And every so often she appeared, waltzing along the pavement in her latest opera costume, breezing past me as if she owned the whole street, knocking over my coin pot, drawing all the attention to herself, virtually scream-ing "Look at me!" to everyone who passed. I hated her and everything she stood for.'

'So you attacked her,' said Bryant.

'I lost my mind. There I was, freezing cold, the only mime working in the street because the tubes weren't run-ning, and there *she* was – even on Christmas Day, the one time you'd think I could get some peace – and again she shot me a filthy look and muttered something under her breath as she passed – and I just snapped. I jumped down from my podium and ran after her, but I couldn't move quickly because the outfit is hard to balance. I really only wanted to confront her but the headpiece weighed me down and tipped me over, so that I fell on top of her. I threw out my arm and tore her costume, and we landed on top of this stupid sparkly reindeer. The whole thing was ridiculous, grotesque. Luckily there was now nobody around to see us. When she fell she banged her head and passed out. One of her necklaces was caught up in the reindeer's lights. I pulled off my glove and tried to free it, but all I did was leave it broken inside the reindeer with my fingerprints all over it. I had a pen-knife in my pocket – the suit sheds and sometimes has to be trimmed so I can get the zip open – so I cut the reindeer free, squashed it flat and fled with it under my arm. I knew that my coin belt had spilled its contents on the pavement but I didn't think anyone would trace me through a handful of small change. That's how you found me, isn't it?'

'No,' said May. 'My partner here saw a constellation where I only saw stars.'

Oluwa furrowed his brow. 'I suppose you will prosecute me now and I will lose even the low standing I possess.'

The detectives stepped outside and spoke quietly between themselves for a minute. Oluwa silently awaited a verdict.

'How did you know it was him?' asked May, puzzled.

Bryant made marks in the air. 'Covent Garden has tourists. Mimes have costumes and small change. Madame was missing a necklace. The only reason for taking the reindeer was because it held incriminating evidence.'

They went back into the interview room.

'Mr May and I have reached a decision,' said Bryant finally. 'The only way we can drop the case is by telling Anna Perigorde that we can't find you. That means you must leave James Street and never come back.'

Oluwa had tears in his eyes. 'I don't know how to make a living for myself any other way.'

Bryant withdrew the Christmas card Janice Longbright had given him and turned it over, writing on the back. In doing so he wiped rainbow glitter all over his pug nose. 'You made the suit yourself, yes? Did you ever make any others like it?'

'Of course,' said Oluwa. 'They wear out quickly. Almost every penny I earn goes towards making the next one. I am very good.'

'Then call these people,' said Bryant, handing him the Christmas card. 'They run a special-effects company based in Bristol. I'll have a word with them. I have a feeling they could use a fellow with your talents. If you agree to this, we'll set you free.'

Oluwa still looked fearful as he cautiously rose to leave.

'It's all right,' Bryant assured him. 'Take the suit with you. You'll need to show them some of your handiwork.'

'I don't know how to thank you,' Oluwa began.

'You don't have to,' said Bryant. 'It's what everyone should do at this time of year. It's Christmas.' The detective's nose sparkled. He might have been the seventh reindeer himself.

BRYANT & MAY'S DAY OFF

There are post-war London smells which have now been lost: the mildew in sailors' clothes long packed away, the scent of tobacco sweetened with amber, the mustiness of horsehair cinema seats. Arthur Bryant smelled them all, mainly because he smelled *of* them all. He was a man born for winter, and like many born Londoners a hot summer day only served to confuse him.

He had found ways to fill the morning, breakfasting at the Lyons' Corner House on the Strand, visiting Joseph Wright's painting *An Experiment on a Bird in the Air Pump* at the National Gallery, clambering through the tops of the planes and elms of the Embankment's tree walk, its boards hung about with Chinese lanterns, and now he was bored. It was rare that he had a day off and he hated them, especially in August.

The morning had begun with a summer storm that had deflated the Zeppelin-sized clouds above the city, leaving the sun to steam them into wisps. Now the light was diamond blue and it felt hot enough to fry an egg on the pavement.

There was something about a hot day in London that made you feel you had to put your skin into sunlight in case there wasn't another fine day before the onset of autumn. It was absurd to feel so pressured. Londoners were daisies, forever phototropically craning their heads to brightness.

Mooching towards the river, he wished he had not worn his thick winter vest. Dressed in the kind of scratchy tweeds his father usually wore to go to the races, he reluctantly decided that looking smart was less essential than being comfortable. He was surrounded by floral summer dresses and businessmen in shirt sleeves, jackets slung nonchalantly over their shoulders. The air around the Thames was humid and still, and smelled of warm bricks.

Bryant pinched off his hat and fanned his face. Although the war was now a distant memory it still seemed as if no one remembered how to dress. The ladies expressed more originality, altering their old summer frocks by adding pleats and bows and silk flowers, but half the men were still in demob suits, an army of grey and brown-clad civilians on the march from their baking offices, looking for somewhere shady to eat their packed lunches.

There were so few cars on the Strand one could be forgiven for thinking that petrol rationing was still in place. Bryant's father missed being able to trade coupons for clothes on Warren Street's black market, where deals were sealed with a nod and a handshake in shop doorways. The war had been good to men like him.

'I thought you were in some kind of experimental unit,' his old man had complained, 'not a bloody copper.' It shamed him to think that there might be a male in the household willing to follow the line of the law.

'Science involves detection, and the reverse is increasingly the case,' Bryant explained, but his father did not want to know. Bert refused to hear about his son's career and eventually went to his grave resentful and bewildered. The day of the funeral had been hot, too, tactless weather for mourning.

'I say, there you are.' John May came charging up the crowded pavement. 'I was calling out but you were miles away. You forgot these.' He handed over a greaseproof packet of cheese and pickle sandwiches. May had not long been working with Bryant but was already discovering his strange ways, one of which was placing an order of priority on his forgetfulness so that considerations of lesser importance, like office politics, food, courtesy and deference were deleted in favour of the things he actually cared about. 'I didn't think you were coming in today, but someone saw you leave these on a desk.'

'I only popped my head around the door, purely because I was passing.' Bryant accepted the sandwiches and stuffed them into his pocket.

'Gosh, aren't you boiling in that old suit?' May was bounding alongside him, being annoyingly puppyish, a long lean Labrador of a man, far too ready to think kindly of others.

'This is a Harris Tweed, hand-woven in the Outer Hebrides and made from pure virgin wool,' Bryant said, dodging the question. He could have explained that he owned no summer suit and would not have been able to afford one if he had the inclination to make such a purchase. John May came from a better-off background and probably took it for granted that seasonal clothing could be unearthed according to the climate.

'It just looks so heavy. It's seventy-five degrees, you know, probably more if you measure it from the Air Ministry roof. You picked the right day to have off.'

'I didn't pick it, I was told to take it,' snapped Bryant. 'They think I work too much. Anyway, there's bound to be another storm later. City weather has no stability.'

It was a depressing thought but May had noticed the pattern himself. Although the day had started with a downpour, by eleven the sun was burnishing the copper-edged buildings that hemmed the skyline and softening the tarmac along Lower Thames Street. Ahead the river sparkled like the Mediterranean.

'Don't you have something you should be doing?' Bryant dug a digit beneath his celluloid collar, trying to loosen it, but the blasted thing just stuck out on one side.

'I'm on lunch, but to be honest there's not much going on today. Here, let me get that.' May reached over and pulled the white strip free for him. Unlike others, he never took offence at Bryant's impatient tone. In truth he felt a little sorry for his partner. There had been some kind of tragedy in his life and he often appeared lost and uncared-for. It looked as if he'd slept in his suit. 'I think you don't know what to do with yourself on a day off,' he said. 'Why don't you sit in the park and enjoy the sunshine?'

'Why don't *you* sit in the park? Go on, hop it.' Bryant ploughed on through the lunchtime workers. 'I hate having days off. It just winds me up, wandering about. Why would anyone want to sit sweating in a bandstand deck-chair listening to *Workers' Playtime*?'

'You know, it would improve your efficiency to let that formidable brain relax once in a while,' May pointed out. 'At least let me buy you a lemonade. We could find a bench, roll up our trouser legs and watch the pretty girls go past.'

'With my legs? You must be joking.'

May persevered. 'Don't you ever want to recharge your batteries?'

'All batteries need to make them run is plenty of acid,' Bryant replied, then stopped short, a dog sniffing out a butcher's shop. 'Trouble.'

A rotund man in a waistcoat and pince-nez was wringing his hands in the doorway of his jewellery shop, Lombroso & Sons. Golden necklaces glinted in padded racks of maroon velvet, set within the shop front's old-fashioned black glass frame. Mr Lombroso (for it was the proprietor) searched the street in ill-contained panic.

'We're police officers,' said Bryant, 'can we help?'

'A thief,' said the jeweller, glancing at him with disconcertingly thyroidal eyes. 'Just a minute ago on this very spot.'

'What happened?' Before May could halt his progress, Bryant was already sliding into the dimly lit shop.

'But we have to find him!' cried Mr Lombroso.

'Then explain quickly,' said Bryant.

'A man came in and asked to see a tray of rings in the window. I removed them and allowed him to examine the one he liked. When he mentioned another that his fiancée might prefer I climbed into the window to fetch it. I returned with the ring, he decided against the purchase and left. That was when I saw what he'd done.'

'What had he done?' Bryant asked.

Mr Lombroso held up the tray and removed the ring in the bottom left corner. 'It's painted tin,' he said. 'While I was in the window he switched them. The ring he took is the most valuable one we have in stock.'

'Why did you leave him alone with the tray?' May wondered.

'There has to be trust,' said Mr Lombroso, clearly shocked. 'He introduced himself, although I didn't quite catch the name. And he looked like a gentleman.'

'In what way?'

'He had a very smart suit, double-breasted herringbone with a hand-stitched lining of pale grey silk. I used to be a tailor; I know fine clothes when I see them. Most of the company employees around here wear off-the-peg. We have to hurry.'

'Would you recognize him again?' Bryant asked.

'No, but I'd know the suit anywhere.'

'Is there anything else you remember about him?'

'He was wearing a grey trilby and Oxfords with a fine perforated toecap.'

'But physically?'

'He's probably in his forties but just – ordinary. Clothes make the man.'

'It would have helped if you'd seen his boat race,' said Bryant. 'Which way did he go from the front door?'

'Left, I think.'

'Close the shop,' Bryant commanded. 'We'll help you look.'

'How will we ever find him in these lunchtime crowds?' May asked his partner.

'It's five to two,' Bryant replied. 'Any moment now he'll find himself in empty streets. It's all insurance and account-ants around here: clock-watchers, the lot of 'em. Lower Thames Street is a dead end. He can't get out without entering a building. You've seen what the office workers wear – he'll stick out like a nun in a snowstorm.'

Mr Lombroso hastily pulled down his shutters and pocketed an immense ring of keys. 'I should never have turned my back,' he said, huffing after the detectives, 'but I thought, you know, a doctor, well, he's from the profes-sional classes.'

'Wait a minute, a doctor?' said Bryant. 'You didn't men-tion that.'

'Oh yes, he told me while I was looking in the window. He met his fiancée during the war. He'd seen service as a doctor and she was his nurse. He said it had to be a gold ring – he hated the thought of silver. Well, the finest we have are inset with diamonds of four carats. Do you know what that means?'

'Of course,' said Bryant. 'The word derives from the seeds of the carob tree, which were used by gem traders before the twelfth century to balance scales when weighing a diamond.'

'I didn't realize he was simply telling me a tale to make sure I brought out the best tray.'

'So he's a professional,' said May as they searched the faces around them. 'Do you really remember no physical features at all?'

'He didn't take his hat off and it's dark in the shop,' said the distraught jeweller. 'I think he was rather pale, though.'

'After the summer we've had so is nearly every man in London,' said Bryant, scanning the street. Four secretaries, three bankers in top hats, a clutch of men in bowlers, no thief. They checked each building as they passed, questioning the doormen, several of whom were missing an arm, having taken the only jobs they could find after the war.

'What's at the end of the road?' May asked his partner.

'The river, old bean. And he can't have just— Hold on.'

Bryant all but ran to the far wall, where a great iron gate had been propped open. He looked down on to the Tower Beach and saw masses of semi-naked bodies on the sand, his heart sinking.

In 1934 King George V promised the children of London that they could have 'free access forever' to this specially constructed foreshore, and over the next five years half a million people swam and sunbathed among the vendors and entertainers, hiring threepenny rowing boats to go under Tower Bridge and back. The beach was to remain in place for nearly forty years.

Today the so-called 'London Riviera' was swarming with sunbathers. Colourful towels had been laid out, striped deckchairs rented, grand sandcastles built, and dockers' daughters splashed about with the sons of bankers. Handkerchiefs had been knotted and trouser legs rolled up, but the majority of sun-worshippers had stripped to their woollen bathing trunks and swimsuits. Copies of the *Daily Mirror* had been opened to see whether Jane, the paper's resident cartoon-strip pin-up girl, had also removed her clothes.

'He couldn't have gone anywhere else,' said Bryant. 'He must be down there.'

'But if all we have to go on is a description of his suit, how can we find him in a state of undress?' May asked. 'Look, there must be fifty men in their forties, all in their swimming togs. He hasn't just removed his clothes, he's stripped himself of his identity.'

The detectives looked down in despair as the swimmers frolicked, bathed and dozed. 'What do we do now?' asked Mr Lombroso.

'Wherever there are this many people there's money to be made,' said Bryant mysteriously, waving a hand at the shoreline. He was right; a hokey-pokey man was selling ice cream and another was hawking newspapers. There was even a young lad leading a donkey about for rides. 'He can't know the area. If he did he'd have turned right coming out of the shop. Instead he found himself cornered. He couldn't come back past your window, so my guess is he's hiding out down here for a while.'

He led the way down the steps to the shore and

approached a man in braces and an undershirt who was standing beside a row of grey metal crates. In each of them was a pile of carefully folded clothes. Propped up against one of the crates was a roofing slate upon which had been chalked: 'Harry the Minder – Swimming Trunks 3d'.

'We need to look through these clothes,' Bryant explained.

''Ere, you can't just come down here and rifle through me clients' clobber,' said Harry indignantly. 'I've me reputation to think of.'

'We won't disturb anything.' Bryant showed his police card. 'This gentleman is trying to identify someone.'

'All right, but be quick about it.' The minder shielded the crates from the sunbathers, fearful that his clients might think he was in league with crooks.

Mr Lombroso beetled along the line of crates and stopped before one like a pointer with a partridge. 'Here he is. Double-breasted herringbone, hand-stitched lining.'

Bryant knelt and checked the jacket pockets. The clothes-minder slapped at him. 'Oi, I didn't say you could touch 'em!'

In the trousers, Bryant found the ring. He rose, holding it up as evidence. 'Whose basket is this? Did you rent him trunks as well? What does he look like?'

'I don't know, just another city bloke without clothes,' said Harry with a shrug.

'He's the man who robbed my shop,' said Mr Lombroso heatedly.

'It couldn't have been,' said the minder. 'He had a kid with 'im – a little boy.'

May studied the shoreline. Over half of the men down at the water's edge were with children.

'Where are the boy's clothes?' Bryant was shown another

crate containing shorts, a shirt, underpants, socks and sandals. 'And you really can't point them out to me?' he asked.

'Do you remember the last properly 'ot day we 'ad?' asked the minder. 'Nor can I. I hate the 'eat. My missus gets funny ideas when she has to take 'er stays off. That's why there's so many secketries down there today, flauntin' themselves. Sex mad they are, when a fella just wants to nod off in the sun.'

'Maybe there's someone else down there in the same clothes,' said May.

'No, this is him and he certainly didn't arrive with the child,' said Bryant.

'How do you know?' Mr Lombroso asked.

'It rained until half nine.' Bryant pointed at the crates. 'This man's shoes are still splashed with mud, but the boy came here in socks and sandals. The socks are dry, so they weren't together earlier. He thought he'd put us off the scent by chucking the kid a couple of bob to come down to the beach with him. Probably sent him off to play as soon as they got by the water.'

'Now what?'

'We take a stroll in the sun,' said Bryant. 'Act natural.' As he was wearing a heavy winter suit with a waistcoat and a pocket watch the effect was far from inconspicuous.

'In his early forties. A doctor during the war, if he's to be believed. Wait.' He gripped May's arm and pointed. At first sight the boy could have simply been having a disagreement with his father, but as the detectives approached, they saw how anxious the lad was to escape. 'Let go of me, I don't bloody know you,' he was shouting as a hand gripped his slender wrist.

The question of culpability would be hard to prove,

May knew, but before he could decide what to do Bryant had shot forward with surprising nimbleness and slapped a handcuff over the pale man's wrist. 'What are you doing?' he cried. 'We don't know—'

'Oh, we know all right,' said Bryant. 'I'm arresting you, doctor.'

'That's the man,' Mr Lombroso said. 'I remember now. He came in last week.'

The pale man in blue trunks seemed to consider his options for only a moment. 'Oh hell,' he said, 'what's the use? Nothing has turned out right for me.'

They led him back to Harry the clothes-minder, where he got dressed with some difficulty.

'He should have lied,' said Bryant. 'He might have got away with it.'

'I couldn't find work after the war,' the doctor admitted. 'You have no idea what it's like, not being able to make a living.' He had no idea how close Bryant had come to following his father on to the streets of the East End and into the black market.

They handed their culprit over to a sergeant on Lower Thames Street. 'Blimey, this is Henry Walters,' said the sergeant. 'Was he after diamond rings again? You never give up, do you, Henry?'

'What did you spot that I missed?' May asked.

'It was what I heard,' said Bryant. 'A doctor with an aversion to silver could only mean one thing. Go on, Henry, turn over your hands.'

Now May saw why the boy had been so reluctant to be led about by his benefactor's hand. Walters's palms were an alarming shade of blue.

'I saw small patches of blue on his back,' said Bryant. 'We have penicillin now but colloidal silver was always used to cure infections. The trouble was that it permanently dyed your skin.'

As they headed back out of the Square Mile, Bryant bought ice creams for them both.

'You're in a better mood,' said May, crunching his wafer with relish.

'Of course,' Bryant replied. 'I felt useful again. It's not such a bad day after all.'

'Shall we go to the bandstand and hear a concert?' May suggested.

'Don't push your luck,' said Bryant, popping the end of his cone into his mouth.

BRYANT & MAY AND THE POSTMAN

'You know the problem with you two?' Janice Longbright, joint Operations Director of the Peculiar Crimes Unit, was studying her duty roster.

'Oh please, do tell,' said Arthur Bryant, lowering his stilton and chutney sandwich for a moment. 'You know I can't resist a sentence that starts like that.'

'You go out on too many investigations by yourselves. You should take a female staff member with you more often.'

'What on earth for? Jackson Pollocks.' Bryant had tried to brush chutney from his waistcoat and made a mess.

'Because you only ever get a male-centric perspective, that's why.' Janice sighed. 'It's like this.' She held up a copy of the *Daily Express*. ' "Pretty blonde Stephanie, twenty-two, says . . ." Imagine writing that about a man. "Well-built Colin" or "petite Dan" – it's a ridiculous attitude to hold in this day and age.'

Bryant dismissed the idea. 'That's just the *Daily Express*. Nobody takes it seriously.'

'People do when they're bombarded with this sort of thing all the time. Women do. We get tired of being judged on our looks.' She could tell her words were falling on deaf ears. 'All right, what do you think when you look at me?'

Bryant chewed ruminatively. 'I think your jacket needs to go up a size. Or the buttons need moving.'

Longbright released a groan of frustration.

'Well, I don't know. You're over-familiar to me, like part of the furniture.'

'I mean do you see me as an officer first or as a woman?'

'I certainly never think of you as a woman. More like an escritoire. You know, sturdy and useful.' He hoped this was reassuring, but Janice didn't look happy. Was there no pleasing her?

'You're hopeless,' she said. 'John, tell him, can't you?'

May tore himself away from his phone. 'What Janice means is that as older males we have entrenched viewpoints, and it would be good to get a female perspective on more cases in order to provide a clearer balance.'

'But we've only got two women out of eight staff,' said Bryant, 'unless you count the cat, and she started out as a boy.'

'I rather think that's the point she's making, old sausage.'

'And there's a glass ceiling,' said Janice, pressing the point with a jab of her biro. 'I'll never be appointed to your position.'

'Well, no, because I've got it,' replied Bryant, becoming confused. 'But you could get higher in the Met. The Chief of Police and the head of the Murder Squad are currently both female.'

'I don't want to be in the Met, do I? I'm in this unit.'

'Fair enough,' Bryant conceded. 'I'll put in a word with Raymond and see if we can't implement some changes.'

'Thank you,' said Longbright.

'Now go and put the kettle on. I'm parched.'

May silently signalled to his partner.

'What?'

May waved his hands, pointing back. Comprehension filled Bryant's eyes.

'Ah. Sorry, Janice. Insensitive. Make one for yourself as well. And bring chocolate digestives.'

Here perhaps we should freeze the frame for a moment and caption the gentleman before us, like an information card on the front of a mummy case:

Detective Inspector Arthur St John Aloysius Montmorency Bryant

Species: Arcanum senex

Age: somewhere between prostate and post-mortem

Previous employment: police headquarters on the Strand, Whitechapel, Bow Street, Savile Row, Mornington Crescent and at the North London Serious Crimes Division

Hobbies: scientific experimentation, arcane literature, part-time tour guide for 'London's Peculiar Walks'

Specialist subjects: London and murder

Favourite pipe: Lorenzo Spitfire

Afflictions: arthritis, selective deafness, Luddism, inability to stay on topic, unembarrassability, sarcasm, theatricality, contrariness, obstinacy, periodic hallucinations triggered by unlicensed medication, the peculiar ability to confuse others.

For the full history of this colourful character we would have to explore at least seventeen volumes of his memoirs, available from all good bookshops. For now, though, let it be noted that every story needs a main protagonist, and this is the only one we have.

The Royal Mail van appeared at the same time every day, 11 a.m., which was largely a waste of time as almost everyone was at work, so instead of parcels and packets being accepted at front doors, everyone got a little slip covered in indecipherable writing, informing them that their mail had been taken to a depot two miles away. It infuriated Bryant, so he took to leaving the deliverer little gifts in return, waiting until he left his van and then posting a similar note through his window stating that while he was out he'd missed an important package that could be collected from number 17, Albion House, Harrison Street, Bloomsbury (3rd floor) after 8 p.m.

As soon as the postal worker realized what Mr Bryant was up to, he took to bringing his mail at a later time when there was somebody home. On such small victories are happy lives built.

One day after the leaving of just such a note, the postman failed to appear at Bryant's door even though his van was clearly parked in the forecourt of the flats, and Bryant began to sense that something was wrong.

When the elderly detective next stepped on to his balcony in his tartan carpet slippers to check that the van was still there, the postman passed him vertically, heading down, and hit the ground with quite a thud. His neck was broken upon impact. He died instantly.

It took Bryant a while to get downstairs because he preferred not to attempt the stairs with his knees, flying postman or no flying postman, and he had to wait for the lift, which had a mind of its own.

The postman's name was Adeel Khan. He was thirty-one

years old and had been born in Karachi. He had trained in IT, but had been forced to change jobs after his company introduced cost-cutting measures. He had been a postal worker for four years, and lived in a council flat in Finsbury Park with his wife and a beautiful three-year-old daughter. It was thought that he slipped and fell over the balcony of the fifth floor, although nobody saw what happened.

'Which is absurd,' railed Bryant when he was back in his office the next day. He snatched off his spectacles to reveal another set of spectacles he'd forgotten he had donned earlier. 'That balcony is nearly three and a half feet high. The floor tiles were bone dry. It hasn't rained in a month and Mr Khan was wearing rubber-soled boots. He had never had a drink in his life. It doesn't seem very likely that he could have fallen over.'

'Then what happened?' asked John May, attempting to untangle his partner's many pairs of glasses and put them into different labelled cases. 'We've not had any witnesses come forward. Maybe he had money worries. Has anyone spoken to the wife yet?'

'Jack Renfield spoke to her,' Janice Longbright confirmed. 'Understandably she's in a terrible state of shock. Giles Kershaw ran a preliminary examination on the body. Massive contusion on the skull, fractured vertebrae, several minor abrasions including a small bruise on the chest. According to his wife Khan left the house yesterday morning at six a.m. in a perfectly good mood, the same as always, kissed his daughter goodbye and said he'd be back at eight thirty p.m.'

'A long day,' said May, handing Bryant the right pairs in the right cases. 'I guess he was used to waiting around in order to deliver your packages. It doesn't sound like a case for us.'

'I thought you'd need some visual ID for him if you were

55

going to conduct interviews,' said Longbright, 'but Mrs Khan had no photographs to give Jack and her husband doesn't have a Facebook profile—'

'Wait, wait – conduct interviews?' said Bryant. 'Where are Colin and Meera?'

'Colin's on holiday in Ibiza and Meera's gone to a wedding. I'm swamped with work so you'll have to do them. It wouldn't kill you.'

It was a warm August afternoon at the Peculiar Crimes Unit and the surrounding streets were becalmed. Most local residents refused to trust the London weather and had headed abroad. This usually indicated a quiet time for the PCU, and the unfortunate death of a postman would have passed beneath their attention but for two facts: it had occurred on the detective's doorstep, and despite his protestations Bryant was incorrigibly curious.

He checked his preliminary notes. 'Mr Khan wasn't born here. Does he have Islamist contacts in his home country?'

'His parents left Pakistan for London when he was two,' said May. 'He's entirely naturalized. The Home Office has nothing on him.'

'You know jihadist insurgents bombed Islamabad airport again two days ago, and all flights are suspended.'

'Pakistani officials are saying Afghan fighters are behind the attack,' said May, 'if you can believe them. I don't think his ethnicity's a factor. Let's start with the idea that somebody here had it in for him. We should go and conduct the door-to-doors. I imagine it's been quite a while since you had to do any.'

'Thirty-six years,' said Bryant. 'It was a warm day like this, August the thirteenth. The last person I interviewed was Mrs Margery Allsop at thirty-nine Kensington Gardens, about a young woman in her care who died of a

massive drug overdose, even though there was no immediate evidence of drugs in her passages. It turned out she
was acting as the "banker" for a drug-selling trio, holding
on to the goods. When the Met turned up, acting on a tip-
off, she swallowed everything in small heat-sealed plastic
bags, but because she had been eating oranges the citric
acid ate through the bags and released their contents into
her system.'

'What a phenomenal memory you have,' said May, not
without sarcasm. 'What's the name of your bank?'

'Er – um. Don't prompt me. I know this.'

'Incredible.' He tapped Bryant on the shoulder. 'Get
your coat on, we're going to meet your neighbours.'

As it was sunny they walked around to Harrison Street.
'Look at this lot, an absolute shower,' said Bryant, waving
his walking stick at passers-by with disapproval. 'Why
can't Londoners learn to dress properly in summer? The
Italians and the Spanish drape themselves in elegant light-
weight suits, not leggings and boob tubes. If you've got
skinny white knees and ankles like a stick insect, why
would you think it's a good idea to wear gigantic shorts?'

'Says the man in the moth-eaten tweed overcoat and
scarf,' said May drily.

'It's bound to rain later. Charles the Second described
the English summer as "three fine days and a thunderstorm". Anyway, I've only got a string vest and a shirt on
under this.'

May stopped on the building's staircase to catch his
breath. 'Aren't you tired? Why didn't we get the lift?'

Bryant pulled a face. 'It smells of curry.'

'You'll have to ask the neighbours to be more mindful.'

'No, it was *my* curry. I dropped a takeaway in it last
night. Here we are, the fifth floor.'

May turned to his partner. 'How do you want to do this?'

'Oh, in twos and threes I think, with a break in between,' said Bryant, ringing the first doorbell.

'So you can write them up as you go?'

'No, dicky bladder. I'm not accepting more than three cups of tea.'

They worked their way swiftly along the fifth and fourth floors, puzzling and upsetting the residents in roughly equal measure. Many were migrants, apprehensive and unaccustomed to impromptu calls. Often three generations were present, including grandmothers in emerald and scarlet sarees who spoke little English, and smart westernized children in Nike shirts. Several of their interviewees were able to recall the postal worker, but nobody knew his name.

'Wasn't it Gounod who said that our homes were no longer in the street because the street was in our homes?' Bryant wondered. 'Ahead of his time, that chap. I didn't think I'd like living in a flat as much as I do. And it's good to finally meet the neighbours.' He had conveniently glossed over the fact that they were conducting a possible murder inquiry.

They spoke to one wild-haired old boy who lived alone, answering their knock in a vest and old-fashioned braces. He had an unshaven chin and a rough cockney accent, and stood just outside his flat with the front door left partly open. Bryant felt as awkward as a dinner guest taking too long to say goodbye, but could not resist peering over the man's shoulder. On a narrow hall table were three white long-stem vases, each containing a perfect purple orchid. Above them was a framed monochrome photograph by Henri Cartier-Bresson, of an Arab man standing half in shadow. Who had this fellow once been: a war photographer, an artist, an engineer, a gardener, a poet? Did he seek a tranquil grace in his life that he could never find at work? Did he take pride in the secret knowledge that his sensitive soul was hidden behind a gruff demeanour? *You can never know people until you see how they live*, Bryant thought.

May looked over at his partner. Bryant appeared to have drifted off into a world of his own, and May remembered why he never took him out on interviews.

'How long does it take to become naturalized, do you think?' May wondered, closing his notebook after the last door shut.

'In my book you're a Londoner the moment you start saying sorry when someone bumps into you,' Bryant replied. 'There's a Romanian girl who started six weeks ago in the Ladykillers Café on Caledonian Road. She couldn't speak a word of English when she arrived. Now she's calling everyone "darlin' ". It's the best way to learn, being chucked into the mix.'

May checked his watch. 'Well, that didn't take long, but we're still four flats missing. Let's do your floor as well.'

'I can tell you now, Alma's out,' Bryant warned. 'She's gone to visit her gnu. She's sponsoring animals for charity at the London Zoo. She made me buy a lottery ticket for a frog last week. Patagonian, near extinction: she's trying to save them. She's always out somewhere trying to save someone or something, hence my issue with the postie.'

'Then let's just visit your neighbour,' said May, ringing a bell.

'Oh, I'd rather you didn't—' Bryant began, but the door

was opened by a heavy-set young man in an Arsenal shirt, holding a can of Camden Hells lager in one meaty fist. The sound of a football match could be heard on his television.

'Don't say it,' he warned Bryant, his thick finger pointed menacingly.

'This is Brad Pitt,' Bryant explained, unable to stop himself. 'He works on a construction site and is absolutely brilliant at swearing. I hear him through the wall whenever his team loses. Do share some of your colourful argot with us, Mr Pitt.'

'My name's Joe,' said Joe, reaching forward and shaking May's hand. 'We had a misunderstanding about my name. I can see now that sarcasm was a mistake.'

'John May,' said May. 'I'm Arthur's—'

'I know who you are. I seen you dropping him off at the flats some nights. Is this a professional call?' Joe took a slug of beer.

'Your postal worker—'

'The one who took a swan dive off the balcony,' said Joe, nodding. 'Yeah, I saw the ambulance cart him off. Which reminds me.' He disappeared for a moment and came back with a large cardboard box. 'I'm not your delivery service, Mr Bryant. I don't know what's in here but it smells off. My dog wouldn't leave it alone.'

'It's probably my tumours,' Bryant explained. 'Diseased ones. I'm helping out a colleague.'

'Perhaps you could make sure he wraps them up a bit better next time.' Joe handed the package over as quickly as he could. 'I knew Adeel. He was a nice bloke. We went bowling together once.'

Bryant raised an eyebrow. 'Crown green?'

'No, ten pin, up Bloomsbury Lanes. He had trouble finding shoes that fit him.'

'I suppose huge plates are a hazard of the job,' Bryant surmised.

'You don't honestly reckon he killed himself?'

'Of course not. We wouldn't be here if we did.' Bryant had dismissed that idea at the outset. 'Do you know if he had any enemies?'

'He was a postie, of course he had enemies.' Joe pulled his gusset straight with a remarkable degree of unselfconsciousness. 'Did you speak to everybody?'

'No,' said May, checking his notebook, 'we're missing numbers twenty-three, twenty-seven and thirty-nine.'

'My missus could tell you who's who but she's up the doc's with our littlest. Twenty-seven's Chinese, they don't talk to nobody. Twenty-three's mad as a coot and *he* don't talk to nobody neither. Social services deliver his meals. Thirty-nine gets a lot of deliveries. She's a right stuck-up cow.'

'You seem to know a lot about what goes on around here,' Bryant commented.

'Yeah well, I have – a few deals going on.' Joe shut up fast, remembering that Bryant was more than just an annoying neighbour.

'What's the problem with thirty-nine?' asked Bryant.

'Her name's Parkhill. Adeel tries to be friendly, right,' Joe replied, 'but she just snatches stuff from him, don't answer or nothing, and shuts the door. She's got a right attitude, rude to everyone. Blimey, I could do your job. Anyway, she's a weirdo.'

'Would you care to elucidate further?'

Joe stuck out his bottom lip and furrowed his brow.

'Could you explain more?' said Bryant.

'Oh, right. She collects all this stuff. Little statues, horrible things. And she has a go at everyone. Goes out the same time every night. You can set your clock by her.'

'That doesn't exactly make her weird,' said May.

'Come back in an hour,' Joe told them. 'She should be back from work by then. You'll see.'

Amy Parkhill opened the door a crack and peered at them without speaking. She was tall, pale and overweight, so full of face that her features might have been tentatively sketched on. Her red hair was scraped back from her forehead and tightly tied. She was dressed in black suit trousers and a blue gingham top. Bryant could see a telescopic aluminium stick set against the wall. He had spotted more of these around lately, used as a walking aid by surprisingly young people.

'I wonder if we could have a word with you?' asked May, showing his PCU card. 'It's about the death of a postal worker who was delivering to these flats.'

'Yes, I heard about it.' She affected disinterest.

'So you met Mr Khan?'

'He rings when he has packages for me.'

'Did you know his name or ever talk to him?'

'No, I just signed his book.'

'How did he seem to you?'

She did not bother to consider the question. 'I have really no idea. He was the postman, not a personal friend.'

'Did he have anything for you yesterday?'

'Yes, a package.'

'You spoke to him?'

'Only "Good morning".'

'The package he brought you yesterday—'

'What about it?'

'What was in it?' Bryant persisted.

'I hardly see that it's any business of yours.'

'I'm a policeman, Miss Parkhill, everything is my business.'

'Mrs. I'm divorced.'

'It's just that a neighbour tells me you receive quite a few deliveries.'

'Which neighbour?' Her tone had grown icier.

'That's irrelevant.'

'Is it a crime now, to order items by post, or am I free to purchase what I choose? I was under the impression that this was still a free country.'

'You're entitled to believe what you like. I find your attitude very aggressive,' said Bryant, trying to remember what Longbright had told him about locating a female perspective and failing miserably.

'I am a private person. I have the right to protect my privacy,' Parkhill snapped.

'I wonder,' said Bryant, looking uncomfortable, 'could I possibly use your loo? My last cup of tea's gone right through me and it's a fair walk back to the unit.'

May was left with Parkhill while his partner used the bathroom. 'Is he your father?' she asked, glancing along the hall.

'So, what did you learn by using your female perspective?' asked May as they headed down the stairs and walked away from Albion House.

Bryant thought for a moment. 'You shouldn't wear gingham if you're portly,' he decided.

'I don't think that's quite what Janice meant. Parkhill wanted to know if you were my father.' May was unable to suppress his laughter.

Bryant was incensed. 'Bloody cheek! You're only three years younger than me. You've had an easier life, that's all. I didn't say she was fat, did I? And when I say fat, I mean enormous.'

'She judged your age by your appearance. Do you take Janice's point now?'

'I take her point but I'm struggling with it. Human beings are naturally judgemental.'

'As police officers it's our job to counteract that,' said May.

'But I joined the force in order to be as judgemental as possible,' said Bryant indignantly. 'It's what attracted me most in the first place.'

It sometimes took May a minute or two to realize that his partner was joking.

'We still don't know exactly where he fell from, do we?' said Bryant. 'No scuff marks on the floors of any of the terraces.'

'We know where he'd got to in his deliveries,' May pointed out. 'He'd just reached Parkhill's door. She'd signed his book. His next stop would have been number forty-one, Mr Davies, two letters. Then he'd finished the block.'

'Odd.' Bryant's face scrunched up.

'What?'

'Postal workers usually start at the top and work down, not the other way around. He began at the bottom and had to take the lift down when he'd finished.'

'I don't see how that can have any significance.'

'Don't you?'

'What's that supposed to mean?'

'It's suggestive, that's all. I'd like to know how soon he changed his routine after he'd taken on the Albion House route.'

May held his partner back on the kerb as a lorry passed. 'I don't see what that's going to tell us. We should be finding out who he hung around with when he wasn't with his wife and daughter.'

'That's just it, John. He didn't. He worked, he went home, he saw his parents and grandparents. Oh, and he went bowling once with Mr Pitt. So either he was secretly miserable and decided to end it all on the spur of the moment, or somebody did it for him.' They leaned forward and studied the traffic before crossing the road, like children observing the Green Cross Code.

'What are we missing?' continued Bryant. 'Was he having an affair with one of the women to whom he delivered packages? Gail Sampson at number nine, she was very pretty. Maybe her partner found out and confronted him.'

May shrugged. 'Khan was happily married.'

'Was he? Jack couldn't tell from meeting the wife. Maybe Janice is right. A woman might spot something we've missed. But I have an idea. We'll have to go to Khan's depot.'

They caught a bus to Almeida Street, Islington, and were taken into the crowded duty room, where Khan's colleagues expressed sadness and incomprehension at the death of their colleague.

'He was just a decent sort of bloke, really open and genuine,' said one of the Post Office managers, unlocking a screen on a battered computer. 'We have to run very careful background checks on who we employ, but his came up spotless. Here's his delivery roster for the last three months. It'll tell you the size, type and date of delivery but not what was in any of the packages. Obviously security's a lot higher these days, given the present threat of terrorism, especially in this area, so everything is screened, but parcels from trusted sources are fast-tracked.'

'Have you had any suspect packages in the last year?' May asked.

'No, none that turned out to pose any real threat,' said the manager. 'The usual morons posting drugs to each other, thinking we won't notify you lot. I'll leave you to go through this.'

Working from a single postcode simplified the task, but it still took them several hours. After a while Bryant snatched off his spectacles and rubbed his eyes. 'How do people work at these things all day long? I'm half blind.'

'Yes, but you *are* half blind,' said May. 'I thought you were going to get your cataracts done.'

'The NHS said they won't sort them out until it looks like I'm viewing Victorian postcards. Amy Parkhill received thirteen packages in just over three months, all the same size and shape.'

'Didn't your neighbour say something about her being a collector?' said May. 'I guess she doesn't trawl junk shops.' He read over his partner's shoulder. 'Ten-inch square boxes, one delivered every Thursday.'

'I took a shufti around when I used her loo, and the odd thing was, I didn't see any figurines,' Bryant said. 'Mr Pitt reckoned they were china statues.'

'Perhaps you'd like to go and antagonize her again when you get home.'

'Good idea,' Bryant agreed. 'It's got to be her, but I can't for the life of me see why.'

Amy Parkhill was not pleased to receive a second visit from her neighbour. 'You're back,' she observed, somewhat redundantly. 'Do you need to use my lavatory again?'

'Thank you, I'm not incontinent,' said Bryant, nettled. 'I wanted to ask you about the packages the postman delivered to you every week.'

She gave an annoyed sigh. 'I collect china figures.'

'Ornaments are meant to be put on display, aren't they? I didn't see any left out.'

'They're not ornaments,' she replied, folding her arms against his questions. 'They are collectables.'

'What kind of collectables?'

'If you must know, they're dogs. So when you went to the bathroom you snooped around my flat.'

'I'm naturally suspicious,' Bryant admitted. 'It's a prerequisite of the job. Are you buying them for someone in your family – a niece perhaps?'

'I can tell you where I bought them, if that will satisfy you.'

'We already know that. They came from the Fenton Crafts Online Gift Store. So where are they?'

'That's absolutely none of your business,' she told him, closing the door in his face.

The next morning, Bryant arrived at the unit to be greeted by the two Daves, the Turkish workmen who had come to fit a toilet three years ago and stayed on.

'Mr Bryant, I wonder if we could have a word with you?' asked the Dave with the more luxuriant moustache. 'It's about your dead postman.'

'Has this been reported somewhere?' asked Bryant, amazed. 'Or have you been listening in on our investigation reports again? You do know you're here to fix the electrics and make sure nobody else falls through the floor, don't you?'

'It's just that Dave here' – he indicated the other Dave, who seemed incapable of speaking for himself – 'his ex-sister-in-law's auntie lives down the road from you and she says another one died. A lady postman.'

'We call them postal workers because it's sexist to say lady postman,' Bryant explained proudly.

'Why?'

'I don't know – Janice told me. I think it's about assuming that postal workers are automatically male.'

'Oh, right,' said Dave. 'I'd better make a note of that.'

'Anyway, what about her?'

'She fell off a balcony as well.'

Bryant's patience was ebbing. 'When was this?'

'About eighteen months ago.'

'Why has nobody told me about this? In Harrison Street?'

'No, in Tenerife. She was pissed.'

'What on earth has that got to do with anything?'

'I dunno. We thought you should know.'

'Do I tell you how to repair a ballcock?' Bryant rolled his eyes and made his way to his office, where his partner was waiting for him.

'This just came in,' May said, handing over a page. 'Amy Parkhill has a history of antagonizing her former neighbours. She's narrowly avoided jail a couple of times, once for nuisance calls, once for trying to poison a cat. Of course that doesn't make her a murderer. What I don't understand is why a bad-tempered woman like her would collect cute animal figurines. You met her. What did you think?'

Bryant donned his trifocals and scanned the page. 'Venison.'

'What do you mean?'

'Tough and unpleasant.' His phone rang, making them both jump, as the ringtone was a woman shrieking a high note from *Iolanthe*. Bryant gingerly put it to his ear. A familiar voice boomed out.

'Mr Bryant, is that you? It's Joe. Mr Pitt. Hang on. Oi, Michelle, turn that down a sec. Sorry, you still there? I got your message about was there anything I'd forgotten.'

Bryant turned off the speaker setting and listened. While

he was doing so, Janice entered with further information. 'Here's the full list of purchased products from the manager of Fenton Crafts,' she said. 'She says you can see them all online. They only make china dogs.'

May examined the list of figurines Amy Parkhill had ordered. 'Odd,' he said. 'They're all the same batch number, all the same breed of dog, the British Bulldog, all the same figures.'

Bryant hung up. 'That was my neighbour,' he said. 'He was talking with his wife and she remembered something rather important. It might explain why I didn't find the contents of Parkhill's packages in the flat. She breaks them in half and throws them away.'

'How do you know?'

'Mrs Pitt went out on to the balcony for a smoke one night and saw her neighbour in the kitchen. She had one of the bulldogs on the counter and was cracking it open with a hammer. They're hollow. Then she swept it into the bin. And here's the interesting part. This was over a month ago.'

'Why is that interesting?' May asked.

Bryant shook his head impatiently, as if the answer was obvious. 'She continued ordering them, didn't she? So she smashes them and orders more?'

'Wait.' May checked the page on his desk. 'This has today's date. She just cancelled her standing order for the bulldogs.'

'There you are,' said Bryant. 'She was looking for something inside them and Adeel Khan had figured out what it was. We go back there.'

The third visit was the least comfortable yet. Amy Parkhill was by now extremely agitated. 'What I choose to do with items that belong to me is no business of yours,' she said. 'If I want to blast them to smithereens with a shotgun it is entirely within my rights to do so.'

'Only if you have a permit for the gun, and not in a built-up area,' said Bryant argumentatively.

'I work for Camden Council, and I will raise the matter of the police abusing their powers at the very next meeting.'

May had had enough of this. 'Why did you break them open?' he asked. 'What were you looking for? Did Adeel Khan challenge you about it? You talked to him, didn't you? You got angry with him, frightened that he would turn you in. You pushed him over the balcony.'

'Get away from this flat before I call—'

'The police?' asked May, trying to restore his temper. 'We're already here and we're on to you, Mrs Parkhill.'

'Well, I thought you went a little over the top there,' said Bryant later that evening, when they were back in their office at the PCU.

'I don't like being taken for a fool,' said May. 'I'm surprised you didn't do something.'

'Oh, I did,' said Bryant, reaching under his desk. 'After you stormed off I got my neighbour to knock on her door and ask to borrow a pair of scissors.'

'Why scissors?'

'It was the only thing I could think of that everyone's bound to have. While she went to get them, I got him to steal this.' He laid Parkhill's aluminium walking stick on the desk. It had been carefully wrapped in plastic.

'A totally illegal thing to do, but we'll let that pass,' said May, taking a good look at it. 'Am I missing something?'

'No, we were,' said Bryant. 'It's got Adeel's fingerprints on the lower end.'

'Arthur, I must be tired – I don't know what's going through your brain.'

'You'll see,' said Bryant with a grin. He took off his shoe, reached behind him and knocked on the wall with it. Janice Longbright came in. 'Janice, would you explain to my colleague what happened to Adeel?'

'Mr Khan was backing away from her when she picked up the stick,' Janice explained. 'It was kept beside the front door. It wasn't a premeditated act. She has a temper. We know that from her past problems with the police. She lashed out at him and didn't know her own strength. The small bruise on his chest was made by the end of the stick. He raised his hands like so, clasping the stick.' She demonstrated. 'But he couldn't get any traction. She's a strong woman. He was tall but thin. He was pushed backwards, lost his balance and went straight over. She went back inside, closed the door. End of story.'

'You're sure about this?' asked May. 'Then what am I missing?'

'The female perspective,' said Longbright. 'Amy Parkhill wasn't interested in the figurines. They were simply the first thing she thought of buying that wouldn't fit through the letter box. She smashed them up and threw them away because they weren't what she wanted.'

'Then what did she want?'

'Him. She wanted Adeel Khan to call on her as often as possible.'

'You can't know that,' said May, unconvinced. 'What makes you so sure?'

'Remember I told you that Khan didn't have a Facebook page?' said Longbright. 'He had one once, but had to take it down. Too much trouble with stalkers. Even the newspapers had picked up on the story. I hadn't seen any photographs of him at all.'

'So?'

'Neither of you noticed, but every one of his female Facebook followers did. He was absolutely bloody gorgeous, like an Asian Kit Harington.' Longbright slid a tabloid article across the desk at them. It was headed, '*You've got male! Secrets of London's sexiest postie!*' 'Next time,' she said, 'try taking the female perspective a little further.'

BRYANT & MAY AND
THE DEVIL'S TRIANGLE

'Do you think there are such things as spiritually bad places?' Arthur Bryant raised his head from a dog-eared copy of Stanley's *Through the Dark Continent* and asked the question out of the blue.

'Yes, I suppose so,' John May replied. 'The Big Brother house. Ten Downing Street. Anywhere Kim Kardashian's been. Why?'

'I'm reading about how the Belgians ruined the Congo. It seems as if everything that's happened there since has been tainted by King Leopold's reign of terror. Of course, the Congo was a perfect target: it had unclaimed land, precious minerals, no central government. Whereas Britannia Street has a bike shop, a tattoo parlour and some scruffy rented flats.'

May looked as if he was getting a headache. 'Once again, Arthur, your mind has jumped off the tracks without taking me along. What are you talking about?'

Bryant set the book aside and opened the Ordnance

Survey map he kept on his desk. Removing a biro from behind his ear, he pointed to a road junction. 'You know where Britannia Street meets King's Cross Road?'

'Vaguely.'

'It's just down the road from here. A black spot. It doesn't have one of those signs saying "Accident Black Spot" but it's one nevertheless.'

'Well, there's a lot of traffic whipping around that one-way system.'

'It's not just traffic – it's crime. This part here, the north-west corner' – he tapped his pen on the map – 'has a much higher incidence of criminal activity than anywhere else in the neighbourhood.'

'Just that corner? Are you sure?' May was intrigued, and came around the desk to study the road layout. 'Who lives there?'

'That's the odd thing. There are no problem families, no illegal residents, but the local cop shop has been clocking up incidents there at a rate of one a week since the start of July and it's now' – he looked at his watch – 'September.'

'What kind of incidents?' asked May.

'I'm glad you've asked me that because I've broken them down into groups,' said Bryant.

'Bored, are you?'

'It's been quieter than usual, I'll admit, but look at this, all on one corner.' He pulled out a roll of paper and held it flat with an ashtray and a box of fruit gums. 'Janice noticed it first and printed it out for me. Four burglaries, two fatal car accidents, one lorry mounting the kerb and seriously injuring a pedestrian, a suicide attempt, two cases of arson, one lady killed under a bus and now a violent assault.'

May thought for a moment. 'That's a heavily trafficked area. It's coincidence. What else could it be?'

'That's what I intend to find out,' Bryant said, rising and slipping his arm into his coat sleeve. 'The latest incident took place just over an hour ago. I thought I'd go and take a look.'

May didn't need to be invited along. The pair left the Peculiar Crimes Unit and headed in a south-easterly direction towards Britannia Street. It was a pleasantly sunny morning, which always put Bryant in a good mood because it meant his knees didn't ache.

'What makes you think you're going to find something?' May asked as they crossed the traffic-clogged one-way system.

'Wouldn't you hate to miss out if I do?' Bryant replied, peering at his partner with eyes like the sun on the sea.

The conjunction of roads below King's Cross had a careless, random quality that rendered it virtually invisible. London was now a patchwork of pockets, an elegant Edwardian building here, a forgotten Victorian garden there, stitched together with nondescript thoroughfares and cheaply constructed modern blocks. Although Britannia Street was surrounded by more interesting places – verdant Bloomsbury to the west, the restored customs houses of Granary Square to the north and the oddly elevated Percy Circus to the east – its junction with King's Cross Road was nothing more than a connection point.

The morning sky was clear and bright, a cue for Bryant to wrap himself in so many layers that he looked like the Michelin Man. In the gap between the top of his striped scarf and the brim of his homburg all that could be seen were the tip of his nose and his milk-bottle-thick glasses.

When he needed to look around he had to turn his entire body to do so. 'Over there,' he said, pointing.

May saw a blackened patch of concrete around ten yards long, and at the end some twisted pieces of metal bolted into the concrete: the remains of a railing.

'Somebody torched it,' Bryant explained. 'It was full of motorbikes at the time. One of the petrol tanks caught fire and the whole lot went up. They had to evacuate the building behind it. To date, no one's been charged. On the opposite kerb two people died from collision injuries and a woman shoved her fist through a plate-glass door, slashing her wrist. Thefts, burglaries, assaults – a dog even attacked its owner, putting her in the hospital, all on the same corner. And now this.' He pushed open the door of the tattoo parlour and ventured into the gothic interior. Black velvet swathed the walls and flickering candelabra provided pinpoints of wavering illumination. On the back wall was a purple neon sign: 'Damnation Tattoos'.

'Good heavens, you don't tattoo people under this kind of lighting, do you?' Bryant asked of Alix, the receptionist, a pale, spiderwebbed girl with mauve ropes arranged on her partially shaved head.

'No, this is the consultation zone,' she said in a surprisingly refined voice. 'The surgery is upstairs at the front. Do you have an appointment?'

'I once considered having something on my right bicep but I couldn't make up my mind between Sir Robert Peel and Diana Dors,' Bryant admitted.

'Oh.' In confusion she turned to Bryant's partner. 'Then have you come about Henry Carrell?'

'I don't know,' said May. 'Have we?'

'That's the fellow. What happened, exactly?' asked Bryant, following Alix up the stairs.

'He's only been with us a month,' Alix explained. 'He came highly recommended. His design portfolio was amazing. I haven't moved anything.' She showed them into a room very different to the one downstairs, white-walled and clinically clean, with mirrors and a white-tiled workbench. But where the tattooist's instruments should have been neatly aligned beside a stainless-steel autoclave, they were spread across the floor in a thin trail of blood.

'Henry's client had already approved his design and signed our contract.' Alix remained at the edge of the room. 'It was her second session with him. He had already drawn the outline of the image—'

'Which was what?' asked Bryant.

'A leopard,' said Alix. 'It was a complex piece with a lot of shading. To make a tattoo permanent, the ink has to get into the dermis. The needle Henry was using has eighteen heads. Each type of needle has a different effect.'

'I've always wondered how these things work,' said Bryant, about to bend down and pick up the corded tattooing instrument.

'You'd better not touch it, Arthur,' warned May. 'Perhaps we should get Dan in to take a look.'

'I don't think that will be necessary,' said Bryant. 'There wasn't anyone else here, was there?'

'No, just Henry and the client, and I was downstairs. I heard a thud and thought something was wrong. Then the client started screaming. She tried to take her arm away while he was tattooing, but it was clamped in place.'

'Who was she?' asked May.

'A young woman who already had a couple of designs on her back.'

'So she knew what to expect,' said May.

'She screamed, and he just kind of went crazy, threw his

needles about, thrashed around, hit her in the face, then collapsed. She was taken to University College Hospital with a damaged right forearm – the needle had badly torn her skin – and he's being treated there right now.'

'You came up here when the commotion started, is that right?'

'Yes. She was clutching her arm and he was rolling on the floor over there. The tattooing instrument was pulled out of the wall.'

'Was anything else out of place or different to how it usually was?'

'Not that I can recall,' Alix told them, looking about the room. 'Wait, that was shut.' She pointed to where the window over the street stood wide open.

'Well, what next?' asked May as they left the tattoo parlour.

'I'm going there,' said Bryant, raising a great woolly arm at the Subway sandwich shop across the road.

'Good Lord, you're not going to eat one of those things, are you?'

'No, of course not,' Bryant replied, pulling a face at the thought. 'I want to ask them some questions. Can you go to UCH and check on Henry Carrell and his client? I'll meet you back at the unit.'

The serving girl in Subway examined Bryant's PCU ID card and removed her blue plastic gloves before coming around to his side of the counter. 'I was here when the bikes blew up,' she told him. 'The heat cracked our window. It had to be replaced. People could have been killed. Luckily we were quiet.'

'Did you see anyone nearby?' Bryant asked.

'The police asked me that. They had a theory that

someone was upset with the motorbike shop – most of the bikes belonged to them – but I don't know if they ever caught anyone. Some bikers drove past shortly before it happened but apart from that the street was just . . . normal, you know? It was about eleven in the morning. We had to close up, because of the damaged window and the police cordon. Lately it seems there are always funny things happening around here.'

Bryant stood at the junction with his hands in his voluminous pockets, watching the traffic and the passers-by. King's Cross Road had a rather colourful mix of shops: a fetish rubberwear outfitters, a hipster cocktail bar, a place that sent money orders to Africa and unlocked mobile phones, a student building clad in buckled steel panels that looked like a very bad architect's attempt to copy the Bilbao Guggenheim on a budget. Ahead lay the great concourse of King's Cross Station. Behind him the road wound to Mount Pleasant, then dropped through Clerkenwell to Farringdon and the river. There was no reason he could think of that would make this neglected little corner of London more dangerous than anywhere else, but he could not shake the idea that some unusual force was at work.

To decide the matter he made a phone call.

Maggie Armitage, Grand Order Grade IV White Witch in the Coven of St James the Elder, Kentish Town, said she could be there in ten minutes, as she was just up the road at Euston trying to buy two hundred feet of fishing line and a handbell. Maggie always appeared *en fête*, brightly clothed in primary colours, layered with enough trailing chiffon and silk to stall an escalator. She had dyed her hair cinnamon and pinned a badge-covered bobble hat on the back.

'Isn't that a rather old-fashioned method of registering a ghostly presence?' asked Bryant as they greeted each other and headed into a coffee shop.

'You can do it with lasers now,' Maggie agreed, 'but Dame Maude tried that and nearly took her eye out, so we're taking the old-fashioned route. Two coffees, please.'

'What kind?' asked the barista, not unkindly. There were forty varieties listed on his blackboard, the most complex being a free-trade organic half-whole milk split-quad decaf soy-whip vanilla cinnamon great white with sugar-free syrup.

'The one made with beans.' Bryant turned his attention back to Maggie. 'Why are you still holding séances anyway?' he wondered.

'Easy money, darling,' said Maggie in a rare moment of sanguinity. 'There are still plenty of haunted people out there looking for reassurance. You could say we're deceiving them but I think of it as cheap therapy. Why are we standing on Witches' Cross?'

Bryant looked around in puzzlement. 'What, here? This has an actual name?'

'That's what it used to be called in the late eighteenth century. On the two opposing corners lived two witches, there and there, where the Subway shop and the tattoo parlour are now. Of course, it was all residential around here, and very poor. The old houses have been knocked down and replaced.'

Both properties had been remodelled extensively and unsympathetically above their ground floors. At the junction's four corners, two buildings had been recently rebuilt in their entirety.

'When you say witches . . .' Bryant began.

'You know the two witch mothers of Camden Town, "Red Cap" and "Black Cap"?'

'Of course,' said Bryant. For centuries two public houses had commemorated the Camden witches. The first had changed its name in the 1980s, and the second had only just been closed down.

'Then you'll know they weren't actual witches. Every neighbourhood once had a matriarchal figure who offered marital and sexual advice to the young women in her street. Some people – husbands, mostly – took against them and accused them of witchcraft. It was the same on this corner. Mother Merlin and Mother Green supposedly lived opposite each other. When they were driven out they cursed the site and it became known as Witches' Cross, a black spot where terrible things would always happen.'

'Fine,' said Bryant, 'but there's a difference between folklore and fact.'

Maggie regarded her coffee with suspicion. 'Not in my book.'

'With all due respect, Maggie, you believe your fridge stopped working because you upset it. In the real world, a pedestrian walking under a bus can't be the fault of ghostly manifestations.'

'Excuse me, but you were just charged six pounds sixty for two coffees purely on the basis of their folkloric origin,' she said, indicating the board. 'And you believe in psychogeography, Arthur, I know you do.'

'Yes, but only because of historical factors. Certain sites have always been associated with public assembly. Others are endemically poor.' They seated themselves at a table in the window.

'Oh, absolutely,' Maggie agreed. 'The buildings themselves have architecturally symbolic designs. Squares suggest masculine power, circles represent calmness and femininity, and triangles encourage energy and stimulation. It's why demonstrations and protests occur in squares, people pass fluidly through circles and become restless in triangles.'

Bryant dug a paper bag from his pocket. 'Do you want a Jelly Baby?'

Maggie accepted a yellow one and bit off its head. 'They used to be known as "unclaimed babies" in the nineteenth century,' she said, chewing ruminatively. 'I presume you're wandering around here because a crime has been committed.'

'Possibly. Possibly not.'

This was the kind of conversation Bryant and his old friend had been having for decades, conducted in reverse and sidetracked by irrelevant anecdotes.

'Attack by tattoo needle, over there,' said Bryant. 'Fellow went bonkers; he and his client are both in UCH. The latest in a series of misfortunes that have befallen people at this exact location.'

'How exact?'

'I'd say to within a hundred feet. I don't think it's a witch's curse, though. There was even a dog. Usually placid, suddenly decided to bite its owner.'

'What breed?'

'Welsh, I think.'

'I meant the dog.'

'Oh. Something big with a lot of teeth. I'm thinking telephones.'

'I'm sorry?'

'Up there.' Bryant pointed to a rooftop with his paper bag. 'Phone mast. You know, high-frequency electronic signals. Dogs have a different audio bandwidth, don't they?'

They looked up at the tilted grey slate roofs and the rows of defunct orange chimneypots. There among them stood a sinister steel sentinel, a bundle of ribbed phone masts pointing in all four directions above the crossroads.

'She's been bandaged up and sent home; he's still out cold,' said May, hanging up his jacket. The morning sunshine showed the detectives' office at its worst; dust lay thick across Bryant's collection of rare, abstruse and mouldering books. Spores floated in the sunlight. 'How did you get on?'

'Maggie made as much sense as a cat in a bin,' said Bryant, 'so as there are too many incidents for you and I to handle by ourselves, I've asked everyone else to help.'

'Raymond won't like that,' May warned. 'He wants us to clear our backlog. Something to do with end-of-month targets.'

'I don't know why he stays on here.' Bryant went to the mantelpiece and knocked his pipe out on the beak of a stuffed owl. 'He'd be much happier with a nice little job in a local council, launching endless unworkable health and safety initiatives.'

'You do realize you're not going to find a connection between cases of arson, assault, road rage and a dog attack?' May was amused but sympathetic. Stranger things had made their way into the PCU's case files.

Bryant's azure eye held the gleam of determination. 'Care for a small wager?'

'Not money, I'm broke this month.'

'Heavens, nothing so vulgar.' Bryant rolled his eyes. 'If I find a common culprit, you can buy me a book I've wanted for a little while. If I fail, I'll treat you to dinner at the restaurant of your choice.'

'Fair enough,' May agreed, 'but let's set a time limit on it.' May checked his old Timex. 'It's coming up for noon, so how about twenty-four hours from now?'

'Deal.' They shook hands and May found he had jelly-baby sugar all over his fingers.

Meera Mangeshkar drummed her bitten nails on the counter of the Harley Boys motorcycle centre. She had been waiting in the bike shop for a while now. As the manager wandered past, still ignoring her, she thrust her hand in front of his face. 'Oi, you've got a customer.'

'Yeah – well, I'm a bit busy right now, my love.' According to the stitched lettering on his blue overalls, his name was Gary.

Meera had brought her Kawasaki here to be serviced in the past, only using the place under sufferance because of its proximity to the unit. 'I'm not your love,' she said, 'I'm a police officer. It's a bit sexist, calling this place "Harley Boys".'

'What do you want me to call it – "Girl on a Motorcycle"?'

'It'd be a start. You've been upsetting the customers again, I hear.'

'What you talkin' about?' Gary grabbed a paper towel and smeared oil from a doughy cheek.

'I heard somebody set fire to your bikes,' said Meera.

'Blimey, you're a bit out of date. That was two months ago.'

'Know who it was?'

'I've got a good idea. Your lot never caught him, though.'

'It wasn't my lot. Tell me instead.'

Gary threw the towel into a bin and came to the counter. 'Some geezer wanted a full service on a KTM 390 Duke. Didn't like the way it handled after he got it back so he chucked a paving stone through the window. Two days later he firebombed the bikes we had chained up outside. We lost the lot.'

'If you know who it was, why wasn't he arrested?' asked Meera. The case file was still open.

Gary evaded the question. 'I'm sure it was him.'

'The police didn't agree with you, did they?'

His swagger kept its edge. 'My neighbour says she saw him, but he told the police he was in Cornwall, and could prove it.'

'They must have checked out his story.'

'Eliminated him from their inquiries, that's what they said. He'd bought petrol in Exeter around the time it happened. But I *know*,' he said with the conviction of someone voting without quite knowing why. 'We all know it was him.'

Colin Bimsley was at Easton House, a 1950s council block in Finsbury, meeting with Shazeen Mirial, a middle-aged woman in a blue silk hijab. It took Colin a few moments to realize that she was blind.

'Mrs Foster was very kind to me,' she explained. 'She collected me from the RNIB every other Friday afternoon.'

The Royal National Institute for the Blind was situated in nearby Bloomsbury. The roads around it were busy day and night, so many of its visitors were collected by friends. 'We usually went to the Ladykillers Café for tea afterwards,' Shazeen explained. 'Mrs Foster was always waiting for me. She was so reliable. I finished with my doctor and it was a lovely afternoon, so we decided to go to a different café with outside tables, where I could feel the sun on my face. We got to the end of Britannia Street and – I don't know what happened.' She lowered her head at the memory. 'She should have stopped but she carried on, right into the busy road. I called out to her. I could feel the kerb and hear the bus coming, but she was a bit deaf and didn't answer me. She went under the bus and was killed instantly.' She wiped her eyes. 'So awful. So unlike her.'

The full PCU team gathered in the new operations room with the exception of Raymond Land, who was in his office reading *Caravan Monthly*, and the two Daves, who were in the basement doing something illegal with a universal flush valve.

Arthur Bryant stood before them with his tea mug and a bourbon. 'Thirteen separate incidents in just a few weeks,' he said. 'Do we have any common causal factors at all?'

'All the incidents took place between eleven a.m. and three thirty p.m.,' said Dan Banbury, checking his notes.

'So, daylight attacks. Any organized crime in the area?'

'Quite a lot,' Janice Longbright replied. 'Two big male gangs, both Asian teens, one female gang, mixed-race, all associated with the two council blocks behind Britannia Street.'

'Why's that, do you think?' asked Colin.

'Purely sociological,' said Longbright. 'The flats were built to house young Asian couples back in the early nineties. The idea was that they'd start families and move out to larger properties, but they got caught in the economic downturn and couldn't move. Their kids grew into teenagers, living in flats that were never designed to house four, five or six people, so they ended up hanging out in the communal areas to stop themselves from getting into arguments with their parents, and, as we all know, that leads to territorial disputes.'

'Their wars are purely internecine, yes?' asked May.

'Looks like it,' Colin replied.

'So we rule them out. What else?'

'The number of burglaries isn't any higher than the city average,' said Longbright, 'but there have been a lot of street thefts lately, maybe four times that of the surrounding area, mostly mobiles taken by kids on bikes, but also quite a few lifted wallets. There haven't been any arrests yet. The kids get rid of phones too quickly, but the Mount Pleasant police are on to it.'

'Anyone else?'

'Mr Bryant, why should they be connected at all?' asked Colin, raising a hand.

'Because of this,' said Bryant, unfurling a sheet of graph paper and pinning it to the old school blackboard he had rescued from a rubbish dump. (He had binned the expensive whiteboard Raymond Land had purchased because he couldn't stick drawing pins in it.)

His staff stared at the mishmash of coloured lines in mystification. 'What are we looking at, Mr B.?' asked Banbury.

'These are all of the unusual incidents that have been reported,' Bryant explained. 'Bear in mind there may be others we don't know about. This spike here' – he tapped the blackboard with a pencil – 'shows when and where the highest number of incidents occur, and it's quite specific: just after one p.m. on a weekday. But there are significant gaps. Look, nothing on certain weeks, here, here and here.'

'Yeah, but there's probably a simple reason for that,' said Colin.

'Pray enlighten us, Mr Bimsley.'

'There are a lot more office workers in this area than residents. Look at all the sandwich bars. They come out on the street at lunch hour. And maybe the gaps correspond to school holidays, when they take time off to be with their kids.'

'An intriguing answer, but then why don't attacks rise during the evening rush hour in winter, when it's dark earlier?'

'You're right, it makes no sense,' said May. 'The RNIB is just up the road and yet none of the victims are blind. Surely a blind person is easier to rob than a sighted one? The woman who went under the bus was sighted, and her blind companion stopped on the kerb.'

'As I'm sure you know,' said Bryant, 'chaos theory is about the butterfly effect. It's the branch of mathematics that deals with complex systems whose behaviour is sensitive to small changes in conditions, so that something seemingly innocuous can have surprising consequences.'

'Bryant, can I have a word with you?' Raymond Land had been standing in the doorway and had, he decided, heard quite enough. 'Would you kindly stop filling my employees' heads with all this conspiracy-theory claptrap?'

'They're quite capable of thinking for themselves, Raymondo,' said Bryant cheerily. 'I'm not *infecting* them. These ideas were around five hundred years before Christ. Thales of Miletus theorized about why changes occur in things. Zeno elucidated the nature of paradox. Empedocles rejected the presence of a void. Socrates—'

'I don't care what a bunch of Italians got up to before telly was invented, I want you to stick to the bloody facts. There's no connection between these crimes. London's a crowded place and there are some sketchy geezers about.'

'Is that it? The sum total of your understanding about the nature of causality in modern society? *Some sketchy geezers?* What about usually dependable people stepping under buses? Slashing their wrists on broken glass?'

'Accidents,' said Land dismissively. 'How many people use Oyster cards on the London Underground? If they all turned up in King's Cross Station at eight fifteen on a Monday morning there'd be chaos, except that the law of averages prevents it from happening. OK, sometimes the station has to close because of overcrowding and then you get a spike in the graph, but there's nothing woo-woo about it.' He waved his hand at the street beyond the window. 'What we have out there is managed chaos. It's the best we can ever hope for.'

'Hoping's not good enough,' said Bryant. 'I want to do something about it. Isn't that what we're here for, to try and make a difference?'

'We're here to keep our jobs by shifting investigations off the books as fast as possible,' Land replied. 'You've got nothing, Bryant, so close it down. This is not an official investigation, do you understand? The Met's bringing an important case in tonight and I want the decks clear.'

Bryant and May were back at the junction of King's Cross Road and Britannia Street. The traffic in London now moved more slowly than a Victorian horse and cart, despite the cash-raising congestion charge that had been imposed on drivers. It wasn't a corner that pedestrians lingered on. There was nothing attractive to be seen, and the warm late-summer air was filled with exhaust fumes.

'There's a common cause, I'm sure of it,' said Bryant, breathing through his scarf. 'Statistics don't just jump like this for no reason. Someone living here knows something. They must have seen something.'

'I don't know, Arthur. You hardly ever see the same people twice around here. It's a transitory area.' May looked up at the bare, blank windows of the newly built first and second floors. 'I'm not saying there isn't a link, just that it's perhaps not as exotic as you'd like to imagine it is. I've been reading up on psychogeography too. There are usually physical reasons why neighbourhoods retain certain characteristics. Hedgerows are replaced by paths and roads are filled in with houses, and if they're in low-lying areas water gets in and damp rooms cause infant mortality, and the memories of dead babies give rise to the creation of ghost stories.'

'My goodness, you've been paying attention to me after all,' said Bryant, astonished. 'I would never have guessed.'

May gave a shrug. 'I suppose if you hang around with a Flat-Earther for long enough you start thinking the horizon's wrong.'

'I'm not sure I care for your analogy. But the problem here is an odd one, isn't it, because Britannia Street is at the top of a hill – a low-gradient one, but a hill nevertheless.'

'There's no mythology you can hang on this that will explain a string of unrelated incidents, Arthur. Perhaps you should just let this one go.'

'I was going to say, before you so rudely interrupted me, that there *is* a reason why hills are special. They're often sacred sites because you can see dawn from them, and the arrival of the sun is a sacred moment for pagans. Pentonville, just up the road from here, was one such site. A "penton" was once a head, by which I mean that it was a kind of rounded oval hill roughly in the shape of a human head, man-made and probably designed to point to the sunrise. At least, that's the theory. And on such a hill you would have a sacrificial stone. *Pen* is a Celtic word meaning "high point". We get the words "pinnacle" from it, and "penny", named because the coin has a head on it.'

'So pagans are sacrificing victims to the sun, only during their lunch hour, is that it? I have to say that of all the lunatic ideas you have ever come up with, this is by far the silliest. Look, we've no leads, no motives, no suspects. Your motorcyclist had an ironclad alibi, and there's no one else to consider.'

'Then we'll do it the hard way,' said Bryant stubbornly. 'We'll do door-to-doors.'

'Raymond will go bananas if he finds out.'

'Not if we start right now,' said Bryant, checking his watch. 'It's lunchtime, peak activity hour. If we call the others this minute, we can still all get back to the unit before the new case comes in.'

The staff's respect for Bryant was enough to encourage them to surrender their lunch breaks. Joining the detectives at the junction of Britannia Street and King's Cross Road, they split up and recorded conversations with those who lived and worked in the four buildings. Few of the residents were at home, so they ended up talking mostly to shop workers.

Later that afternoon Janice Longbright gathered their findings into a single spreadsheet. After Raymond Land had left the building (on the stroke of 6 p.m.) the detectives pinned a copy to the common-room blackboard and studied it. Bryant had brought along a box of old books, none of which seemed to have any relevance to the problem, and sat sifting through them, barely paying attention to the proceedings.

'This theft is odd,' said May. 'Three weeks ago a young

woman stopped an older man in the street and stole his laptop from under his arm. Two old dears in the building opposite saw it happen.' He held up a photograph of the girl. 'Paula Machin, a twenty-seven-year-old registered heroin-user. She has a string of priors, mostly antisocial stuff, and a couple of attempted thefts. This time she was successful.'

'Why is it odd?' asked Bryant, looking up from his book and peering over the tops of his trifocals.

'Well, look at her. Five foot nothing, arms like bits of wet string. The old ladies said that the fellow she stopped just stood there and let her take it from him.'

'Perhaps she propositioned him and he was still considering his answer,' said Meera.

'Maybe. He never reported the theft.'

'Wait a minute.' Bryant raised a hand. When his forehead creased in thought you could wedge an envelope in the folds. 'Do any of those buildings have air conditioning?'

Now it was May's turn to look puzzled. 'I don't know. I could find out.'

'And while you're at it, can you check for incidents on the same dates last year? Oh, and get me weather forecasts for every day with an incident?'

'There's something going on behind that wrinkly brow of yours, isn't there?' said May suspiciously.

'Don't blame me,' said Bryant. 'You're the one who came up with the idea.'

'What idea?'

'Also, I was thinking of the Bermuda Triangle,' Bryant replied obliquely as he packed away his books. 'I have to go back there tomorrow at around one.'

'OK, I'll come with you,' said May.

'Not necessary, old thing. Someone has to be here for Raymond's new case. I need to take someone else. I need an expert.'

May was a little miffed. 'Who?' he asked.

'One of the two Daves.' Bryant put a lid on the box and stumped off to his bookshelves.

'Well, this is a treat, Mr B.,' said Dave Two, the Dave with the gigantic black moustache that made him look like a cross between Super Mario and a Ukrainian Cossack. 'I tried to offer my advice on one of your investigations only last week, but Mr Land threatened to have me deported.'

'It's not that we don't value your expertise,' Bryant explained. 'We'd just rather have it about U-bends. Better suited to your training, no?'

'I used to be with the Turkish police,' said Dave Two. 'That was how I learned how to use copper wire and lead piping. Is a joke,' he added hastily. 'I make joke.'

'Forgive me if I use your expertise in a field other than crime-fighting,' said Bryant. 'Woodwork, perhaps. Come along with me.'

It was a perfect September day, hot and bright, with a sea-blue sky that fitted around the low rooftops of King's Cross like a theatre backcloth. These days the seasons seemed to arrive in London a month or so later than they had when Bryant was a child; it felt like early August.

The elderly detective explained what he felt were the key points of the mystery, then looked expectantly at the builder.

'This may take a while,' Dave Two warned. 'I'm not good with people. I'm better with floorboards.'

'Take all the time you want,' said Bryant, inviting him out on to the middle of the pavement. 'I've asked you here specifically because of your area of expertise. I have a theory, and I want to see if you come up with something that fits into it. Think of this as a kind of "Spot the Mistake" puzzle.'

Dave Two screwed up his eyes and looked around. He saw the four corner buildings, the one-way system, the tattoo parlour, the motorbike shop, the café and various pedestrians trying to cross the road. Gradually his focus narrowed to one spot. 'Well, there's one problem that I can see, right there,' he said, pointing.

'And what's that?' asked Bryant, craning forward.

'Hinges,' said Dave Two.

'Has he not come back yet?' asked May, leaning into the common room. 'Has anybody here seen Arthur?'

Colin looked up. 'He went out with one of the Daves. He was telling him something about the Bermuda Triangle.'

May headed down to the black spot and found no sign of his partner or the builder.

'We're up here,' Bryant called, leaning dangerously out of a first-floor window. 'We're about to conduct the experiment. Come up!

'You remember the Bermuda Triangle,' he said excitedly, bouncing about at the top of the stairs as May made his way up. 'It was also known as the Devil's Triangle, although it's a vague sort of region in the western Atlantic. Supposedly aircraft and ships vanished under mysterious circumstances. But it's one of the most heavily travelled shipping lanes in the world, and a huge number of aircraft fly over it.'

'You're saying it's analogous to Witches' Cross or whatever your mad friend told you it was called?' asked May.

'The number of incidents seems high until you set it in

context with the number of people who pass through the junction. Then it seems low. It turns out that planes and ships weren't vanishing in the Devil's Triangle at all. They crashed or went off course or their radar failed for perfectly ordinary reasons. The number of ships and aircraft reported missing in the area was not proportionally greater than in any other part of the ocean. But there *was* a factor that increased their chances of vanishing. It's an area of tropical cyclones. So I began to wonder, what if there is a similar anomaly at work here? Something that might appear to link a variety of different events?' He punched out a number on his phone. 'Are you ready, Dave Two?'

'Ready, Mr B.'

Bryant took his partner by the arm and made him lean out of the window. 'Watch over there,' he said, pointing at the building which stood diagonally opposite. Suddenly there was a flash of dazzling light on the first floor, and another across the same floor of the building on the other side of Britannia Street. A moment later there was a screech and a crash. Below them, an Amazon delivery van had hit a lamp-post. 'Yes!' shouted Bryant, punching the air.

The Amazon driver was not hurt, but his airbag had inflated suddenly and fired his glasses out of the window, so he was not best pleased. Bryant ignored him and took his partner to one side.

'When you said that the blind woman was fine but the sighted one wasn't, you set me thinking. It had to be something they could all see. The last of the new buildings was completed two years ago. There were several accidents that first summer, but not as many as this year. You remember number twenty Fenchurch Street, the Walkie-Talkie building? How its glass curvature caused a so-called "death ray" to set fire to parked cars? I did some checking on Henry Carrell, the tattooist. Unfortunately when you went to see him, he hadn't yet undergone any tests. The doctor says he suffers from photosensitive epilepsy. He lied on his job application. I was sure it had to be something to do with the buildings themselves.

'I thought about the Sir John Soane's Museum, and the way the architect had redirected light through his dark building with the aid of hinged mirrors. Dave Two here spotted the problem. When the builders finished those two office blocks' – he pointed out the pair of ugly red-brick boxes that stood on the opposite corners of King's Cross Road – 'they hinged the mirrored windows on the wrong sides. As a result, when the sun is at a certain height and both sets of windows are opened out, a shaft of light bounces between them and down into the street. And on some days when it's hot and very bright, the beam also hits that student block, intensifying its power.' He indicated the building clad in warped sheets of shiny steel.

'The light blinded Mrs Foster, heated up the tank of one of the motorbikes, caused traffic accidents, sent a dog into a rage and even made a woman walk into a plate-glass window. But the worst part was that most of this could have been prevented. The various cases were written up by different officers on different forces. There's a demarcation line running right across the roadway here. As a result, no one person ever read all the statements, or they would have realized that several of the victims recalled seeing a flash of light.'

'So it was human error, not psychogeography,' said May.

'Was it though?' Bryant replied with a grin. 'Those two buildings are where Mother Merlin and Mother Green once had their houses.'

'So, do I get to be on the unit now?' asked Dave Two, proudly smoothing his great moustache as he joined them.

'No, it's back to sinks for you,' said Bryant.

The builder shrugged. 'I'll go after the contract to put their windows in the right way around. The pay will be better,' he replied, sauntering off.

'As I won the bet,' said Bryant, 'there's a very rare edition of the plays of Aeschylus that I'd like . . .'

'You didn't win,' May pointed out. 'You said, and I quote, if you found a common culprit. I think you'll find that the dictionary definition of a culprit is "a *person* who is responsible for a crime or other misdeed". You found a thing. I'd like to have dinner at "Dinner", the Heston Blumenthal restaurant.'

Bryant considered the idea as they headed back to the unit. 'I think in this instance you'll have to settle for a kebab from "Kebabs" on King's Cross Road. I'm not on a builder's salary.'

BRYANT & MAY AND THE ANTICHRIST

' "Devils have no power at all, save by a certain subtle art," ' Arthur Bryant muttered darkly from behind an enormous leather-bound volume.

'What are you reading?' asked John May, tapping at the pudgy fingers he could see curled around the gold-edged pages opposite him. They were seated in Bryant's Bloomsbury flat amid the detritus of a late Sunday-morning breakfast that had involved kippers, Lincolnshire sausages and baked beans.

'It's a quote from the *Malleus Maleficarum*, the *Hammer of Witches*,' replied Bryant matter-of-factly. 'Not the 1486 edition of course, just a facsimile. It was designed as a guidebook for inquisitors to aid them in the identification of witches.'

'I'm sorry?'

Bryant started explaining again. May wondered how many times he could ask his partner to repeat what he was saying before he gave up and tuned out. Bryant's enthusiasm for esoteric subjects could be trying. It was like having a complicated joke explained to you by an earnest child while looking for your turn-off in heavy traffic.

'And that's why midwives were burned at the stake,' Bryant finished blithely. 'The point being that the Devil's "subtle art" lies in his insidious power to influence the way you think.'

May set his *Sunday Times* aside. 'Why don't you read something normal for once? A novel, a newspaper, a Batman comic or something. Do a crossword. You'd relax more.'

'I don't want to relax, thank you.'

May threw the newspaper across. 'Read the obituaries, then. You like those.'

'No, they never tell you how the subject died. Painfully, happily, in a freak accident, filled with regret for lost loves? Surely that's the best bit.' He tapped the cover of the *Malleus Maleficarum*. 'Millions carked it because of this book. Anyone who didn't fit the standard image of a pious Christian, anyone who was poor or old or simply different. It's a lesson we've still not learned.'

'And you're reading it now because . . . ?'

Lowering the volume, Bryant raised his eyebrows and furrowed his chin as if the answer was painfully obvious. 'Manoj Haranai has come back.'

'Haranai? This is the hate preacher who got kicked out of Islington a few years ago?'

'Yes, and I think he's up to his old tricks again.' Bryant put down the book and removed his boots from the table.

'Is that why you made me come and see you on a Sunday morning?'

'He's reinvented himself as another type of fire-and-brimstone preacher.' Bryant poured himself a fresh cup of tea. 'If there's one thing I really hate, it's preachers taking money from gullible believers.'

'You hate a lot of things, Arthur,' May reminded him.

Over their years of being partnered at the Peculiar Crimes Unit, the pair had developed an ever-increasing list of pet hates. May's included disorder, officialdom, committees, radio DJs, chain restaurants, selfies, uncomfortable English furniture, musicals and restaurant critics.

Bryant's list was somewhat more extensive, including authority, hypocrisy, parochialism, cowardice, complicated cocktails, people who stood outside stations with megaphones telling him to heed the word of Jesus, Transport for London calling passengers 'customers', signs that warned him the end of the escalator was approaching, bad sculpture (specifically Paul Day's embracing lovers at St Pancras Station and Maggi Hambling's Oscar Wilde coffin near Trafalgar Square), men who talked about cars, television producers, press releases, twenty-somethings with beards who weren't sea captains and all music written after 1975 except EDM, although typically there were a great many changes, updates, exceptions, cavils and footnotes to his choices.

May was the kind of man who listened to others and amended his opinions accordingly. Bryant nurtured his list of grievances and fantasized about Jacobean methods of revenge. Happily, their likes continued to outweigh their dislikes, which at least kept them mentally fresh and employable.

'But here's the odd thing,' Bryant continued, climbing to his feet and lighting his pipe beside the window, although it would have helped if he'd bothered to open it. 'So far there have been no reports of him ripping anyone off, which makes me think that he's on to a new type of scam. He's back on his old beat, just up the road from here.'

'Then he must be up to something that stays below our radar.'

'The Met haven't picked up on anything, so they can't act. Which is why I think it may be our job to keep an eye on him.'

'What do you want to do about it?' asked May. Watching his partner smoke made him want to pat his pocket for a cigarette until he remembered that he'd quit again.

'I think we should go to church,' Bryant replied brightly.

Their meeting with the preacher occurred on a normal London day, which is to say it was veiled with rain and as grey as a sock. That Sunday morning the whole of King's Cross had a hangover. Nothing was open, there was hardly any traffic and the only sound came from suitcases being rolled back to the station by sodden football supporters.

By contrast, the little church on Pentonville Road was flourishing. It hid among the usual array of low-rent stores, a filthy betting office, a shop that sold elderly Turkish pastries, a run-down bar full of obese men in three-quarter-length trousers and baseball caps who looked like giant toddlers, an old-fashioned minicab company, a place that unlocked stolen phones and mailed money orders overseas and a partially burned-down nightclub called 'Cocks & Hens'.

The congregation stood patiently outside the hall waiting for the doors to open, and were attired for a wedding. Nearly all of the worshippers were of Caribbean and West African extraction, and most were women over forty. Among them was Alma Sorrowbridge, Arthur Bryant's landlady. Her usual church in Finsbury Park had been temporarily closed down by the council, but nobody had been able to tell her why. She suspected it was being sold off for flats. Regular churchgoers had been redirected to a number of smaller chapels, including this one, the Brotherhood of the Rejoicing Heart.

'Did you ever read the official profile on this fellow?' Bryant asked May as they slipped in behind Alma. 'He's a piece of work, a lay preacher who supposedly studied a hotchpotch of sketchy belief systems. He's been pulled in many times for causing an affray, public nuisance, cyber-fraud, money laundering, even a couple of B & Es.'

'So he got deported?'

'No, he left ahead of an official push.' Bryant brushed at a ketchup stain on his shirt. 'There was a story going around that the Met lacked the hard evidence they needed for a formal prosecution. Haranai plays the long game. I guess he laid low for a while. A bit of a charmer in his time, especially with lonely widows. He beat a bigamy charge by arguing that within his religion it was legal. The psychiatric report diagnosed him with a host of disorders including paranoid schizophrenia.'

May was surprised. 'Yet he still got back into the country?'

'Oh, he knows the ropes, whom to talk to and what to say. Let's see what he's got to say this time.'

The church had been decked out with red nylon curtains and Christmas lights so that it looked more like a fringe theatre than a place of worship. As the lights dimmed, the detectives seated themselves behind Alma, who did her best to ignore them. For all his much-professed atheism, Bryant found his landlady's faith touching. She had a powerful, optimistic belief that everything happened for a purpose. Nothing seemed to depress her.

A small gospel choir robed in purple rose from folding chairs and sang angelically. They were followed by a fat little motivational speaker who talked in vague, wide-ranging terms about the Kingdom of Heaven. Manoj Haranai had clearly been held back as the headline act. He was a larger-than-life presence who commanded the audience from the moment he entered, walking gravely to the front of the stage to deliver his address, then roaming through the congregation as he drove each point home, warning each of the attendees with a laser stare.

Bryant leaned in to May's ear. 'I'm surprised anyone believes in all this rubbish.'

'I don't, Mr Bryant,' said Alma, overhearing him, 'but one of my ladies does. She says his soul shines forth.'

'That's not his soul, it's sweat. Look at him, he's making the stage wet.'

Haranai was ranting now. 'DENY the kingdom of the LORD and you will invite SATAN into YOUR home!' Back and forth he strode, thrusting an accusing forefinger at members of the audience.

'I'm here to represent her,' Alma confided.

Bryant craned forward. 'Your friend? Why isn't she here?'

'She's at home resting. She had a nasty shock yesterday evening. She's very upset.'

'Wait, does this have something to do with Mr Haranai?'

'I'm not sure,' Alma whispered. 'When she got home from the shops she found she'd been burgled. She lost all her savings, poor thing.'

The audience rose to its feet and applauded loudly. Apparently this part of the event was at an end. 'What happens now?' asked Bryant.

'He does individual consultations,' Alma replied.

'And of course he charges a fee.' A thought struck him. 'Did your friend have a consultation with him?'

'Yes, she told Mr Haranai where she lived.'

'What, and you thought you'd come and investigate this by yourself? You do remember you share a flat with a detective, don't you?'

'I didn't like to bother you with something like this, so I went to Islington Police Station.'

Bryant's exasperation grew. 'Why would you do that?'

Alma looked at him with shame in her face. 'I thought it might be better to talk to a younger officer from, you know, a more ethnic background.'

'What, instead of the old white bloke who couldn't possibly begin to understand your friend's problem? Where does this gullible old trout live, anyway?'

It was a red rag to a bull, of course. To think that his own landlady wouldn't avail herself of his services! As soon as the performance was fully at an end, Bryant made Alma give him the address and the detectives headed to Canonbury to visit Mrs Eustacia Granville.

Stepping away from the Caledonian Road, a thoroughfare of dry-cleaners, minimarts and shops with mystifying window displays, they soon found themselves in an elegant street of terraced houses with Ionic pilasters and Doric columns, to which had been added sphinxes and obelisks.

'They were built about a hundred and eighty years ago when Britain was very concerned about Egypt and Syria,' said Bryant. 'Nothing really changes, does it? That must be the place, just there.'

Between the villas stood a new block of flats with meanly proportioned balconies of grey steel. The gated entrance had a large illuminated key pad and a porter call button. Mrs Granville had clearly been informed that the detectives were coming to visit, because she had set out tea with the best china and arranged a choice of lurid, unappetizing cakes. The flat was crammed with far too much furniture, all of it purchased for a more spacious property.

'I knew as soon as I opened the door,' Mrs Granville explained, ducking between them to wipe a spot of spilt tea from a polished tabletop.

May looked around. Judging by the way her clothes hung on her Mrs Granville had been larger than she now was, and quite recently; the clothes were still fairly new. She was tentative and dainty of manner; she needed to be, in order to avoid breaking anything in the overcrowded flat. A stack of metal rails stood in one corner, cardboard boxes in another. May surmised that the Granvilles had not long ago moved from a house to this flat. The support rails had been removed from the bathroom and the toilet following the recent illness and death of Mr Granville. The living room looked like a stage set minus one of the principal cast members. May had seen such makeshift arrangements in many a newly widowed woman's home, and the sight always made him sad.

'There was a cup lying on the floor,' she explained. 'A single cup. Nothing else was out of place. You feel so invaded. I was too frightened to go all the way in so I called on my neighbour, but she was out. There's never anyone at home in this building. I should never have moved here.'

'What was missing?' May asked, looking around at the immaculately tidy shelves.

'I keep my money in my bedside table. I don't trust banks these days. It was all gone. Nearly seven thousand pounds.'

'Could you show me where you kept it?' He followed her to the polished table beside the bed and its forlornly empty drawer.

'It had been opened and pushed shut after, very neatly.'

'Why did you have so much on the premises?'

'I got three thousand, two hundred pounds for our car.

My husband died, Mr May, and I don't drive. The rest is my savings – all the money I have. I can't even pay next month's bills.'

'You told the police about this?'

'No, because what can they do? When I had my phone snatched by some boys on bikes they did nothing. I told them they lived just up the road, that I'd seen them before, but we don't even have a local constable around here any more. The money won't be found, will it? They'd just come in and make a mess and do nothing except tell me off for keeping it here in the flat. It's all so humiliating.'

The local police had a poor success rate with burglaries. Even when they took someone into custody they rarely managed to return goods and never recovered cash. Clearly, Mrs Granville valued her privacy above all else.

'How did he get in?' called Bryant, examining the jamb of the front door. 'This hasn't been forced.'

Mrs Granville came back and pointed to a small, fiddly box of grey brushed metal attached to the wall outside the front door. There were a dozen illuminated buttons arranged in rows of three, numbered one to twelve.

'There are twelve flats,' Mrs Granville explained. 'The main gate has a similar key pad. It's terribly annoying because when visitors call flats eleven and twelve they often try to put the numbers in separately. Everybody knows the main entrance code because all the delivery lads use it. So I have this as well. It's a key box. There's a separate four-digit code for it. When you enter the code, a spare door key is released. It's in case I ever lose my keys. I changed the code earlier in the week.'

'What's the number for the key pad at the main gate?'

'I don't need to keep that one written down because it

only changes once a year. It's two – eleven – seven – nine.'

'What was your old code for the key box, and what did you change it to?' asked May.

She thought for a moment, a hand tapping nervously at her neck. 'All I can remember is that I changed it.'

'When?'

'On Wednesday, I think. Let me see.' She rummaged in the magazines on her table and produced a minuscule slip of paper. 'There. It's two – eleven – four – six now.'

'Please think very carefully, Mrs Granville. Did you change it before or after the burglary?'

'Before.'

'Who else has the code to this box?'

'Nobody except me.'

Bryant narrowed his eyes. 'You haven't shared it with anyone?'

'Not a soul.'

'But if the door wasn't forced, someone else must have known the number. What about the porter – does he have it?'

'No. I swear to you, I haven't given it to anybody else. William, my husband, told me never to share such things with anyone. We moved here so he wouldn't have to climb stairs, but he died soon after we arrived.'

'When did you last see Mr Haranai?'

'Four days ago.'

'Why do you think he is involved?'

'I went to his evening service and talked to him over coffee, and he asked me all about where I lived. I didn't think anything of it at the time.' Mrs Granville's hand flapped at her chest like a moth behind glass. 'He wanted to know all about this place.'

'Why?'

'He said it helped him to understand more about his parishioners. I told him some of the things I didn't like about the block. Afterwards Alma ticked me off for being so open with him. I didn't see the harm – after all, he *is* a pastor – but then I did wonder about some of his questions.' She looked flustered. 'I don't want to point the finger of blame at anyone. That would be wrong. But it seems such a coincidence, me describing my home and then being burgled.'

'You didn't tell him you kept money here, did you?'

'Well, no, not in so many words. But I may have implied . . . Oh, I don't know.' She tapped at her neck again.

'Would you say you're a regular at Mr Haranai's services?' asked May.

'Yes. I've been going several times a week for the last two months. Since I lost William I've found it a great comfort.'

'And you're absolutely sure you didn't give Mr Haranai your code in any of your meetings?'

'I'm very careful about that sort of thing. I'm a private person, Mr Bryant. Besides, I changed the front-door code just after I saw him. He couldn't have known what it was.'

'I think we need to change it for you again, just to be on the safe side. You don't think there's any way Mr Haranai could have got information from you without you realizing it?'

'I don't see how. I never normally write the number down. I wish I could remember what I changed it from. It was something to do with the Bible, I'm sure. Everything has been so confused. How could I have lost my life savings? I've been such a stupid old fool.' She passed a hand across her face. 'I have nothing left. Nothing.'

'Then we have a conundrum to unravel.' Bryant got to his feet. 'Is there anyone who can help you, Mrs Granville?'

'No one,' she said forlornly. 'In any case, I couldn't accept help. I feel so ashamed.'

'You have nothing to feel ashamed about, believe me. Thank you for your hospitality.' He signalled to May. 'John, perhaps you could help Mrs Granville conduct a thorough search here, just in case.' *In case she's made a mistake and the money's still here somewhere*, he implied. 'I'll let you know how I get on. It's time I paid Mr Haranai a visit.'

The vaulted church hall was empty now and the lights were turned up, revealing peeling green paintwork and tattered red drapes. Old smells stung his nostrils: mildew, beer, something darker; the space had previously been used as a meeting house, a bar, a sex club and a cinema. At first he thought the stage was empty, but then a sliver of shadow rose and came towards him.

'Mr Bryant – well, well, this is a surprise.' Manoj Haranai had his hand outstretched. Bryant found it hard not to flinch. He had always been astounded by the gullibility of the general public. There was nothing about Haranai that rang true, even for a moment. The lay preacher's smile was so mask-like that it should have made even the most naïve member of his congregation uncomfortable. 'Would you like me to get you a chair, old chap? You look so tired.'

'I'm quite capable of standing, thank you.' Bryant looked around. 'You've come down in the world.'

'From little acorns, isn't that the expression?' Haranai's smile widened but his eyes remained hard and cold. 'Every new ministry has to start somewhere.'

'Well, I'd rather it didn't start in my back yard.' Bryant looked up at the peeling ceiling.

'I can do some good here. This is a deprived area.'

'Yes, and I don't want you depriving them of anything else. I hear you're back in the game.'

'To which game are you referring?'

'The confidence game, Manoj. I don't want you practising it here, or anywhere else.'

Haranai threw his hands high. 'I am trying to give the people hope.'

'It's what you're taking from them that worries me. You were a street hypnotist once, remember?'

'I did a lot of things to get by, Mr Bryant.' Haranai's smile never wavered. 'And you know it's impossible to get anyone to do something that's against their will.'

'I know that,' Bryant agreed. 'You talked to a Mrs Eustacia Granville the other day.'

'I talked to many of my parishioners.' The word still jarred with Bryant; it sounded as if Haranai was attempting to align himself with properly trained ministers.

'You see them in private consultations. Why is that?'

'There are things they feel uncomfortable discussing in front of the rest of the congregation,' Haranai explained reasonably.

'These consultations.' Bryant swiped at the air as if trying to locate the thought. 'Are they based in theology, psychology, what?'

'They're just chats,' said Haranai. 'You should know, Mr Bryant; the people of London once shared their problems with their neighbours, but now they have no one to talk to. I encourage them to open their hearts.'

'And wallets, no doubt. Mrs Granville has neighbours.'

'She tells me they are never there. Often she is the only person living in her building. Loneliness is a terrible modern disease.'

'What did you tell her was the cure?' asked Bryant.

'What do you think?' replied Haranai, pushing the detective to argue with him.

'I think he read her mind,' said Bryant as they strolled towards Piebury Corner, the white-tiled pie shop on the Caledonian Road.

That was enough to stop May in his tracks. 'Please don't drag the supernatural into this,' he warned. 'I searched Mrs Granville's flat and there was no sign of the money. If Haranai stole it, there has to be a simple, logical explanation.'

'First of all, mind-reading involves increased perception, not ghosts. And (*b*), there are proven techniques.'

'Like what?' May asked, pushing open the pie shop's door.

'You start with observational clues about what the other person is thinking,' said Bryant. 'People get more enthused when they discuss their personal interests. It becomes easier to ask them questions. You decode the non-verbal signs to see where their passions lie. Millennials don't like expressing personal opinions face-to-face because they've grown up glued to their screens and walkie-phones. Older people can often be more confident and challenging because they're used to giving opinions.'

'So you're an expert on neurolinguistic programming now, are you?' asked May sceptically.

'There are hundreds of techniques you can study,' Bryant explained. 'There's a thing called the Barnum Effect, where you watch your subject's reaction to a series of seemingly bland statements and slowly refine your diagnosis. We employ over three thousand different micro-expressions a day – well, Raymond doesn't; he probably has about four – but an expert can ascribe precise meanings to them.

Haranai started out as a street hypnotist. There's a very simple "interrupted handshake" technique that wide boys were using in the West End just after the war. You can find instructions for it all over the interweb. I could do it on you right now. You don't have to put anyone in a trance to get them to do as you say.'

'So you could hypnotize me?'

'Watch.' Bryant grabbed his partner's right hand and stared into his eyes. 'You hear nothing but the sound of my voice.' He waved his free hand over the counter. 'You are going to pay for my pie.'

'Didn't work,' said May, pulling his hand free. 'How do you think Haranai does it?'

'I think he just engages subjects and gently leads them to tell him more than they intend. When he's not performing, he stays very still and watches everything. I'm sure he extracted some nugget of information from Mrs Granville and used it against her.'

'What, he came up with a way to get into her flat? What did they talk about, for heaven's sake?'

'The Devil.' Bryant studied the menu. 'What are you having?'

'Steak and oyster pie,' said May.

'I knew it,' said Bryant.

The following week, as soon as he opened the door of number 17, Albion House, Harrison Street, Bryant knew that something was wrong. Alma always baked on Sunday afternoons but today there was no scent of warm spices coming from the kitchen. He found her in the living room, snuffling around the fireplace.

'What's the matter?' he asked. 'I thought you were going to bake gingerbread pudding today.'

When she turned to him, he saw that she had been crying. 'Eustacia,' she said, and started crying again. He
accepted a hug and, not knowing what was expected of
him, patted her gently on the head.

'She took sleeping pills,' Bryant explained over the phone.
'There's no suspicion of foul play. I think it's clear why she
did it. She'd lost her husband and her life savings.'

'What if it wasn't Haranai?' May asked. 'Did you
consider that? The evidence against him is purely circum-
stantial.'

'Alma says she was Mrs Granville's only friend. Nobody
got on with the husband.' Bryant put one finger in his ear.
'What is that dreadful noise?'

'I'm in a pub.'

'Well, can you step outside?'

'The street is noisier.'

'There's no CCTV near the entrance to the flats. If only
we could find proof that she gave Haranai the entry-code
details. What about the porter? He wasn't in his booth
when we met her.'

'Arthur, you may have to let this one go,' said May.
'Haranai's an old pro. He won't let us bring him in without a very good reason. All you have is a confused,
vulnerable old lady who was depressed over the death of
her husband. I don't see how we can make any further
advances.'

'He's a manipulator,' said Bryant doggedly. 'You
searched her flat and I questioned Alma, and we both
came up blank. So let's swap places.'

Rain was sifting gently across the road as Bryant approached
the flat in Canonbury. When he reached the outer door of

the block, he entered the code of 2 – 11 – 7 – 9 into the key pad and was automatically buzzed inside. Before entering, he ducked back and stared at the panel for a moment. 'Interesting.'

Then he headed to see the porter, a young Indian man who sat in a claustrophobically small glass booth, like a plant in a terrarium. 'Did Mrs Granville have many visitors?' he asked. 'Do you keep a logbook?'

'No,' replied the porter. 'Nobody came to see her much. Another old lady, once or twice, but not for a while now.'

'Do you know her name?'

'No.'

'What about this fellow?' Bryant slapped a photograph of Manoj Haranai against the glass.

'No, I've not seen him, sir. I'm on every day until six but sometimes I'm away from the desk.'

'You're a smoker,' Bryant noted.

'I need a break from that glass box sometimes.' The porter let him into the apartment.

'I don't suppose you know what Mrs Granville changed her spare-key code to last week, do you?'

'I'm afraid not, sir.' With his smoking habit exposed, the porter was now anxious to get back to his post. 'The residents are encouraged not to share their codes with anyone.'

'Of course not. Very sensible.' Bryant paused. 'Did you talk to her much?'

'Not very often. She was – private. Very religious.'

'What makes you think that?'

'She gave me this.' He felt inside his shirt and produced a tiny gold crucifix. 'She was giving them to everyone. You know how old ladies get funny ideas.'

'Can I see?' Bryant examined the cross, which was made of gold-sprayed plastic. 'What sort of funny ideas?'

'She told me we had to keep the Devil away,' the porter explained. 'She was worried that Satan would invade the building.'

'Why would she think that?'

'I don't know. I think she was easily influenced by what people told her. She believed everything she read in the papers. She asked for the outer-door code to be changed. I told her I couldn't do it. Then she gave me the neck-chain and made me put it on.'

There was nothing out of the ordinary about the cross that he could see. After the porter left, he took a pair of leather gloves from his pocket and tried to use the spare-key box next to the front door. Then he walked around the flat for a while, re-enacting the theft that had caused an ashamed old lady to take her life. Bryant left the building a little less mystified than he had been when he arrived.

After a verdict of suicide was recorded the case was closed, and although no evidence came to light that Manoj Haranai was in any way responsible for the robbery, the detectives in their stubbornness presumed it was simply unprovable. Such cases were splinters that remained embedded in the flesh, impossible to dislodge. A few weeks later, news filtered through that Haranai was moving to a new ministry in West London.

'We should see him one last time, just to pay our respects,' said Bryant doggedly. 'The church is only around the corner. It would be rude not to.'

'All right, but I don't know what you think we're going

to find,' said May, knowing it was easier to go along with his partner than try to change his mind.

Bryant was thinking back to a conversation he'd had with Alma the night before at King's Cross tube station. They were going to see a horror film in the West End, and he had needed to use the ATM on the station concourse.

'How on earth do you manage to remember your pin number?' Alma had asked, watching him input the numerals without thinking. 'You can't remember our home phone number.'

'That's because I never use it myself,' Bryant had explained. 'I've more important things to remember.'

'Like what?'

'Thirteen twenty-nine,' Bryant had replied, as if it was obvious. 'The year that gave us the phrase "small fry". The mayor brought in laws to protect overfishing in the Thames by expanding the size of the holes in fishermen's nets so that the small fish, or "fry", could escape. I rather like knowing useless facts like that.'

'So that's your pin number?' Alma had asked.

'No, it's five – two – four – five,' Bryant had replied, tapping the side of his nose, and as Alma had long since given up trying to understand how her lodger's mind worked, she stumped off to pick up a copy of the *Evening Standard* while he collected his cash.

'What if we were thinking about it wrongly?' said Bryant now as the detectives approached the hall on Pentonville Road.

'How do you mean?' asked May.

'We can't prove that Haranai extracted the entry code from Mrs Granville, but suppose he found a way to give her a new code that he was sure she'd use? We know his powers of persuasion are formidable.'

'You mean some kind of subconscious suggestion? Good luck getting that into a court of law.'

'I don't suppose we'll ever be able to do that, but it would be satisfying to at least know, wouldn't it?'

Haranai was far from pleased to see them. 'This is harassment,' he complained.

'My dear Manoj, seeing you twice in six weeks is hardly harassment,' Bryant pointed out. 'I suppose you heard about Mrs Granville.'

'Sometimes the protection of the Lord is not strong enough to keep Satan out,' Haranai replied.

'You gave her some crucifixes, I understand.'

'I hand them out to everyone who attends my sermons.'

'To ward off evil, like holding up garlic to a vampire. You told her to do something else to keep Satan at bay, didn't you?'

'I don't know what you mean,' snapped Haranai. 'I'm leaving today, Mr Bryant, so if you'll excuse me, there is much still to do.'

'This will only take a minute,' said Bryant. 'It's the oddest thing. Everyone knew the code to the main gate of Mrs Granville's building. It's two – eleven – seven – nine. But nobody had the code to her spare front-door key, not even you. She told us that she changed it just after she saw you, before she was robbed. Why would she do that?'

'How would I know?' Haranai was growing increasingly impatient.

'Because I think you planted it in her head,' said Bryant simply.

'Arthur, I'm not sure where you're going with this,' May began in warning. To his knowledge Haranai had broken no law.

Bryant knew there was little chance of forcing an

admission of guilt, but he wanted Haranai to know that his every move would be watched from now on. He thought back to the previous evening, when he had explained his choice of an ATM pin number to Alma.

'Five – two – four – five?' she had said, puzzled. 'That's not a date.'

'No.' Bryant had traced a pudgy finger in the air. 'It's a right-angle triangle. I can't remember the number so I remember the pattern.'

He thought back to the susceptible, friendless widow confiding in the bogus pastor, and became more convinced than ever of his guilt. 'Why did you ask her where she lived?'

Haranai shrugged as if the answer was obvious. 'There are a lot of robberies in her neighbourhood. I concern myself with the spiritual wellbeing of my flock.'

'You warned her that the Devil was nearby.'

'And he is. Sadly my warning came too late.' He rose to show the detectives out. 'If only there was something I could do, but I'm leaving tonight and taking up residence in a new chapel.'

Bryant also rose but paused. 'Perhaps there is one thing you can do. Submit to a DNA test.'

May knew his partner was bluffing. The unit could not afford to call in tests after a case was closed. 'Arthur,' he said, 'I think we should be going.'

'Nonsense. If Mr Haranai really wishes to help us he'll let us eliminate him from our inquiries.'

An air of hesitation shimmered over Haranai's eyes and then was gone. 'Of course,' he said finally. 'Anything to help.'

'A piece of evidence has come to light, making the move necessary,' said Bryant casually.

Haranai's ever-confident smile faltered.

'She knew it was you who burgled her, of course,' Bryant continued. 'If I'd have thought a little faster I'd have realized the truth and might have saved her life. She was telling the truth. She didn't give you the key code; you gave it to her.'

'I didn't give her anything, Mr Bryant.'

'Not the physical number, no. But you made her fearful enough to go home and revise the sequence.' He dug in his pocket and removed the sliver of paper on which Mrs Granville had written her new code. 'This is the code she used after the burglary: two – eleven – four – six.'

'I fail to see what any of this has to do with me,' snapped Haranai.

'That's the thing about old ladies,' Bryant pointed out. 'They do love bits of paper.' Turning over the scrap, he showed Haranai the other side. 'Mrs Granville kept the drawing you made for her, the one you used to explain why she should change her number.'

He flattened the paper on the tabletop between them. On the reverse were two tiny pencil diagrams, one of an inverted crucifix, and one the right way up.

'You pointed out that if you draw lines through the numbers of the main gate's code, which everyone knew, it forms a symbol of the Antichrist, an inverted cross. That's why she asked the porter to change it, even though it wasn't within his power to do so. It could only be done by the managing agent. I must say it was smart thinking on your part, coming up with that one. You suggested that she could keep the Devil at bay by changing her front-door code to make the universally recognized sign of the cross. Then all you had to do was wait a while and try it for yourself while she was out.'

'This is ridiculous,' said Haranai. 'She must have done this herself. You cannot prove—'

Bryant raised an interrupting hand. 'One other point. It was clear to me that the burglar wore gloves when using the key pad to open the box, and inside the flat, but he would have had to take them off to get the actual key out of its box – it's such a fiddly little thing.' Bryant smiled innocently. 'I tried to remove it several times and failed. We don't even need a DNA match for you, just a finger-print. You killed her, Haranai.'

'The power of suggestion,' muttered Bryant, poking a thumbful of Old Mariner's Filthy Shag into the bowl of his pipe. 'Without it there would have been no need for the *Malleus Maleficarum*. It was a weapon cruelly wielded against the trusting innocent. Some editions had a pent-acle adorning the cover. I suppose a man like Haranai is always on the lookout for signs and portents that will help him take advantage of others. If Mrs Granville's entry code had consisted of six numerals instead of four, it might have been ten – six – four – twelve – two – ten.'

'Why,' asked May, 'what would that have been?'

'You tell me,' Bryant replied with a smile, sitting back to enjoy his pipe. 'Draw it out.'

BRYANT & MAY AND
THE INVISIBLE WOMAN

'You *said* I could have an *ice cream*.' The boy aggressively pulled against his mother's hand.

'I said you could have one after we'd been around the gallery.' Her grip tightened. The rain was seeping in veils now. She hung on to her partially collapsed umbrella with the other hand, trying to keep them both dry.

'The gallery's deadly boring. It's just bits of rope and wood.'

'It's not deadly boring, it's the Tate Modern.' She slowly dragged him towards the corner of the building. 'Mummy wants to see the Rothkos.'

The little boy rolled pleading eyes. 'I'll just stay here without moving until you've finished.'

That's what I say to your father, she thought. Aloud she said, 'It's tipping down. You'll catch your death if you stay here. You're coming with me.'

He pouted and puffed and dug in his heels. 'But it's so *deadly boring*.'

At that moment the Tate Modern became somewhat less boring when a body hurtled past them and smacked into the concrete walkway, spattering them both with blood.

The boy looked up at the building, stunned into silence, his jaw slack with wonderment. A man had apparently fallen from the sky. All thoughts of ice cream had evaporated. As the mother looked down at the crimson speckles covering her fawn raincoat, then at her son, all she could think was, *His school trousers are ruined*. Moments later there were security guards everywhere. The shattered body was hastily covered with a red blanket and a police car was pulling up on to the pedestrian walkway with its blue lights revolving, but no siren.

When the mother realized they could both have been killed if her son had not held her back, she felt a rush of released tension sweep over her, and hugged him to her, overwhelmed by the preciousness of life.

'A fifty-two-year-old Caucasian male named Mark Scott,' DS Renfield informed Arthur Bryant and John May, handing them photographs because he knew Bryant was unlikely to open his email attachments. 'He did a swan dive from the open-sided viewing gallery of the new Tate extension. Nearly killed a couple of bystanders, a mother and her son.'

'Dead, I presume,' said May.

'As he fell six storeys on to his head, I'd say yes,' Renfield pointed out.

'What were you doing there?' asked Bryant.

'I was out on patrol with a mate of mine in the Met when the call came in,' Renfield explained. 'He was about to end his shift so we were going for a drink.'

'And this was last night, so why are you telling us now?'

'Blimey, I'm trying to do you a favour. I thought you'd be interested.' He shot a look at Janice Longbright. The pair had come into the detectives' office at the PCU thinking it was the kind of case that would excite their interest.

'We're very busy,' Bryant complained. 'We've got a dead woman found in a locked garden in Holland Park, and no leads. Now is not the time to . . . Why do you think it's one for us? This isn't our jurisdiction.'

'We've got the woman who killed him, plus a witness who saw the whole thing.'

'Then what do you need us for?' Bryant pointed out of the window with a stick of liquorice. 'Have you seen the plaque on our building? "PCU", it says. "Peculiar Crimes Unit". I don't call that peculiar, I call it a two-inch double column in the *Evening Standard*. Early edition, replaced by a piece about a baking show.'

'You really have no empathy at all, have you?' said May in perpetual wonderment at his partner's insensitivity.

'I have something more important – curiosity.' Bryant turned to Renfield. 'All right, I'll bite. Why did she do it?'

'This is where the peculiar part comes in,' warned Renfield. 'The killer is Rebecca Hope, Scott's partner, and the witness is a woman she met a few minutes earlier at the gallery. No one else was up on the deck at that moment and there's a camera above the main door. Hope rode back with us after being taken into custody and talked all the way. She admitted killing him. I couldn't shut her up. She spent the night at Snow Hill. The admitting officer took an initial statement from the witness, but I imagine you'll want to take another one.'

'Nothing Hope said in the car is admissible,' said May. 'She has to make a statement under supervision and without coercion.'

'I know,' said Renfield. 'She's on her way here. The HSCC* think we might be more suited to dealing with her.'

'Oh, they do, do they? Who's running the local Murder Investigation Team for that area?'

'An old pal of yours, Rupert Harmsworth. He says he has his hands full at the moment.'

'*Ça explique tout*,' said Bryant. 'The only thing he knows about work is how to work the system. From the sound of things we won't have a problem getting a statement out of her.'

'What, so we're going to take this on in the middle of another case, are we?' asked May, nettled.

'Good heavens, you can manage more than one thing at the same time, can't you? Look at Janice, she does half a dozen things at once. What did Hope say in the car?'

'That she'd met him soon after his wife died. That she loved him with all her heart but had to kill him, and that's all we needed to know.'

'Interesting,' said Bryant. 'It says a lot.'

Renfield looked mystified. 'Does it? I don't see how.'

Bryant already had the bit between his teeth. 'Janice, pull out everything you can find on her history, will you? And look into his background. John, can you handle the statement?'

'You know you *can* sit in on interviews yourself, Arthur.' May knew that his partner had an aversion to them.

Bryant waved the idea aside. 'I don't need to. You'll only tell me off for leading the suspect. Just make sure she's

---

* Homicide and Serious Crime Command.

relaxed and feels safe, and let her talk for as long as she likes. The answers always come when the recorder is turned off, so don't turn it off.'

'Arthur, she's a suspect, not a witness,' May reminded him.

Bryant wasn't listening. 'Send someone to get a statement from the witness. I'll read the finished documents when you've collated them. It'll be faster that way. Maybe we can get this done while we're waiting for the Holland Park case to break.'

Renfield and May went to the interview room and made arrangements.

Excerpt from the transcribed statement of Rebecca Hope, taken at the Peculiar Crimes Unit, 231 Caledonian Road, King's Cross, on 19 November at 10.30 a.m.

I was standing before a painting by Salvador Dalí called *The Image Disappears*. It's not very big, maybe fifty centimetres square, rendered in ochre and amber oils. It shows a young woman reading a letter by a window. She's very clearly painted; you can see her hair, her nails, the folds of her dress. But when I stepped back a little and studied it again, the girl had vanished and had been replaced by the face of a stern-looking man. I feel like that now. Like I'll disappear to let the man appear.

The panel on the wall said that Dalí had painted a number of these optical-illusion pictures in the 1930s. I wanted to see others but the rest of the room was filled with bits of wood and coils of wire. The exhibition at the new Tate Modern extension was called *Seeing Is Not Believing*. It was a private view, very dressy, so I had glammed up for the occasion. We were going to go together, Mark and I.

An awkwardly tall blonde woman was standing beside me sipping white wine from a plastic cup. 'I have no idea what that's meant to be,' she said. 'I don't come here to look at the art.'

'So why are you here?' I studied her from the side. She had one of those upside-down mouths that couldn't smile, and the kind of thin skin you get from counting calories and pushing salads around plates in expensive restaurants.

'I'm looking for a date,' she said, wiping maroon lipstick from the rim of her cup. 'A lot of my friends come here to meet men. You know they're going to be cultured, right? Look at that one over there. He's carrying a book. That's a good sign.'

She pointed to a man in a beautiful grey suit, dark-haired, a little thinning on top, brown shoes, expensive but the wrong colour. He had his back to us, so I couldn't see how she could tell if he was dating material. 'That's my partner,' I told her. As if sensing that she was talking about him, Mark moved out of range.

'This wine is rubbish,' said the blonde, draining her cup. 'I need a refill. Wish me happy hunting.'

I followed Mark upstairs to the viewing deck. He was walking just a little way ahead of me, a paperback in his right hand. The lifts were too crowded to board so I continued up the stairs to the deck. I pushed open the glass panel to the exterior walkway. It was darker and mistier now, and the river air smelled brackish and dank. I remember the concrete floor was soaked and puddled in places, which made it slippery. It was too murky to see out over the city.

Mark was walking a little way ahead. The paperback was Dickens' *Our Mutual Friend*. The blonde downstairs would probably have approved.

I called out to Mark, 'Hey, you.'

He raised his head and looked around, waiting apprehensively while I caught up. For a moment I thought he'd failed to recognize me. There was a faraway look in his eyes. A gust of wind brought more rain over the balcony. At that height London weather plays havoc with your hair. The event was invitation-only and glamorous, so I hadn't dressed for warmth. There weren't enough lights working on the deck, so I stood beneath one where he could see me.

The cold night air didn't seem to bother him. I wasn't sure what else was left to say. I knew things were as bad between us as they could ever get.

He asked me what I thought of the exhibition, almost as if I was a perfect stranger.

I told him I liked some of the paintings but to be honest a lot of it was lost on me. One room was full of ductwork and cables. I thought the workmen were still finishing the ceiling but it turned out to be an installation about Syria.

I remember looking out into the sky and thinking the clouds had jaundice – light pollution, I suppose. I was glad there were no real stars to be seen above the city, only the red pinprick lights of cranes. Stars make me feel lonely.

'I'm not sure we're supposed to be out here,' he said, leaning back against the railing. 'It looks like they're still working on the exterior. They were rushing to get it finished for the opening. I thought they were going to glass the whole thing in. Someone could fall over . . .'

We stood there a little longer, just looking at each other. He was always so reasonable, so pleasant, so *English*, and at first it had worked. He had always made me want to be kind in return.

Behind us someone came up to the glass doors and looked at the bad weather, but was driven outside by the need for a cigarette. Then I heard her footsteps, high heels on concrete. It was the woman I'd been speaking to downstairs.

I looked back at Mark. I was sick of arguing with him. I was defensive and angry. I don't remember much about what happened next. I saw my hand hitting his shoulder, and Mark's expensive brown shoes slipping on the wet concrete. I raised my arms and put my hands on both his shoulders, and pushed as hard as I possibly could. I heard him cry out, and then he was gone. The beautiful grey suit blurred with the falling rain and simply vanished over the edge. The paperback fell on to the wet floor.

I stared at the railing that was too low, the safety barrier he had fretted about, and realized I was left with the other woman who stood there struck dumb by what I had done. Then she turned and ran away. She wanted nothing to do with it. He disappeared in seconds. The observation deck was filled with swirling rain. I couldn't even see Mark's footprints any more.

I remember the accusing looks of people lining the staircase as I made my way down, soaked and shaking violently.

As I passed the room with the Dalí painting I briefly caught sight of it again, and this time I couldn't see the woman in it. I later found out that it isn't about a woman at all, but two men, Vermeer and Velázquez. The woman in the picture is just a trick, a phantom. The woman was never real.

Only I know what happened between us, and the pain will never go away. I think there are always some things that should be held back. There's only one person who should know everything about you, and that's the person you love the most. Not a police officer who looks at you with suspicion and spends all his time trying to catch you out.

If I told you how much I suffered because of him, would that make it any better? His daughter and I, we only ever wanted what was best for him. Mark was so self-destructive, I'd always thought that there was nothing we could do. But last night I realized that there was something I could do. I could kill him.

'Am I missing something?' Longbright asked. 'I didn't hear any mention of a motive.'

'That's the problem,' May replied, turning the page around and studying it again. 'When I asked her why she did it, she said she didn't know. All she'll admit is that she needed to do it for his sake, and that she's glad she did.'

'That makes no sense. I've got some background history on them.'

Bryant looked around Longbright's desk. 'Where's the file?'

'I emailed it to you.'

'But you know I like you to print it out.'

Longbright adopted her don't-mess-with-me look. 'You know we're paper-free, Mr Bryant.'

'You may be, I'm not. What happens to my file if the power fails, like it did last week?'

'It only failed because you blew up the junction box,' May pointed out.

'John, can you print out the document for him?' asked Longbright. 'There's something odd about the whole set-up.'

Excerpt from the transcribed statement of Lisa Harper, taken at Snow Hill Police Station, 5 Snow Hill EC1, on 18 November at 8.37 p.m.

I met the woman I now know to be Rebecca Hope at an exhibition at the Tate Modern called *Seeing Is Not Believing*, which I suppose is appropriate, considering what I saw earlier tonight. It was a private view and the press were there and some of the artists were in attendance. She and I got talking; I can't remember how. She was wearing a beautiful black cocktail dress – vintage I think, because it was high-necked with a backless triangle but had sleeves, very 1930s. I'm in fashion, I notice these things. I pointed out a nice-looking man carrying a book, something by Charles Dickens, I think, and she said it was her partner. Then she went off. I remember thinking she seemed very agitated. I thought it was odd, him standing over there and her over by me, almost as if they didn't know each other. It wasn't as if either of them were off talking to other people. They were just standing . . . apart. I thought, *Either she's lying or they've had a fight.*

I wanted a cigarette, but perhaps it wasn't entirely an accident that I went up to the viewing deck. I saw him heading up the stairs, with her some way behind him. I don't know if you've been to the new Tate extension, but it's terribly awkward, spatially. There's a bank of lifts, hopelessly inadequate, and this big staircase, terrible

feng shui, and there's been a huge row over the viewing deck because it overlooks some very expensive
apartments with floor-to-ceiling glass walls, and the
residents are complaining that they're being gawped at
all day.

Anyway, I suppose I followed them. I must admit I
was a little bit curious, and I was by myself with nothing
better to do . . . When I got upstairs I saw that it was still
raining. I pushed open the glass door and there were the
two of them, out by the wall arguing. I say arguing, I
couldn't hear them because there was a traffic helicopter
somewhere overhead, but it looked very aggressive; I
could tell by the way they were standing. And she had
spoken so glowingly about him to me just minutes before, I thought it was odd that her mood could change
so quickly.

The light's not good up there. I suppose they keep
them low because of the neighbouring buildings, and so
you can see across London, but there wasn't much to see
tonight. He was facing me with his back against the railing, which is surprisingly low considering how high up
you are, and she was facing him so she had her back to
me, and suddenly he went over. I couldn't see how her
hands were placed but he was like – you know when you
sit on the edge of a swimming pool and just sort of drop
backwards into the water? That's how he went, like
that. And I thought, *My God, she's crazy*, and headed
for the doorway back to the stairs, then I heard her
scream very angrily, and as I ran down the stairs I could
hear her behind me, and for a moment I thought she was
coming after me as well.

She took the stairs all the way down, but when she
got to the bottom she just stopped and waited, and then

the police arrived, and she walked calmly up to them – I remember thinking how tranquil she suddenly seemed, as if she was fully accepting of what would happen – and she spoke very softly to them. And that was that.

Someone had already covered the body. It had just missed a little boy and his mother. The whole thing – it was just so strange. I suppose the thing that bothered me most was that I couldn't associate this woman I'd been chatting to earlier with someone who would shove her lover over the side of a building.

Longbright sent May the remaining documents she had collated, and laboriously printed them out for his partner. Half an hour later, May found Bryant standing on his smoking terrace, a tiny wooden balcony that faced into the central courtyard of the PCU building. Far from keeping his pipe smoke away from everyone it had the effect of distributing the aroma to all the offices.

'Dan's got some footage for us to watch,' said May. 'Is this thing safe? I take it you read Janice's notes.'

'Not all of them, but I took away the salient points,' Bryant replied, puffing thoughtfully.

'So you know that Scott's first wife died twelve years ago and that he has a daughter by her.'

'I think I missed that part. What else did I miss?'

'He and Miss Hope got together not long after the first wife died. The phrase "whirlwind romance" came up a few times in Janice's calls to the families. His daughter Emily is eighteen and devastated, but for a reason we'll come to. Rebecca Hope ran a number of different businesses, although they fared badly during the economic downturn, leaving her broke. Mark Scott owns a large house in Hampstead overlooking the Heath, which he was given by his parents. He'd been treated for depression for a number of years, and was on a pretty severe medication regime. Lately Hope had also been prescribed similar medication. It sounds like the relationship was in trouble. They weren't married, but apparently he changed his will leaving everything to her, cutting the daughter out entirely because lately he and Emily had argued. Janice is tracking down other family members, but so far she says the most obvious and noticeable element of the relationship between Rebecca and Mark is the great love they had for one another.'

'Which only deepens the mystery as to why she would want to kill him,' said Bryant.

'Whether they were happy or not I guess we'll find out when Janice talks to their friends later today. In the longer version of her statement, Miss Hope reiterates that she loved him very much. What she doesn't do is show any regret for what happened.'

'Then why would she shove him off a building?'

'That's the question, isn't it? He comes from an upper-class family, father in the House of Lords, owns land in Hampshire, that sort of thing. She alienated his family at an early point in their relationship – I don't suppose it took much, as her parents ran a bakery in Leeds. In my experience rich families can be extraordinarily unpleasant about attractive women wanting to marry their favourite sons.'

'You see, this is where your Facebook and your Tweety thing can't help,' said Bryant vehemently. 'All this information flying around the stratosphere, all these selfies and texts, and yet they're useless when you really want to get at the truth. You can sit there playing *Call of Nature* all day—'

'I think you mean *Call of Duty.*'

'—and it doesn't tell us a thing about who you really are.' He took a last drag at his pipe and knocked it out on the railing, mindless of the burning ashes that scattered themselves throughout the courtyard. 'Let's take a look at that footage.'

'You don't all have to huddle around my laptop,' said Dan Banbury irritably. 'I've sent the file to everyone.'

'Can't open it,' said Bryant. 'Just play the blasted thing.'

'You haven't even tried, have you?' Banbury sighed and hit play. The monochrome footage had a granular gloom that turned figures into blossoms of soot. It showed an angled patch of concrete with a two-legged shape at one end.

'Can you enhance it?' asked May.

'This isn't a Tom Cruise film, John. I can't just hit a button and zoom it into crystal sharpness. It's a poorly positioned out-of-date closed-circuit camera with dust over its globe. But I'm pretty sure that's Mark Scott. Watch this part.' He fast-forwarded to a later point in the recording. A second figure, much smaller, ran into the frame. She wore a tight black gown with a sequinned hem. The tops of both their heads were cut off, but it was obvious that some kind of confrontation was taking place. 'See, he steps back, closer to the wall, almost like he's afraid of her, she comes forward, they're still not engaging directly, then . . .' He slowed the image down.

The detectives watched as the smaller figure stepped so close to the larger one that they overlapped and became one. A moment later, only one pair of legs could be seen. 'And over he goes,' said Banbury.

Another figure, clearly female, passed closer to the

camera, heading for the deck's doorway. 'And there goes Lisa Harper, anxious to keep clear and get the hell out. I'd say that was pretty conclusive evidence, wouldn't you?'

'It seems that way,' said Bryant grudgingly.

'Is it admissible evidence?' asked May. 'The quality's not good.'

'We'll have to take advice on that.' Banbury shut down the footage. 'What do you think?'

'The witness clearly stayed in her corner beneath the camera, so she's in the clear,' said Bryant.

'She was never under suspicion,' said May.

'She still needed to be ruled out,' Bryant replied. 'Lisa Harper was tall and blonde. Rebecca Hope is slender and fairly short. I wonder why he moved like that?'

'Like what?'

'Back and forth, almost as if they were sparring. There was something strange going on between them. Hope doesn't seem the devious type. Perhaps she's not lying to us so much as omitting a crucial part of the story.'

'Why can't we just accept her testimony?' asked Renfield. 'She pushed him over and that's that?'

'Because she can't give us a reason for having done it,' said Bryant.

'He could have annoyed her, forcing her to act in anger, purely on the spur of the moment. That's how it appears to me.'

Bryant looked around at the others. 'Anyone else have an idea of how to proceed?'

'Can we get hold of the dress Rebecca Hope was wearing last night?' asked Longbright.

'You'll split the seams, you're too big-boned,' said Bryant rudely.

Longbright had a genetic predisposition towards heft.

She was not, however, like those larger women who looked as if not all of their body would follow them when they came to a sudden stop, but was pleasingly firm-muscled.

'I'd like to match it to that footage,' she said, 'just to be sure that it's what we're seeing in the shot.'

'I think we need to schedule another interview with Hope,' said May. 'It sounded to me as if she was sticking to a script.'

Because the Holland Park murder case was occupying so much of their time, they didn't get back to Rebecca Hope until late in the evening, by which time she had been in custody for almost twenty-four hours. As they hadn't been able to apply for an extension, the detectives knew that they would shortly have to release her unless she was charged.

Before they entered, they studied her through the small window of the interview room. She sat motionless, facing away from them, small and so still that she might have been carved from wood. The basement room had fierce, flat strip lighting and a single window that opened into a locked stairwell leading up to the street. There was nothing to look at, and she continued staring straight ahead as they entered. There were tired creases above her eyes. She had refused to eat, and had only sipped at a glass of water. Clearly she was under great emotional strain.

'Miss Hope, we need to talk a little more about what happened,' said May gently.

There was no reply.

'If there's nothing more you can tell us, we have to take your statement as it stands, and that means you'll be charged accordingly,' Bryant explained.

'I'd much rather you just got it over with,' she said in a small, soft voice. 'I'm ready to accept the responsibility.

There's nothing more to be said, I'm afraid. You know what happened. You must do your job.'

Bryant shot his partner a look. *This is going to be an uphill battle.* 'We still have a few minutes,' he said. 'Let's go back to the beginning.'

Upstairs, Janice Longbright had taken receipt of a package and was unwrapping it when Meera Mangeshkar came in.

'You're working late,' said Longbright, cutting open the box with a paperknife.

'Colin and I are still collating the witness statements on Holland Park. What's that?'

'Have a look.' Longbright carefully unfolded the black evening dress and held it up. 'It weighs nothing. No wonder she was cold.'

'Is that Rebecca Hope's gown?' Meera, a girl who rarely strayed from Dr Marten boots, leggings and sweatshirts, studied the dress with interest. 'Blimey, there's nothing of it.'

'Haute couture, my dear.' Janice pressed the material against her chest. 'I don't know how women get into things like this.'

'No outfit is worth freezing your tits off for,' said Meera.

'Have you ever worn a vintage dress?' asked Longbright.

Meera looked at her as if she had just asked why the DC never took holidays on the moon. 'Of course not. Why would I?'

'Well, say you have somewhere smart to go—'

'Can I just stop you there? The smartest place Colin's ever taken me is the Mecca Bingo hall in Tooting.'

'Every woman should own a little black number.'

'Why?'

'To make you feel good when you're fed up. Don't tell me this job never gets to you.'

'Of course it does.'

'What do you do when it does?'

'I get pissed.'

Janice released a sigh of despair. 'Try the dress.'

'I don't think I'd fit it. I'm a size six, mostly.'

'What do you mean, mostly?'

'I spend too much time at the gym. Upper body strength.'

Janice checked the label. 'This is a six so you should be fine.'

Meera looked horrified. 'I'm not trying that on; it looks like it'd fall apart. What's it made out of, anyway?'

'It's satin and crêpe de Chine. I used to model clothes like this.'

'What, before you ended up stripping?' Meera held up the dress and poked at it.

'I was never an ecdysiast, I was a hostess.'

'Sure you were. All right,' said Meera, pulling off her sweater, 'but don't laugh.'

'If you could just describe what was going through your head when he went over the edge,' said May, checking his watch. 'Just give us something, Miss Hope, and we may be able to have the charge mitigated.'

'I wouldn't want that,' said Hope flatly.

'You must have had a reason,' snapped Bryant. 'You didn't leave home to go to the exhibition together; he left first and you caught him up. Why?'

Hope looked down at the floor, refusing to catch his eye. 'You have to charge me with murder or let me go.'

'Arthur, we're out of time,' said May. 'I can't get an extension without Raymond's approval and he's gone off somewhere.'

'There must be someone in the Murder Investigation Team who can grant approval.'

'They need Land's signature.'

'Charge me,' Hope challenged. 'You have to do it.'

Bryant looked at the page that lay between them. On top of it was a black biro. All that was needed now were two signatures.

The alarm on May's phone made them both jump. Hope remained immobile. Realizing what the tone signified, she suddenly looked more peaceful. 'That's it,' said May, reaching across and picking up the pen. He uncapped it and started to sign the charge sheet.

The door to the interview room slammed open. 'Don't sign it!' Longbright cried. 'She didn't do it.'

'You know nothing,' replied Hope.

'I know you couldn't have killed him.' Longbright set the dress down on the interview table. 'It's a size six from 1935. The satin is worn thin.'

'It was my grandmother's,' said Hope, looking uncomfortable.

'Mr Bryant, Meera is a size six. She just tried the dress on,' Longbright explained. 'It fitted her perfectly, but people were slimmer when it was made. It's physically impossible to raise your arms above waist height. She couldn't have pushed Scott in the way she described without tearing the sleeves to pieces.'

'If you didn't push him, what did you do?' asked May.

Hope's shoulders sagged forward. She gnawed at a knuckle, thinking through the implications of her response. The room remained silent. Finally she spoke. 'I didn't do anything,' she said.

'Then how did he—' May began.

'He jumped,' said Bryant. 'She followed him there because she knew he was going to try.' He turned to Hope. 'That's why you and he were standing on opposite sides of the gallery's reception room, wasn't it? He hadn't seen you until that moment.'

Her voice was so quiet now that they could hear the rain falling into the basement stairwell, and had to strain forward to hear her. 'Have you ever dealt with someone who's severely depressed, any of you?' she asked. 'There's no rationality to it. There's nothing you can say or do that will make them feel better. He suffered from bouts of depression all through his life,' she went on. 'He'd tried to kill himself before. I had always managed to stop him. But we reached a point where he just wanted to die. He had stopped taking his meds, and wouldn't allow me to get him any more help. You don't understand what the strain of living with someone like that does to you. The more time we spent together, the more this – thing – took over our lives, until I had all but disappeared.'

She rose and walked unsteadily to the window, where raindrops were cutting through the dirt on the panes.

'I knew he was determined to do it this time. He wouldn't alter his will to favour Emily. He wanted to leave everything to me. I followed him up to the observation deck, and I knew there was nothing I could do to stop him. Then that blonde woman followed us up. As he moved towards the railing I knew I had to make it look like murder, so I closed in on him, knowing she would back up my story.'

'You knew what would happen afterwards,' said Bryant.

'What?' asked May. 'I don't understand.'

'You can't inherit from somebody you've murdered if it can be proved you had something to gain, and the will was made in Miss Hope's favour,' said Bryant. 'The house in Hampstead would pass to his daughter. That's right, isn't it, Miss Hope?'

'He wouldn't change the will, and there was a clause in it preventing me from passing it to her,' she said numbly. 'But she would inherit if I couldn't.'

'A loophole,' said Bryant. 'You didn't plan this. You wouldn't have worn the dress if you had.'

She looked up at them, wiping her eyes. 'The thought occurred to me when I was up there, standing before him, listening to him explain yet again why I would be doing him a favour by letting him end it all. I suddenly thought: *This time I don't have to beg and plead*. This time Emily could be protected, and perhaps the court would show me mercy when the facts surrounding his medical history emerged.'

'You needn't have taken that route,' said Bryant. 'You're a declared bankrupt. If you receive an inheritance after filing for bankruptcy, it usually becomes part of your bankruptcy estate. The property would most likely have passed to Emily anyway.'

Longbright handed Hope a handkerchief.

'If you can't inherit and Mr Scott's daughter is protected, there is no reason why you should be charged,' said Bryant. 'You can have your life back.'

'We still have to file a report,' said May. 'But we're an autonomous unit, we don't report to the HSCC. You should be with Emily now.'

Longbright took her by the arm and led her out.

'The dress,' said Bryant, 'you can take it with you.'

'Give it to the officer who fitted it,' said Hope. 'I never want to see it again.'

As Rebecca Hope was met by her stepdaughter and led

off into the rain, May turned away from the window of their office and tore up the charge sheet. 'I hope we did the right thing,' he said. 'We'll get hell for this.'

'Probably,' Bryant agreed. 'Too much of this job is about taking things away from people. It feels good to give something back. Perhaps we restored her to visibility.'

BRYANT & MAY AND
THE CONSUL'S SON

In the damp, unlit basement of number 231 Caledonian
Road, King's Cross, Central London, a workman shouted
across to his mate. Confusingly, they were both called
Dave. The basement smelled of drains and fungus and
something rich and dark from the river below that prick-
led the skin and cleared the sinuses.

'I think we've got a problem,' said Dave, stepping over
the flooded areas of the basement floor. 'Look.' He ran his
torch beam across the stone, where a foot-wide channel
reflected slow-moving, brackish water. The stream disappeared into an iron grate set in the stone slabs. Long
smears cut through the green slime that had formed on the
floor.

The other Dave scratched his backside with the end of a
bradawl, knelt down, stuck his forefinger in the water,
tasted it and spat. 'It's sort of fresh.'

'What do you mean, "sort of"?'

'Not sewage.' He rose and spat again. 'Nasty though.

Freezing cold. It's probably coming from the River Fleet. Half of the old buildings around here still have wells in their basements.'

'Is that how this place gets its drinking water? It would explain a lot about the nutters upstairs. Lead in the pipes.'

'No, they're on Thames Water here.' Dave Two shone the torch across the far wall, lighting up a modern steel door. 'That shouldn't be there. Two entrances to the same basement?'

'That must belong to the joint next door. Maybe it was all one big building, then got flogged off separately.'

'What's next door?'

'The Ladykillers Café and a bar. It looks like they're storing their stock down here.' He waved his torch beam over wine racks and crates.

The second Dave poked about in his tool bag and found a claw hammer. 'Did you ever go to Becky's Dive Bar in Borough, under the Hop Exchange?' He stepped across the channel and checked out the far side of the room. 'Becky's barman had the biggest belly in London. To reach the loos you had to step across an underground river cut into the floor, exactly like this.'

'Blimey. Is it still there?'

'What, the bar? No, I think she got closed down for selling tainted sausages. What's that?'

In the centre of the river-damp floor sat a striated concrete box, approximately eight feet long and three feet wide.

'It can't be a substation,' said the first Dave. 'Not with a concrete lid. That's Portland stone. Half of London was once made out of it. Comes from the Isle of Portland in Dorset. White limestone. They used it to build St Paul's Cathedral. And Buckingham Palace.'

'How do you know all that?'

'My old man was a stonemason.' Dave One sidled over with a cage lamp and set it down. Taking his place at the corner of the lid, he indicated that Dave Two should do the same at the other end. Together they strained to lift it off. The slab proved too heavy to raise so they were forced to slide it over. Even then it would only move inch by painful inch.

After a few minutes they had managed to shift it half-way, but then it reached its tipping point and dropped, slamming to the floor. The Daves jumped out of the way to avoid having their toes crushed.

One of them crept forward with the cage light and gingerly lowered it over the edge.

'Is there something inside?' asked Dave One, straining to see.

'Not something,' replied Dave Two. 'Some*one*.'

They peered in together. Within was a slender body wrapped in a red plastic tablecloth covered in purple hyacinths. 'Blimey,' said Dave One. 'Is he alive?'

Dave Two gave a gesture of despair. 'Of course he's not bloody alive, he had half a ton of Portland stone on top of him.'

Dave One considered the point. 'Then how did he get in there?'

They walked around the tomb, their torch beams criss-crossing. 'Here.' Dave Two crouched down and ran his hand along the side of the box. 'This bit's a different colour. Painted wood.' He pushed against it and found that the upper edge had a sprung swing-hinge. 'The body could have been pushed in.' Rising, he studied the box from a little further back. 'What's it for? You wouldn't make a junction box out of stone. All the electrics are up on the ground floor.'

'It's like an altar or something,' said Dave One. 'I thought we'd find some gas meters and a pump, not a corpse in a tablecloth. My missus has one just like that.'

'Maybe she did it, then.'

Dave One looked back at the staircase. 'The PCU's main entrance has facial recognition software, so he couldn't have come that way. How did it get here?'

His partner pointed back at the steel door in the far wall. 'There's another method of egress.'

'*Egress?*'

'Going in and out.' Dave Two gave himself another scratch with the bradawl. 'I think there are bugs down here. You know the first thing I'd do? Check with the owners of the café, find out where the key to that door is.'

'Which sounds like a perfectly viable plan until you remember you're not a detective like them upstairs, but a builder-decorator with a certificate in plumbing.'

Dave Two began to pack up his tools with a deep sigh. 'I'm wasted in this job,' he said.

Some weeks later, Janice Longbright was looking around the PCU's ground-floor waiting room, trying to summon an inner reserve of patience that she knew she did not possess. Part of the unit's new commitment to accountability involved encouraging members of the public to come forward and talk to local officers in the weekly clinic, and today it was her turn to deal with them.

The routine was simple. You listened, filled out a form and directed them to another department. It achieved nothing and helped no one. If you were lucky, they didn't come back. Sometimes she ended up giving them money from her own purse. She studied the core of familiar faces. They fell into three distinct groups: people undergoing genuine hardship; complainers to whom Raymond Land referred as 'squeaky wheels'; and lonely men and women who had no one left to talk to but shopkeepers and public officials. There were six waiting to see her, one of whom was wrapped in a red nylon sleeping bag and cradling a sickly-looking terrier.

She checked her list. 'Mr Jamel Raif?'

The one in the sleeping bag raised his hand. She beckoned him to follow, waiting while he climbed out of the bag. He had no trousers. Taking him into the overheated interview room, she wedged open the window to let some fresh air in. Raif smelled rank. 'Please take a seat. Do you have any clothes?'

He looked forlornly down at the dog. 'Somebody stole my holdall.'

'Is that why you're here?'

'No, I can get clothes at Cally Road Worship. My work jeans are in the wash right now.' There was an evangelical hall nearby that gave out clothes on Sunday mornings. Raif modestly folded the sleeping bag over his boxers. The terrier stared at her expectantly. 'A friend of mine has gone missing.'

'You still sleeping on the street?' She had seen this one before, living in a red nylon tent under the canal bridge at Royal College Street.

'Nearly a year now.'

'That's a long time. Are you—'

'Don't worry about me, I've got myself a job, I work nights cleaning up at the Vinyl Café over by the Tileyard Studios. I just don't have a home. This is about Jerry. That's what I call him. His name is Jericho.'

'Jericho.' Longbright opened a drawer and took out a notepad. A pen and paper were still best for interviews. 'When and where did your friend go missing?'

'Just up the road, around five months ago. August.' He handed over a crumpled photograph. It showed a lean-bodied young man with shoulder-length blond hair, a wispy blond beard and no shirt, leaning against the side of a camper van brushing his teeth. He had wooden beads around his neck and the sun in his eyes.

Longbright tapped a crimson nail against her teeth. She knew where the shot had been taken. Students used to sell their gap-year utility vehicles there until the police stopped them. 'This is on Market Road, near Cally Road tube station, isn't it?'

'He had an old VW camper van,' Raif explained. 'He was going to get rid of it, but he had an accident and couldn't afford to get it fixed. I saw him most mornings. Then one night he just disappeared.'

'One *night*. How do you know that?'

'I was trying to get some kip – my sleeping bag was against the wall behind his van. His light was on. It went off some time after midnight, then I heard the side doors open and close. The van is still there. The council took all the other abandoned vehicles away but they had trouble trying to move the VW.'

'You haven't seen him since this was taken?'

'No.'

'Why did you wait so long to report him missing?'

'I didn't know you were running the clinic again. The old King's Cross station closed down.'

'There are constables covering your area.'

'We don't have a good relationship with them, because of the girls.'

Ah yes, the 'girls', she thought, remembering the hard-boiled line-up of gender-fluid ladies who stalked the street after midnight. A few of the roughest ones still worked the lower end of the road. 'You've been around here a long time now.'

'I want to get settled but they keep moving me over the border,' said Raif sadly. Camden and Islington had a habit of shifting transients across the line that separated the two boroughs.

'How do you know your friend didn't just go travelling again?'

'He had connections but no money. Really, like no money at all.'

'Do you remember the exact date he went missing?'

'I didn't see him after the beginning of August.'

'Does Vice still do round-ups?'

'Not so often now. Most of the girls have moved on. They come by once in a while.'

'Do you have anything that would help me find Jericho?'

'Just the picture. He never told me his last name. Maybe Camden still has the van. I think they sell them at auction.'

Longbright checked the clock above the door. 'And this is all you have?'

'I can give you a physical description. And I can draw him for you. I went to art college. Not that a degree in fine art can get you a job.'

'It could help us identify him. I'll check for the vehicle. If you leave details of where we can contact you . . .' She walked to the door and opened it; the queue in the waiting room had built up considerably.

'You already know where to find me.' Raif shuffled to his feet and held the sleeping bag over himself. The dog watched him anxiously. 'There was one thing,' he said. 'He told me about his father, like it was a big deal, but I don't know if it's true.'

'What about his father?'

'You're going to think I'm crazy.' Raif shook his head in disbelief. 'He said his old man was the American consul in London. He couldn't get anyone to believe him. He said they'd fallen out and the old man wouldn't speak to him or give him any more money.'

She pointed a finger at him. 'You, don't go anywhere.' She grabbed a phone and called John May's extension. 'John, it looks like we have a lead on the boy they found in our basement.'

Longbright stood just beyond the doorway of Raymond Land's office.

'Don't hover at the threshold,' called Land irritably. 'You're not Dracula waiting to be invited in.'

The two Daves had assured him they would find a door that fitted properly and fix it in place. So far they had come up with a pair of hinged brackets and an indentation chiselled into the frame for a strike-plate, but no actual door. Now that his divorce was through, Land's New Year resolution had been to become technically adept on hand-held devices so that he could register to start online dating, but filling in the profile had utterly defeated him. Lately he had been feeling increasingly useless. He couldn't even get his office door fixed.

'What do you need me for?' he snapped.

'Last month our workmen discovered the body of a twenty-two-year-old man called Jericho Flint in our basement, yes?' Longbright slipped a sheet of paper on to Land's eerily tidy desk. 'His head had been bashed in and he was wrapped in a tablecloth. The body went to Giles Kershaw over at the St Pancras Mortuary, but was taken away from him before he could conduct a preliminary examination.'

'I've been meaning to ask you about that,' said Land unconvincingly. 'Where did it go?'

'He was identified as the son of Howard Flint, the US consul in London, the one who recently left office.'

'They all leave office,' replied Land. 'They have to be gone before the next inauguration day. What do you mean, already identified?'

'Apparently two men turned up at the mortuary flashing US secret service accreditation and took the corpse away with them.'

'How did they know he was there, for heaven's sake?'

'I always assume the Americans know everything. It's safer that way.'

'Wait, this is the consul who told the press he was sick of being served lamb and was looking forward to having hamburgers again?'

'I don't think he enjoyed his time in the job. You probably want to know how the body was identified.'

The thought had not occurred to Land but he nodded gratefully.

'He had some sensitive documents inside his jacket. Mr Flint was on hand to identify his son. The lad had joined him here in London after completing a gap year. Apparently Flint Senior and Junior weren't on speaking terms. The father had cut off the boy's trust fund.' Longbright handed Land a hard copy of a press clipping. 'I had to pull this from a tabloid. Information on the family is hard to come by.'

Land skimmed the page. 'Why's that?'

'There's some kind of press embargo on their personal lives, so the only articles out there are bits of society gossip. Reading between the lines you get a bit more of a picture. The father is a hawkish Republican; the son was an artistic counter-culturalist. Jericho was interviewed by the paper nine months ago. At that time he was living in Hackney, smoking dope, selling paintings to earn a living. He'd settled in London because it was one of his father's conditions for being granted any sort of an income. Flint Senior wanted the boy where he could keep an eye on him. They argued and the money tap was finally switched off. That much seems common knowledge.'

Land handed back the article. 'Tell me about the part that isn't.'

'It looks like Jericho Flint was in financial trouble. He lost his flat and borrowed from everyone, so he probably made a few enemies. I spoke to a mate of his who was pretty sure that something bad had happened to him.'

'Why does he think that?'

'If Flint had been so short of cash he would have sold his van, even though the engine needed to be repaired. Instead he vanished overnight, leaving the vehicle behind. It's only a fifteen-minute walk from Tufnell Park to our building, so how did he end up in the basement?'

'It's not our job to answer that any more,' said Land wearily. 'I'm sure the US Embassy has plenty of granite-faced agents looking into it right now.'

'Then I guess you haven't seen this,' said Longbright, passing him a letter. 'The Home Office is handing us the responsibility.'

Land was horrified. 'They can't just do that – can they?'

'His body was found on our premises, Raymond. As you can see, they feel it's incumbent upon us to lead an investigation and avoid souring our so-called "special rela-tionship". We're waiting for their coroner's report.'

Land's eyes widened. 'You've spoken to them?'

'I just had them on the phone.'

He slapped the desk purposefully. 'Then get Bryant and May in here.'

'They're tied up with another case.'

'This is more important. I don't want the Americans saying we can't handle it.' Land's hand went to his lips. 'No, wait. If I bring Bryant in he'll start involving witches and shamans. We'll become a laughing stock.' There crept upon his face the anxiety of an Englishman stricken with indecision. It was a look you could see every day in Pret A Manger when middle managers struggled to choose sandwich fillings.

'Then don't officially involve him,' said Longbright. 'It would be better if the embassy didn't see their names on the investigation team. Let them think Jack and I are handling it.'

'Do you think you're up to it, Janice?'

Longbright shot back a look that could have cracked a window.

'All right, I'll keep their names out of the official report. See what you can do.'

'I'll need to talk to Mr Bryant about how the body was found.'

Land sighed. 'This is how it always starts. First we ask his opinion, then a couple of days later the unit is overrun with members of the maniac community. I don't want him reporting to the Yanks that Flint was ritually sacrificed by druids. That weird illness he had made him worse than he was before.'

'Mr Bryant was suffering the after-effects of having been poisoned,' Longbright reminded her boss. 'He's back to normal now.'

'He was never normal,' said Land forlornly. 'He is the thorn in my paw, the stone in my shoe, the fly in my ointment. You think Her Majesty's Government causes trouble for us? Wait until you see what the Americans can do. They won't appreciate some superannuated Harry Potter interfering with international policy. You have to keep him as far away from them as possible, do you understand?'

'I just thought you should be kept in the picture. I didn't think you'd seen the letter.'

Longbright took her leave, although not before Land noticed that she had failed to agree to his terms.

One of the Daves stuck his head around the door of the detectives' office.

'Bugger off,' Bryant warned. 'We can't have you two electrifying things while we're trying to work.'

'Sorry to bother you,' said Dave One. 'It's just that me and my colleague were talking about that lad whose body we found in the basement. We heard you've been asked to investigate the case.'

'How do you get your information so fast?' asked May impatiently. 'Is there some kind of underground network we should be aware of?'

'They *did* find him,' Bryant reminded his partner. 'You'd better come in.'

Dave One stepped across the threshold and scratched at his scrubby beard. 'The basement door was locked when we went down there. We were the first to open it. But there's another way in from the building next door.'

'You mean Flint could have come in from the other side?'

'It's just that you wouldn't hide a body down there, because of the difficulty getting it down the stairs, right?' Dave One looked at his boots, embarrassed. 'I know it sounds daft—'

'No, it doesn't at all,' said Bryant, enthused. 'You think he was killed down there. It means he could have met someone in the Ladykillers Café or the bar, and there was an altercation.'

'We thought you should talk to the owners.'

'You can't, Arthur,' warned May. 'We can't be seen to be working on the case.'

'What, you think the Yanks have got spies out watching the building? Surely they won't stop me going for a cuppa and a cake.' He rose to his feet. 'Come on, I've had my eye on their Victoria sponge for a while.'

Jack Renfield was careful not to smile too much. He had been racking his brain trying to think of a way to win back Longbright, and now the opportunity had presented itself. As he had been teamed with her once more, he would be able to show her how thoughtful and supportive he could be. It had been quite a learning curve for the former desk sergeant from being the confused butt of everyone's jokes to reinstatement as a trusted member of the PCU. He tried not to appear too dog-like when gazing at her.

'There's not much to go on.' Longbright turned the pages on her notepad. 'We know Howard Flint was estranged from his son. The CIA brief says that he knew the boy was still living in London but wished to have no further contact with him. Jericho Flint was last seen on the evening of August the tenth. It means that whoever stashed him in our basement did so right under our noses.'

'Either he was killed here, or brought in already dead,' said Renfield. 'I know we're lax on security but there's no way someone could have carried a corpse through this building. The electronic entry system was installed at the main door as soon as we arrived.'

'But the Daves say there's another way in,' Longbright said.

He caught her eye just as she had the same thought. 'Let's see for ourselves.'

Number 231 Caledonian Road occupied the end-of-terrace position on a sliver of land that had formerly hosted (in reverse order) a public house, temperance rooms, a chapel, a brothel, a boarding house and a private residence. When the Hoop & Grapes lost its licence and closed down, the property remained derelict for several years before being converted into offices that were purchased by the Home Office to house the Specialist Operations Directorate. The PCU jumped the queue because it urgently needed to be rehoused, Arthur Bryant having managed to burn down their old unit at Mornington Crescent.

The basement was much older than the late-Victorian edifice that had been constructed over it. A painted wooden door at the rear of the ground floor led to the basement staircase.

'Dan reckons the lower floor was laid after 1824. Something about the mass manufacture of concrete. It was built over a tributary of the River Fleet and used to store beer barrels.' Longbright stopped before a riveted iron door edged with yellow and black striped tape. 'The Daves were meant to put some lights in but didn't get around to it.'

'Here, let me.' Renfield squeezed past her. Gripping the handle in a meaty fist, he dragged the door open.

'The US Embassy brought in members of their own team to stay with Flint's body. They spent an afternoon at the unit, but didn't allow anyone else downstairs.' She turned on her cage light and held it high. 'After they removed the remains, they taped up the door with specific instructions that no one should enter the basement. Obviously they forgot to tell the Daves.'

'This part looks a lot older than the building above,' said Renfield.

Longbright's light fell on the eight-foot-long stone box that had contained the consul's son. 'The lid is a single piece of Portland stone.' She pointed to the great slab that leaned against the container. 'It took two of them to push it off.'

'Whoever brought him down here must have known about the box,' said Renfield. 'You don't just stumble on something like this. How come nobody came down to the basement when we first moved in?'

'Raymond told us it belonged to the building next door. I checked the lease, and it turns out he was wrong – as usual.'

'If Flint was already dead there had to be at least two others with him, putting him in the casket while we were working upstairs.' He pressed his hand against the box and felt the damp, cold stone on his skin. 'What's it doing here anyway? How *could* anyone have known about it?'

Longbright led the way over to the door in the partition. She leaned close to the wood. 'I can hear something moving about on the other side.'

Renfield placed his ear against the door as well. 'Maybe it's rats.'

The door suddenly opened outwards and Bryant stepped in. 'The café has a cocktail bar downstairs,' he explained as May followed him in. 'They have a very good selection of gins. It appears several of these basements were once connected. If this is the way they brought him in, they'd still have had to pass through a busy bar.'

'Why would anyone go to so much trouble?' Renfield asked. 'What do you gain by hiding a body down here?'

Longbright shone her torch at the empty sarcophagus. 'Who's going to look for it in a cop shop?' she replied.

'How would you like to not smell of cabbages any more?' Longbright asked brightly.

Meera Mangeshkar regarded her with suspicion.

'I'm talking about taking you off bin duty.'

Meera scrunched her lips. She might have been trying to imagine elephants in outer space. 'Me and Colin always get the bin searches. There's no one else to do them.'

'Perhaps I could persuade Raymond to outsource the dirtiest jobs. You've both been doing them for long enough.'

Mangeshkar's mistrustful eyes narrowed still further. 'What's the catch?'

'No catch. Jack and I could do with your help. The consul's son hung out with a young crowd. They won't open up to us, but they might to you.'

'You're a police officer. You can get them in here and scare the shit out of them.'

'That isn't how we do things, Meera, you know that.'

'You're saying we should go undercover?'

'Jericho Flint was sleeping in a camper van on Market Road. There's a healthy counter-culture scene around there. There's also a big recording studio complex nearby that has a twenty-four-hour café used by sound engineers and musicians. I've sent you and Colin some profile notes. Find out who Flint's friends were. His father wants to know what his son had been up to.'

'Why? It says here he hadn't seen him for a year. Why didn't they speak? What's missing from the notes?'

'That's what I'm going to find out,' Longbright replied. 'Jack and I have an appointment with the US consul tonight.'

'They're moving the embassy from Grosvenor Square to Nine Elms,' said Meera. 'The new one looks like a fortress with swords on the top and a moat.'

'I imagine that's pretty much what it is. Apparently they didn't think much of the security in this place. We're meeting Mr Flint tonight in a "soft secure" building in Mayfair, but I can't get you in. Only two of us are getting clearance for entry. If we're given any further information I'll feed it through, but you can start right now by going to the Vinyl Café. Try not to look like coppers.'

'What do you mean?' Meera seemed aggrieved.

'The boots.'

'I don't know what else to wear.'

'Look around you. Try dressing like a normal girl for once.'

'There are so many things wrong with that sentence I don't know where to begin. I've seen the old photos of you in your low-cut gold lamé gown down the strip club, dressed like Marilyn Monroe.'

'Diana Dors, actually.'

Meera shrugged. 'I don't know who that is, presumably someone old. I'll go undercover but I'm not wearing a dress over black leggings or doing anything weird with my hair.'

Longbright considered her. 'I don't think I've ever seen you out of uniform. You don't have the fashion gene, do you?'

'No, I have the climbing-in-and-out-of-bins gene, thanks to being stuck on rubbish duty for ages. You're the glamorous one, but I agree you're pushing it age-wise so I'll give it a go.' She looked down at her ribbed navy PCU sweater. 'Colin will be all right, he always fits in.'

'You two seem to be getting on pretty well these days.'

'I'm waiting for him to underestimate me. That'll be fun.'

'You know he's in love with you, right?'

Meera rolled her eyes. 'I'm not thick. He just needs to slow down a bit.'

Janice laid a hand on her arm. 'Don't hurt him, Meera. He's not as strong as you.'

'Yeah, well. Ta for the advice. Not sure you're the one to be giving it.'

'Because of me and Jack?'

'Yeah. On, off, nobody knows where you stand.'

'It comes with the job.' Janice gathered her notes and pulled a pencil out of her hair with some difficulty.

'You mean the job comes first. Like Superman not marrying Lois Lane.'

'They got married.'

'Only in one timeline. Then ended up single in another.'

'Then I guess that'll be like me and Jack.' She waved Meera away. 'What is this with the personal stuff? Nobody around here ever discusses their personal life.'

'That's because most of us don't have one,' Meera pointed out.

'Go on, get out of here, before I change my mind.'

Jack Renfield studied the address on his phone. The bay-windowed Victorian houses in Mount Street hid their true identities. It was hard to tell which was a private club, an expensive restaurant, a consulate, a sultan's apartment. Many were merely elegant shells for shifting money around the world.

'I read some pretty brutal comments from Howard Flint about the British police,' said Renfield, checking the door numbers. 'Didn't he accuse us of being soft on terrorism? I thought consuls are meant to be non-partisan.'

'They are, and so is the ambassador. It's here.' Longbright climbed the tiled steps to an elegant red-brick mansion with closed grey blinds. 'He's heading back to Boston soon. We're lucky we caught him.'

The door was opened before they could ring the bell.

'We're from—' Jack began.

'We know who you are,' said a secret service agent, stepping back. Longbright raised an eyebrow at Renfield and stepped inside. The black and white tiled hall and oak-panelled rooms beyond offered the perfect simulacrum of a wealthy Mayfair house in the 1930s, but there were tell-tale signs of hidden technology. Sharp-blue LEDs were embedded in the skirting boards, and tiny black cameras winked from the corners of the ceilings.

'DI Longbright, DS Renfield, come through.' Howard Flint beckoned to them with a welcoming smile that did not reach as far as his eyes. He had the air of a harried diplomat trying to organize the evacuation of a colonial outpost before the eruption of a volcano. His untidily parted red hair almost hid the white plastic button in his right ear. Every now and again he paused, listening to it, before glancing back at them. 'We were expecting somebody more senior. I can't spare you much time tonight. Everything I have to say is in the official report. I'm putting my wife on to you.' He made it sound like a threat. Leading the way to a bare office where two chairs had been placed before a desk, he indicated that they should sit, then left the room.

'Awkward,' Renfield mouthed at Longbright. A gold

antique carriage clock pinged on a black marble mantel-
piece. The door opened and in came Kate Flint. Longbright
goggled and thought, *This woman means business*; hair
set hard, jaw set firm, a square-collared grey moiré two-
piece suit, discreet pearls, clear nail varnish, patent-leather
heels. If her home was a fortress, she was definitely its
guardian. Janice realized she was much younger than
her fashion sense suggested, certainly a generation later
than her husband. Formal introductions were effected.
The consul's wife tapped her foot and appraised each of
them unnervingly.

'There were a few points not covered in the report,'
Longbright began.

'Why don't I just talk,' replied Kate Flint, not phrasing
a question. She paced the room, leaving them to twist
about in their seats. 'My husband and my son were not in
contact with one another. Jericho chose to remain in London after his gap year rather than return home to begin
an internship in a legal firm. During this interim period
neither of us maintained close contact with him, although
my husband made extensive inquiries as to his whereabouts. We held on to his passport because he could not be
trusted to take care of himself. We need to know what
happened to him between August tenth and the discovery
of his remains on your premises. We should have been
apprised of your role in his death, how he gained admission to your building and which of your officers may be
culpable.'

'I don't think you understand the situation, Mrs Flint,'
Longbright interrupted. 'Your husband's tenure in the consulate has now expired, so while we will still do everything
within our power to help you discover the truth about your
son, we have to conduct the investigation in accordance

with our own jurisprudence and the procedures set down by London's Homicide and Serious Crime Command.'

Flint stared at her in brutal silence for a few moments, then continued as if she hadn't spoken. 'What we need you to do is find out who killed our son and why, and to do so before his official service so that we may grieve with closure. We will need a full timeline of your unit's accountability in this matter, and further to that we will need—'

'You are required to aid us in the official investigation, Mrs Flint,' said Longbright, raising her voice. 'We'll have questions concerning your relationship with your son. For example, why did you have no contact with him?'

Flint's face stayed emotionless. 'Our relationship with Jericho is no concern of yours. What should worry you more is that he was found dead inside your unit, which places every member of your staff under suspicion of direct involvement in his death.'

Renfield tried to calm the situation. 'When can we expect to be informed about the findings in the coroner's report, ma'am?' he asked.

'My husband has decided that you should not be allowed access to the report, as it was conducted outside of your jurisdiction.'

'That could be seen as obstruction,' warned Longbright.

'Howard never wanted you to handle the case. Apart from the ethical issues raised by a potentially culpable department investigating itself, your unit's track record is a matter of grave concern to us. Your senior detectives are past retirement age. They fail to run their investigations according to national statutory regulations. They have a history of evidence contamination and rights abuses. They openly share privileged information with undesirables and have been the subject of countless internal investigations. I understand they've repeatedly ignored Home Office guidelines and were prosecuted for releasing illegal aliens into the community.'

'They get results, Mrs Flint,' said Renfield.

'They burned down their own unit, didn't they? Yet somehow, despite all of this, they've managed to renew their charter and continue in office. Clearly they have some kind of special relationship with the City of London Police Commission.' Like her husband, she had mastered the art of the menacing smile, which she now used to devastating effect. 'Under the circumstances, we are unable to share any information concerning our own independent investigation, and feel it is better that you reach your own conclusions. Your detectives will find out that their network of special relationships does not extend to the international consulate of the United States of America. We are leaving at the end of the week. You have until then to submit your own findings.'

Dismissing them with a brief raising of her hand, she left the room.

'Blimey,' said Renfield as they left, 'was she trying to put the frighteners on us or what? What do you think was going on there?'

'Either she thinks we're complete morons or they've got something to hide,' Longbright replied as they crossed the road. 'It's going to be tricky working without the coroner's report. I wonder what will happen if we apply for their phone records.'

'Janice, we're on our own. Whatever happens, they're going to hang us out to dry. If you think they haven't already reached their own conclusions you're underestimating them. Our investigation is a technicality, nothing more.'

'Then we'll have to surprise them,' said Longbright, setting her jaw.

Bimsley and Mangeshkar had changed from their black PCU uniforms into jeans, sweaters and dark jackets. Market Road had a wild, unkempt look. It was the kind of area where you kept your phone in your pocket. They stopped before the only remaining vehicle parked at the kerb. Colin cleaned a patch of glass with his fist and peered through the filthy windscreen.

'VW Dormobile, 1971. It would have been blue and white originally, probably worth about twelve grand after a bit of panel work. It was found unlocked. Someone's nicked the tyres.' He opened the door and slid it back. 'Blimey, it's a bit fragrant inside.'

'He was living in it,' Meera replied. 'I'm sure others have been since then.'

Once, the street that ran between Tufnell Park and Pentonville had been lined with gap-year camper vans up for resale, just as Warren Street had once been filled with used cars. Both markets had existed on the borderline of legality and had been closed down.

The interior of the vehicle was plastered with colourful pages from art books. Colin poked his fingertip into the corner of the dashboard and showed it to her. 'Print powder. Looks like Mr Flint's team has been over the interior. Their tech is probably better than Dan's. We won't find anything here.'

'How can we determine a cause of death without the body? If his people have already conducted their own investigation, why use the PCU at all? And how are we expected to file a report when someone else has already trodden over the evidence?'

'As I see it, the PCU has one advantage.' Colin climbed out and dusted himself down. 'We don't work the same way. We take our cue from a couple of detectives who don't just think outside the box, they tear off its hinges, smash it flat, stamp on it and start the investigation somewhere else. Sort of thing.'

'Thank you, Colin, for that erudite explanation of the unit's philosophy,' Meera said, pulling the van door shut. 'Let's try the Vinyl Café.'

It was a ten-minute walk to Tileyard Road, a dead end of new orange-brick boxes that existed on the fault line between Pentonville and Somers Town, an odd no-man's-land created by a rough triangle of railway cuts, embankments and arterial roads. It was an area that had long been suited to grey skies and rain, but lately the factories and warehouses had been replaced by rows of cloned apartments.

'My dad wouldn't recognize this place now,' Colin said. 'The air's almost clean.'

'What did he do?' asked Meera.

Colin smiled to himself. 'He was a patterer. That's what my great-granddad used to call it. A newspaper-seller. They shouted out the headlines, and the gorier they made the stories sound the more papers they sold. He had the gift of the gab all right. That's why my mum fell for him.'

'It's funny, you don't have that at all, do you?' said Meera.

'Are you saying I'm inarticulate?'

'No, I'm saying you're honest.'

'He had other jobs but they were all a bit sketchy.'

'Sounds like Mr Bryant's old man. No wonder you two get on so well.'

The Vinyl Café was clearly operating in its own creative ecosystem. The customers were unpretentiously fashionable, with the easy-going air of industry creatives who had seen it all before.

They headed to the coffee counter. 'Glad I found this place,' Meera told the barista. 'A mate of mine recommended it. Jericho Flint, used to come in here sometimes, do you know him?'

'Meera, what's the point of us being undercover if you act like a copper?' Colin whispered.

The girl handed over two soy decaf flat whites. 'This is my first week.'

'Who's been here longer? What about your regular customers?'

The barista pointed to a table in the corner. 'They're session musicians, been coming here since it opened.'

'Cheers.' Meera dropped some coins into her tip saucer and beckoned Colin to follow.

'Who am I supposed to be?' he asked as they approached the table.

'You don't have to be anyone, we're not making small talk. Hi. Can I have a word?' She waved at the table and dropped on to a spare chair without asking. Colin hovered awkwardly behind her. The group broke off its various conversations and studied her. 'My name is Meera, and I'm looking for this guy.' She thumbed open the photograph on her phone and showed it to them. 'We think he used to come in here sometimes.'

'That's the artist,' said a young girl with a blue ponytail and one side of her head shaved. Elegant tendrils of a pastoral tattoo crept up her right arm and over one bare shoulder. 'I'm Abi, I'm one of the sound engineers here.' She raised a hand. 'He used to come around selling his paintings. Sort of like surreal circus posters. Very cool. I bought one.'

'How long ago was this?' asked Meera.

'Are you friends of his? He's a nice guy. I wouldn't want—'

'We're police officers,' Colin announced.

The temperature around the table dropped a degree or two. Meera mentally slapped a hand on her forehead. 'Do you remember his name?' she asked.

'Jericho,' Abi replied. 'Not a name you forget. I haven't seen him for a while.'

'When was the last time?'

'August, maybe. Definitely summer.' She looked to the others for confirmation. 'Is he missing?'

'I'm afraid he died,' said Colin. 'We know very little about the circumstances. We're trying to help his parents.' It wasn't a lie. 'Did he have any friends, anyone he came in with?'

'No, he was always alone,' said Abi. 'Wish I could help you.'

'Abi, he sold a painting to the café,' said one of the session musicians. 'It's in the other room.' Abi shot him a poisonous look.

They trooped through to the tables by the hot food counter, behind which were arranged dozens of pictures. Meera spotted the primary-coloured poster at once: a human rhinoceros in chains, surrounded by cobra women. 'Is that one of his? Quite a vivid imagination.'

'He had a whole portfolio of artwork like that,' said one of the other engineers. 'They're based on old Barnum & Bailey posters but they all feature mythical creatures.'

Colin turned the poster on its hook and looked at the back. In the corner was a sticker. 'He had an agent?'

'I wouldn't think so,' Abi replied. 'He was selling them in pubs and cafés. I saw him in the Star of Kings one evening with a portfolio full of photocopies.'

'That's the framer's sticker,' said Meera. She knew the place well, just under the arches opposite the platforms of St Pancras Station.

It took ten minutes to walk to Bill & Ben's Framing Emporium. Within the Victorian red-brick arches were a handful of dusty old shops, including the frame-makers. Opposite, the modern glass-tiled wall of the station rose up, two halves separated by a century and united by a single road.

'It makes sense,' Colin said. 'He was living in the van and selling his work in the same area. He had no transport so he would have used the nearest place.'

'We should have been allowed to file the first report.'

'Meera, we're the crime scene.' Colin pushed open the door in the arch and stepped into a chaotic geometry of hanging frames. 'Afterwards they'll compare the two investigations. It's an old tech trick, setting up a duplicate procedure to keep your own data clean.'

Bill and Ben were obviously brothers, working beside each other in old-fashioned brown carpenters' aprons in the shop's cluttered studio. They scrutinized the picture on Colin's phone and conferred.

'He came in here quite often,' said Bill. 'Music-hall posters, circuses, strange artwork. Produced guerrilla street art as well. The council paid him to brighten up some of the tunnels around Waterloo. Wasn't very struck by those pieces myself. He looked a bit on his beam-ends, didn't he?'

'Yes, living rough,' Ben agreed. 'You know how people get a sort of frayed look after a while? But clean, though, and always cheerful. Young, of course. American. We must have framed half a dozen of these for him. We did floaters and box frames with natural veneer finishes, a couple with nice mouldings. He was selling them and making a living, I'll tell you that.'

Bill opened the order book on the counter and turned it around. 'Business must have been picking up, because he started coming in regularly last summer. And he was choosing more expensive frames.'

Colin showed them the photograph again. 'Would you go on record with an identification?'

'It's definitely him,' replied Ben. 'I remember because he always sent his girlfriend to collect the finished pictures.'

'She was a real looker,' said Bill. 'Young, though. Probably not much more than eighteen or nineteen.'

'He had a girlfriend?' Meera was surprised. No one at the Vinyl Café had mentioned her.

'We haven't seen either of them for a while now.'

'How long?'

They consulted again. 'A few months?' said one, and the other nodded. 'A few months. August or September.'

'How were the frames paid for?' asked Colin.

'Cash, she always paid cash.'

'Can you give us a description of her?' Meera asked.

'Long dark hair, fancy dresser,' said Bill. 'There's never much you can say about pretty people, is there?'

'She had an accent,' said Ben. 'She sounded Eastern European.'

'Did you find out her name?'

'It might be on one of the old receipts. She had to sign to collect.' He checked the counterfoils in the receipt book. 'Here you go. Rose something. Bill, what does that say?'

They all studied the handwriting. 'What is that last name? Clavi, Slavi?'

'I think the first letter is a C,' said Meera.

The rest of the receipt read: 'For collection 7 September.'
'She never picked it up. It's still here. Hang on, I'll get it for you.'

Bill came back with a small bubble-wrapped rectangle eighteen inches by twenty-six inches, then cut it open with a Stanley knife. The artwork showed a bikini-clad girl on a Lambretta scooter, 1950s-style. Her glossy black hair was tied back in a ponytail.

'That's her,' said Ben. 'It's a really good likeness.'

'So his girlfriend modelled for him. Can we take this with us?'

'Sure, if you pay a hundred and twenty quid.'

'Keep the frame – the picture's evidence.'

After looking uncertainly at his brother, Bill turned over the painting and set to work. 'You know, we just knew him as Jerry. A nice lad.' Bill removed the picture and rolled it up.

'If anyone comes in asking for this, give them our number.' Colin handed Bill his PCU card.

'We know you guys,' he said, showing his brother the card. 'We own the antiques shop next door. I sold Mr Bryant some bits and pieces just the other day.'

'What sorts of bits and pieces?'

'A rifle-range target, a ventriloquist's dummy and a grate.'

'Why am I not surprised?' muttered Meera.

'Has this girl done something wrong?' asked Ben.

'Why?' Colin countered. 'Did she look the type?'

'Frankly,' replied Bill as his brother nodded vigorously, 'yes.'

'Let's get back.' Colin held the door open for Meera. 'We can't go any further without some help.'

*

PCU DEBRIEF – UNEDITED TRANSCRIPT

DAN BANBURY The CCTV above the bus stop on Pancras Road recorded the girlfriend leaving the framers on July the sixteenth, heading in the direction of Market Road. We're trying to trace her whereabouts but we don't have much to go on.

MEERA MANGESHKAR You have her full name.

BANBURY I've had no luck so far so I'm trying other spellings. We've got one receipt signature that's open to interpretation. There are five postcodes around here: N7, N19, NW5, N1 and now N1C. Do you know how many residents aren't on the electoral register?

JOHN MAY And there's no one left at Market Road who might recall seeing her.

COLIN BIMSLEY The cops cleared them all away, and there are no residential properties on that stretch, just football pitches. Meera and I figured they had to eat, so we took the screen grab and the poster to the nearest supermarkets on Camden Road. There are five minimarts on that stretch. One guy recalled seeing her around the same time she collected the picture.

MAY Really? Why would he remember her?

BIMSLEY She used to come in regularly. He had to write the customer's name on the coffee cup, and saw that she had a red rose tattooed on her upper arm. It's a kind of vegan-organic place called Butterfly, the only place like it in the area – a lot of the musicians go there.

ARTHUR BRYANT So much for rock 'n' roll. Have they all gone gluten-free now?

MANGESHKAR We're running a check on ink parlours but it'll take some time. There are dozens, and a red rose is one of the most common tats.

BRYANT Anything else?

MANGESHKAR That's all we have at the moment.

BRYANT Because you're going about it backwards.

BANBURY Sorry, Mr B.?

BRYANT Are there any biscuits? Something I can dunk. Not Lincolns, they fall apart. Something a little more robust, Bourbons, perhaps. Oh, wait, I have these.'

Janice Longbright paused her recorder while the unit's most senior detective emptied a bag of Barratt's Shrimps, Love Hearts and Milk Gums all over the table.

MAY Perhaps we could steer you back on to the conversational highway, Arthur?

BRYANT Jack, how did the US consul seem to you?

JACK RENFIELD Angry. Impatient. We only saw him for a moment.

JANICE LONGBRIGHT He didn't want anything to do with us.

BRYANT So how would you proceed?

RENFIELD What, me? I'd take a good look at how Jericho Flint spent his time. Maybe he found himself caught up in something he couldn't get out of.

BRYANT I'm sure that was the first thought to pass through his father's mind. But there's nothing on record about Jericho Flint, is there? No online profile, no political affiliations?

LONGBRIGHT Not that we've found so far. Of course, they could easily have been removed.

BRYANT During the time Howard Flint's team had the case they filed a coroner's report plus all their findings on us, the victim and the circumstances surrounding his death. The consul's wife told you their investigation is not subject to UK jurisdiction. So what do you do? You immediately follow in their footsteps.

LONGBRIGHT You're saying we should start somewhere else?

BRYANT I'm saying you should do what this unit does best. Go with the gut instead of the brain. They used deductive logic, technology and common sense.

MAY Not weapons that usually exist in our arsenal.

BRYANT I assume they studied the boy's movements and got to his friends. They may even have tracked his final hours. Yet they still came up with nothing.

RENFIELD We don't know that.

LONGBRIGHT We wouldn't have been given the case otherwise, Jack. They'd have informed the Home Office that the investigation was satisfactorily concluded.

BRYANT Exactly. So there's no point in trying to reproduce their investigation without the same resources. You need to start at the other end. What's the key thing we know about the consul and his son?

LONGBRIGHT They fell out.

BRYANT Why?

LONGBRIGHT Personal differences, I imagine.

BRYANT Opposing ideologies, really? I had nothing in common with my parents but we stayed close.

RENFIELD But a Republican consul and an artistic dropout? The old man must have been disappointed. Maybe he didn't approve of the girlfriend.

BRYANT Forget the friends. Forget the politics. Start with the girl. She's the only one we may be able to find.

MAY You won't get very far. I already ran some online searches. Every single piece of information on the case can be traced back to a central government source.

Neither the consul nor his wife have a Facebook page or a Twitter account. The son had both for a while when he first arrived but they were deactivated long ago.

BRYANT The government only wants an official version out there. That's why we need a new approach. I appreciate that this is your baby. John and I won't interfere in any way. I don't want to influence you. *Cherchez la femme.*

LONGBRIGHT How?

BRYANT An attractive young girl always has friends. Find them.

Bryant stood on the staircase leading to the basement of the Ladykillers Café. The entrance to the cocktail bar was lit with crimson neon handwriting: 'The Wilberforce'.

He wandered in, sucking at his unlit pipe, and took a look around. There were red leather bar stools, framed 1950s posters of Ealing comedies and a still of Mrs Wilberforce herself, Katie Johnson, posing with her parrot, General Gordon.

A scenario was forming in his head. Soon after midnight on 10 August, Jericho Flint had left his van on Market Road. Perhaps he had arranged to meet Rose Clavi. If they were looking for somewhere to drink, their best option would have been to head south towards King's Cross. Here they would have had the choice of at least six bars and two private members' clubs.

Bryant seated himself on a bar stool and swung it around. The posters and photographs of King's Cross in 1955 passed him again and again. The years fell away. King's Cross had had hidden bars and clubs in the basements of its buildings for as long as he could remember. Bottled beers, cheap gins, the spoor of perfume and tobacco, Matt Monro and Kathy Kirby on the jukebox, the smell of urine and Dettol wafting in from tiled toilets.

The decades drifted. The stools became vacant as barflies died off, décor changed, the jukebox vanished. The bumble of banter was etched into the walls: Macmillan, Wilson, Heath and Thatcher; Man U, Arsenal, Chelsea and Spurs; the Maltese, the Krays, the Great Train Robbery; Tommy Steele, Alma Cogan, Frank Ifield and Dusty Springfield. He was cursed with a memory for ephemera: the times and places, the characters and their conversations. So vivid was the past that the present seemed insubstantial and ghostly by comparison.

He helped himself to a shot of rum and downed it in one. He tried to imagine a young man with shaggy blond hair perched on the next bar stool.

Jericho Flint, estranged from his wealthy, powerful parents, painting surreal scenes of a London that never was, in love with the dark-eyed retro-hippy Rose, who collected his frames and stayed over in his cramped VW van until one night – what?

What brought you here? he wondered.

He slid from the stool and walked out into the corridor. There were three doors: two for the toilets and a third which led to the basement that connected to the PCU.

The basement floor was wet with river water. Between the stacks of yellow plastic crates was a cleared path leading to the door that opened to the unit's stairs. There before him stood the stone casket.

He thought about the contours and patterns of the water-riven neighbourhood. The Canal Museum was just two streets away, situated further along the course of an underground stream. In its basement was a circular stone ice cave, built in the mid-nineteenth century. Everyone who visited the basement commented on the lowered temperature. Barges had come from Norway to deliver vast slabs of ice via the canal system to Carlo Gatti, the Swiss-Italian who first brought ice cream to London. The wharf in the next street was named in his honour.

The stone box that stood before him was not a sarcophagus but an ice-holder, unusual anywhere else but once ubiquitous in this part of North London, the first place in the city to have fresh ice delivered.

To reach the box required passing through three doors: the main entrance to the Ladykillers Café, the door to the Wilberforce cocktail bar and the downstairs basement door. But it was still a more likely route than getting past the locked entrance and video identification system of the PCU.

Someone knew about the ice box. They had drawn Flint down here, killed him and shoved him inside it, knowing that there was little chance of anyone finding him. The cold would delay the body's decomposition.

The café and club were part of the new sleaze-free, upmarket King's Cross. The days of protection rackets, bent coppers and working girls had passed. The cocktail bar held ironically hip knitting parties, for God's sake. He had met the owners and spoken with them. Their lease for the premises had been paid from the Bank of Mum and Dad. They rarely visited their own property. But what about the managers? They were there every evening.

There were only two ways to lure a man into the dark: by force or deception. Suddenly it became obvious that he needed to find the girlfriend, Rose. A scenario came into focus: a betrayal, a smile in the shadows, a desperate girl using a gullible dropout to get herself out of trouble, a situation that resulted in Jericho Flint losing his life.

The Wilberforce's bar manager would live by night and know all the regulars. Rose Clavi was a regular; she had to be in order to know about the ice box in the basement. Everything depended on finding her.

As the wet streets cleared in King's Cross, the lights of the PCU burned on beyond midnight. Raymond Land was wandering from room to room stifling yawns, a habit that spread like measles.

In the common room Meera Mangeshkar had made vast amounts of chai and Turkish coffee to keep everyone awake. Bimsley was doing stretches at the window to try and stop his back from seizing up. Renfield and Long-bright were staring at laptop screens that had now switched to night mode. The others were hourly adding to the progress boards that stood against the rear wall of the common room. Only the two Daves were missing.

'Where is she?' asked Jack Renfield, scrolling through onscreen pages of missing persons. 'Rose Clavi. It's not a common name.'

'There's a mid-length haircut called a Clavi-Cut online, but that's about all,' said Janice, sitting back and repinning her hair. 'We shouldn't be relying on Google searches. We should have the same resources as the Met's MIT.'

'Bees,' said Bryant, looking for somewhere to bash out his pipe bowl. 'That's all I've got. *Hoplitis claviventris*. They're known to nest in rose bushes. Common to the North of England and some of the Midlands. They're univoltine. Rather like my downstairs neighbour.' He spotted blank looks. 'They produce offspring every year.'

'You think she's named after an insect?' Banbury scoffed. 'Sorry, Mr B., think you're barking up the wrong tree.'

'Barking is right,' muttered Raymond Land, sticking a

tube of Vicks up his left nostril. 'There must be something else on Jericho Flint. Good God, the Yanks can't have buried everything. Any luck with the bar manager?'

'He left in October,' Longbright replied. 'Kharmel Hunter. He was there for seven months. Paid off the books, cash in hand. He's dodgy.'

'What do you mean?' asked May.

Longbright ran a nail down the screen. 'A history of small-scale trouble, some odd gaps in his timeline, a couple of suspect associates. Jobs include debt collection, bouncer, security.' She added him to the list as a Person of Interest.

The night was mild despite the drifting rain that glossed the neon-crazed pavements. They sat beneath the red and green striped awning of Simmons Bar on the Cally Road as Meera came outside with three bottles of pale ale.

'Colin was telling me that when you first turned up you were meant to be undercover, but he forgot to keep it a secret,' said Abi, the engineer from the Vinyl Café.

'Yeah, he has the honesty gene.' Meera shot him a look. 'We have another lead on Jericho Flint and wondered if it might trigger any more memories. We hear he had a girl-friend called Rose. Young, hippyish, long dark hair. She probably stayed in the camper van with him. Did you ever see someone like that?'

Abi thought for a minute. 'She came into the Vinyl Café with him a couple of times. Very pretty. They had match-ing tattoos. I remember thinking they must be in love. They were very attentive towards each other.'

'What about after August the tenth, when Jericho was last seen? Did you see her again?'

'She came in alone once or twice, just for lunch. She kept pretty much to herself.'

'Can you remember exactly when?'

'I don't know, late autumn, November maybe. She was in winter clothes but it was still mild out.'

'Can you think back and try to remember any conversation at all that passed between you?' Colin asked. 'What did she order?'

Abi took a slug of ale. 'A beer. Maybe a salad. I don't remember anything else.'

'Hey, Abi.' A slender Japanese boy with tied-back dreadlocks was standing beside their table. Unable to stay still, he shifted constantly as if responding to the music in his head.

'Hey.' Abi didn't seem pleased to see him. She turned to the others. 'This is Finchley. He works in the Vinyl Café.'

'Finchley?' Colin repeated.

'People call me Finch.'

'Where'd you get that from?'

'My mother went into labour on the platform of Finchley Central tube station.'

'Blimey, it's a good job she didn't drop you at Cockfosters.'

'I remember the girl. The one you're talking about.' Finchley hopped from one foot to the other, drumming his fingers on the edge of the table. 'She had a rose on her upper arm, yeah?'

'You don't know what we're talking about, Finch,' said Abi.

'Yeah I do.' Finchley smiled at the memory. 'She was outside the café when I closed up one night. You'd gone home, Abi.' He turned to Colin and Meera. 'She was upset about something. I thought she might need someone to talk to.'

'What was the problem?' asked Colin.

'She'd just had a big bust-up with her boyfriend. I guess

it must have been a really big fight 'cause there were drops of blood on her dress. She said they were his.'

'Do you know what the fight was about?'

'She said she was leaving him. Something about some pictures.'

'He was an artist,' said Colin.

The bar door swung open, releasing a gale of laughter from within. 'I walked with her a little way, trying to be sympathetic and that,' said Finchley. 'I asked her if she wanted to go for a drink and she said no.'

'That was sensitive of you, Finch, trying to pull her while she was distraught. I guess she was lucky you didn't pour chloroform into a Kleenex.' Abi folded her arms in annoyance.

'She didn't say where this fight had taken place?' asked Meera.

'No, but it must have happened somewhere near because she pointed back, over her shoulder.'

'When was this?'

'I guess it was August because I remember a lot of the studio engineers who use the café were away on holiday.'

'Is there anything else you can recall about her?'

Finchley shook his head. 'Do you know how many customers we get in there? There's no time to stop and hold a conversation. She seemed kind of paranoid. It put me off her a bit. You know when girls—'

'Careful,' warned Abi.

'Yeah, well, I left her at the corner on York Way.'

'And was that the last you saw of her?' Meera asked.

'No, there was one more time. It must have been just before Christmas. She was in that organic place, Butterfly. She looked great, very together.'

'How?'

BRYANT & MAY: ENGLAND'S FINEST

'Dressed like a grown-up, like she was in a career as opposed to a job? I said hi but she left. I guess she had to be somewhere.' Finchley slapped at the table, beating out a rhythm.

'So her boyfriend vanishes off the face of the earth and she looks radiant,' said Meera, catching Colin's eye.

'She couldn't have done it,' said Colin. 'Getting a body into a stone coffin – a strong bloke could barely manage it.'

'Then maybe she had an accomplice,' said Meera.

Back at the unit, Renfield and Longbright were having no luck. All they had on the Flint family were a couple of suspiciously tidy CVs, a handful of inconsequential criticisms from political journalists, nothing remotely libellous. 'They're holding the party line,' said Janice. 'The whole thing feels stage-managed. Have you ever googled Madonna? You get exactly the same thing. Most of the results have been removed under European data protection law. How can we find out anything about their relationship with their son?'

Jack thought for a minute. 'Every family has a black sheep. Brothers are usually disastrous to high-fliers. Jimmy Carter had Billy, Richard Nixon had Donald.'

'There's a cousin,' said Janice. 'Jericho has Nathan.' She scrolled her screen, peering close.

'There's no one around to see that you wear glasses,' said Jack gently.

Longbright batted the thought aside. 'He escaped accusations of insider trading and the harassment of a female work colleague.'

Jack leaned closer and stole one of her chocolate digestives. 'See if he has a Facebook page.'

'Don't eat those, they're fattening. Nathan Landry

Mandell. Jackpot.' She tinked the screen with a lacquered nail. 'The cousin's the wild card. Dropped out of college, busted for possession, DUI and sex with a minor, although he was just sixteen and she was one week from legality. Parents kicked him out so he came to Europe. There are shots of him working in the outdoors in a uniform.' She sped through the sidebar of photographs. 'This is why I never post on Facebook. I can tell you exactly where he is.'

Jack brightened. 'How?'

She enlarged one of the photographs. 'That white curve in the corner of the shot is a giveaway. It's the ramp of the Lubetkin Penguin Pool at London Zoo.'

'You think he and Jericho kept in touch?'

'It's worth a try,' said Bryant, wandering past. For a man with a faulty hearing aid he seemed to pick up on everything. 'John and I can head there as soon as the staff arrive for work.'

They went to the zoo together a little after eight the next morning, taking May's BMW to Regent's Park. Bryant was in fine garrulous form, having managed to grab a couple of hours' sleep on the PCU's ratty sofa bed. May was suffering. He had not been sleeping well lately and had stayed up with Longbright and Renfield through the night. Now he felt distanced and disconnected from his surroundings.

London Zoo had been the brainchild of the founder of Singapore, Stamford Raffles, and was the world's oldest scientific zoo, having begun life as a place for the study of natural history. The animals from the menagerie at the Tower of London were moved in, and a peculiar range of neo-Georgian pavilions, galleries and kiosks took their place beside the streamlined sweep of the art deco penguin pool and the mountainous outback-themed Mappin Ter-races. Here elephant rides and chimps' tea parties delighted children for decades until the tide of public opinion turned against them.

They found Nathan Mandell in the Nightlife area, a day-for-night world of bats, rats, lorises and blind-eyed cave creatures. Mandell wore the red sweater of a volun-teer, and was attempting to slide a sheet of glass back in place over a tank of lizards. Rotund and flushed, he lacked the bloodless hauteur of the Flint clan. For a moment it looked as if he might turn and run, so startled was he to be approached without warning.

'It's all right, we only want to ask you a few questions,' said May, raising a calming hand containing his identifica-tion. 'Is there somewhere we can go?'

'Sure, I guess.' Mandell put the glass back in place and stepped down from the edge of the lizard cabinet. Behind him, fruit bats hanging from a tree branch unfurled their spidery wings and rewrapped themselves.

Mandell lowered his bulk on to a plastic chair in the zoo's café and patted his thinning sandy hair into place. He glanced apprehensively from one detective to the other. 'I don't have anything to do with them. Not Howard or Kate, or Jerry. We used to play together as kids – everyone called us Tom and Jerry, you know? But I was kind of wild and he dropped out to recreate himself. That's what he told me: "I'm going to recreate myself. I'm not like my parents. I'm going to be an artist." I thought maybe we'd get to hang out, being in the same country and all, but he didn't want to stay in touch. He's kind of a loner.'

'How did you end up working here?' asked May.

'I like animals. I look after the pygmy slow lorises and some of the lizards. Animals don't have agendas or ambitions. Everybody in my family has a hidden agenda. They don't talk, they negotiate deals with you, and you always come out worse off.'

'When was the last time you saw Jericho Flint?'

'Over a year ago. We had a family gathering, rented some grand old manor in Kent called Tavistock Hall. It was my aunt's eightieth birthday. She lives over here. Jerry didn't get an invite but he turned up anyway. We talked for a few minutes. He didn't stay.'

'Why not?'

'His father, man. Howard hates him.'

'Why?' Bryant cut in.

Mandell gave a small laugh. 'Where do I start with that one? Let's see now. He refused to stick to the family plan and get himself into law school. He chose to live like a bum and turned down his father's handouts. He didn't want to be obligated to his old man. That's what Howard does, he ties everyone to his side with favours.'

'How did his son manage without his father's offer of money?'

'He sold a lot of commercial art at first, but then he did some crazy stuff – "terrorist graffiti", he called it. He hacked a bunch of personal files on MPs and corporate chiefs, and spray-painted their dirty secrets all around Spitalfields. He did these caricatures in the style of old circus posters, really sinister. Howard kept him out of jail.' His face clouded with concern. 'What's happened?'

'He's dead,' said Bryant. 'We need to know who was close to him.'

'Well, not me. But still, that's a shame. He was kind of a lost soul.'

'Do you think he made enemies over his terrorist art?'

'He certainly upset his father. Jerry painted a huge

picture of him, just off Brick Lane. You can still see it on the wall there, next to the Pride of Spitalfields pub on Heneage Street.'

'What happened?'

'I don't know. Jerry laughed about it. There were others, one outside the Star of Bombay Balti House, and one on Bacon Street, but both those buildings got knocked down.'

'Did you and Jericho Flint have any friends in common?' asked May.

'We were both the black sheep of the family but that didn't make us bosom buddies. How did he die?'

'We don't know yet. The day of your aunt's birthday, did he bring his girlfriend?'

'Who, Rose?' Mandell shook his head. 'No, he said he wanted to introduce her but he changed his mind when the old man announced he was attending. I guess Jerry didn't want to make her feel uncomfortable. He knew Howard would humiliate her.'

'Do you think he got into some kind of trouble he couldn't tell his parents about?'

'He was free-spirited but he didn't hang out with bad people. He wanted to be left to live his own life, just like I did. It caused a lot of fights between all of them. I told him, you can't argue with the old man, you just have to say your goodbyes and get out. I thought me and Jerry would be friends. He was smart. He didn't think I was smart. He didn't want to be around me.'

'You can do something for him, Nathan,' Bryant suggested. 'We need to find the girl. We have to report back to the consulate by the end of the week, and right now I don't have any information to give them.'

Mandell stabbed a finger at him. 'Be careful of Howard Flint. He always gets what he wants. If you let him down in any way he'll destroy you. I asked him for help. I'd gotten myself into a bad situation and needed a hand. I almost went down on my knees and begged him.' He looked around at the almost deserted café. 'He doesn't know it but he did me a favour. I'm happier here. There's no pressure. I'll never have to see any of them again. Poor Jerry. He was the only one I ever liked.'

'He wasn't much help,' said May as they left the zoo and walked back to the car park.

Bryant batted some weeds with his walking stick. 'We're either asking the wrong questions or being taken for fools.'

'Not by Mandell,' said May. 'I don't think he's smart enough to pull the wool over anyone's eyes.'

'Imagine, John, you're offered a position in the family dynasty. You can have anything you want so long as you behave in a manner that befits your status. Instead you turn it all down and choose to live as a penniless artist. Your art earns you some notoriety, so your family breaks off all contact with you. You're off the grating—'

'You mean off the grid.'

'Yes, that too, and you sell paintings to make ends meet. You're on the way to joining other artists who died in poverty. Blake, Toulouse-Lautrec, El Greco, Rembrandt, Vermeer – but you don't have enemies. You fight with your girlfriend. Where is she? We need someone who can place them both near the unit on the night he died.'

May looked away. The clouds had formed a great tilting lid of blue above a silver-pink sky. 'We could do a knock along Market Road, see if anyone remembers him. I know it was over five months ago—'

'We don't have the time or the resources for that.'

'What about this picture he did of his father?'

'It may have been painted over but there might be something left,' said Bryant.

'Want me to come?'

'Go and get some sleep. You look like you've been dynamited.'

'And I suppose you feel fine,' May grumbled.

'Of course I feel fine,' said Bryant, swinging his stick. 'I'm working.'

While Bryant headed off to study the site where Jericho Flint had painted his father, Colin and Meera went to find Kharmel Hunter, the former manager of the Wilberforce.

The Commercial Tavern, Spitalfields, would not be opening its doors for another two hours, but the staff were already on site. The pub was classically schizophrenic, full of garrulous locals at lunchtime, seated with their elbows on the bar and pints of cloudy bitter before them, and piratically bearded Shoreditch hipsters in the evening, sipping craft ales and discussing video games. The décor was equally divided, being traditional and solidly Victorian without, whackily collaged within: a magpie mix of artwork pasted from old Janet and John books, with one entire wall covered in jigsaw pieces attached to the plaster by plastic clothing tags. Catering to mismatched clienteles had doubled its revenue.

When Kharmel Hunter looked up and saw Meera and Colin coming towards him, he knew at once that they were police officers, mainly because he had seen them in the Ladykillers Café. Hunter was built for strength, not speed, and remained in place, quietly continuing with the stocktake.

Hunter was much older than Meera had expected him to be. In the lines of his face were the tracks of the music industry, riffing from Pink Floyd through prog rock to punk.

He kept his answers to a minimum, knowing that the more he said the more they would suspect him, but he could not stay silent on the subject of why he was fired from the Wilberforce. 'You've been to the bar, you know what it's like. There's a cold room at the back where they keep the spirits and mixers. It never had a lock on it the whole time I was there.'

'So punters stole from it?' asked Meera.

'No, they went in there to conduct business. You have to go through the bar to reach the toilets and the stockroom. They'd come down and order a drink, then go through to the back and buy a couple of grams. Small-time stuff.'

'You didn't report them or try to stop them?'

'I threw a few out, but only if I was sure they wouldn't come back later. I had no back-up behind the bar. I told the management agency that we needed locks but they didn't do anything. I had to keep a tight watch on the customers after that.'

'If you did your job so well, why did they kick you out?' Meera asked.

'Some cases of Scotch went missing. I explained that it couldn't have happened on my watch.'

'Do you remember a young woman and a man in the bar on the night of August the tenth last year, sometime after midnight?'

'Yes.' He looked from one to the other.

Colin and Meera looked at one another. '*Yes?*'

'She was in her early twenties, long dark hair, hippyish. They went in the back, but only the girl came out.'

'Wait, how could you remember this?' Meera asked.

'It's simple,' Hunter replied. 'On August the tenth the

bar was closed for a private party. Mine. It was my birthday.'

'So they tried to gatecrash?'

'Yeah, they downed a few drinks and disappeared, then she came back by herself. I figured he couldn't have left without me seeing him go past.'

'You didn't think that was odd?' asked Meera.

'It was a party,' said Hunter, slowly and clearly.

'Was this the girl?' Colin held up a photocopy of the painting.

'Definitely, that's her.'

'And the guy?' He found a shot of Jericho Flint on his phone and turned it around.

Hunter looked puzzled. 'No, that's not him. He was in his late thirties – and bald.'

Arthur Bryant stood before the poster-covered wall on Heneage Street and tried to find any trace of painted brick-work. It was still raining hard, and the brim of his trilby had decided to channel water down the back of his neck.

He looked up at the wall and studied it carefully. There were brash ads for bands, clubs and art installations that meant nothing to him or to anyone else outside of the immediate area. He might have been looking at a wall from an earlier century. Beneath so much fly-posting, Jericho Flint's rendition of his father had been obliterated.

The posters were an inch thick. It sounded as if Jericho Flint's portrait of his father had been painted straight on to the brickwork. Seizing a corner of the pasted layers, Bryant pulled hard. The paper had set solid at some point, but the constant rain had softened the glue.

Bryant raised a boot and braced it against the wall, pulling harder at the corner. The compacted posters started to tear. They came off in a single great panel, falling on top of him and sending him sprawling. When he finally managed to fight himself clear and climb to his feet, Bryant found himself looking up at Jericho Flint's original painting.

'We need a photo ID of any bald male working for the consul,' said May.

'You know we don't have access to that kind of information,' Longbright reminded him.

May thought for a moment. 'Dan, can you pull CCTV footage from the street cams opposite the consulate?'

'I should be able to,' Banbury told him. 'They were installed by Metropolitan Police Directorate, not Westminster Council. What period of time do you want to cover?'

'Flint's team started moving out at the beginning of the week, didn't they? You need to go back four months from then.'

'We have a facial-recognition system that can handle that.' Banbury made a call to Anjan Dutta at the King's Cross Surveillance Centre.

'I hope it's better than the one you put in on our front door.' Everyone turned as Bryant arrived in the doorway of the common room.

'What happened to you?' asked May, astonished.

Bryant had leaves, train tickets, pieces of paper, chicken bones, cigarette ends and other assorted bits of street trash stuck all over his coat, trousers and hat. There was a dog-end cemented to his left ear. He looked as if he had been magnetized.

'Glue,' he explained. 'I tried to get some posters off a wall and they fell on me. The rain had melted their paste.' He sank into his armchair. 'I went to Spitalfields. I found

Jericho Flint's original painting. Could somebody get me a cup of tea?'

Longbright and Banbury came through with results at the same time. Just as the crime scene manager's laptop received a photograph of a bald man in his late thirties leaving the consulate, Longbright nailed the ID. 'Samuel Fellowes, former head of Manchester special constabulary, now seconded to Howard Flint. Take a look.'

Bryant discovered that he could not get up. He was forced to slide himself out of his overcoat and leave it stuck to the armchair.

'I took a picture,' he said, passing over his phone. 'That's Jericho Flint's painting. It's what this has all been about.'

'I don't understand,' said May, trying to unstick his hand from the phone's screen.

'You will,' Bryant promised. 'I just need one more thing to prove my point.'

'What's that?' asked May.

'A biography of Marcel Duchamp,' Bryant replied cheerfully.

At first the consul refused to take their calls, but finally agreed to visit the unit after Bryant had a few quiet words with him. Seated in the common room in a grey Gieves & Hawkes suit, he looked as out of place as a racehorse in a greyhound stadium.

'Welcome to the unit's nerve centre,' Bryant said. 'Don't sit there. That armchair's got glue all over it.'

Flint made no protestation as he was steered to a desk, but made it clear that he found his surroundings repellent. 'Well, this had better be good,' he warned, checking his watch. 'I have a flight to catch.'

'I'm not sure that will be possible,' said Bryant, handing

over a printout of the photograph he'd taken in Spital-fields. 'I imagine you thought you'd seen the last of this.'

Flint studied the page and tried to hand it back dismissively, but it stuck to his fingers. 'My son had a warped imagination, that's all.' He pulled at the page and managed to stick it to the desk.

'He wanted to shame you into doing something about it.'

The consul's face did not move a muscle.

'His reinvention as an artist was more than just an embarrassment, though, wasn't it? Perhaps I can focus your attention on the strings of numbers at the top and bottom of the picture. Those are bank deposit account codes, aren't they? Actually, I don't know why I'm asking you because we've already checked them out. Jericho Flint wasn't just painting retro circus posters on walls, he was humiliating the rich and powerful by airing their secrets in public. And in your case, he was exposing the accounts you kept hidden. You sent Samuel Fellowes to threaten him into silence.'

'I asked Sam to have a word with him, that's all,' said Flint. 'He was embarrassing himself.'

'So you weren't embarrassed by the series of posters he painted depicting you as an object of ridicule?'

Flint remained silent.

'Arthur, where are you going with this?' asked May quietly.

'You're not an art lover, I take it,' Bryant asked the consul. 'The name Rose Clavi means nothing to you.'

Flint got to his feet. 'This is going nowhere, and I have important business to attend to. File your report, and we'll take the action we deem appropriate.'

'Jack, stand by the door and make sure he doesn't get out,' said Bryant.

'You have no right—' Flint began.

'Probably not, but you will do us the courtesy of hearing what the unit is going to put in its report. Please sit down.'

Flint stayed where he was.

'Your son told everyone he had reinvented himself as an artist, and the artist was a woman. Rose Clavi. Here was the consul's son, painting scurrilous portraits, dressing as a female and refusing to accept what you saw as his adult responsibilities. His van was filled with colour plates torn from old art books. Marcel Duchamp had an alter-ego. Rose Sélavy – a terrible pun: Rose C'est La Vie. He taunted you, pushed you and pushed you again. Finally you sent in your enforcer, Sam Fellowes. He went to find Jericho at the Wilberforce cocktail bar, and found himself in the company of a young woman. I wonder how long it took him to realize it was Jericho. I imagine that as soon as he twigged, a little bit of unconscious sexism kicked in and he thought his job would be a lot easier. There was a party going on in the bar, so he forced Jericho through the back door into the basement.'

'If you think I'm going to stand here while you accuse me—'

'You can sit if you want,' said Bryant. 'I'm not accusing you of anything. You sent Mr Fellowes to talk some sense into your son, and get back any incriminating data he had on you. You didn't know that the river was going to play its part.'

'What are you talking about?'

Bryant pointed down at the floor. 'The River Fleet, Mr Flint. It's little more than an underground stream now, but it passes through the basement beneath us. And it makes the stonework slippery. Our workmen noticed footmarks in the slime. There was a scuffle and your man slipped over, cracking his head on the ice box. Your son thought fast. He put the documents he was carrying into Fellowes's jacket and rolled him into the box, covering him with a cloth that was left in one of the café's catering packs. Ice keeps things fresh. He bought himself some time. Then he left. As soon as you saw the body, you knew exactly what had happened. Your son wasn't capable of physically hurting anyone. You thought you'd use us to find him, knowing he couldn't reveal himself because you had declared him dead. So what you could do, Mr Flint, is leave your son alone now, and let him be free.'

'You don't know that's what happened,' said Flint. 'You're guessing.'

'I'm guessing, but I'm right,' Bryant replied.

The consul studied each of them with distaste, an explorer stumbling across an alien species. 'You Brits,' he said finally. 'You're nothing in the world any more, just warm beer and wet weather.'

Bryant and May went to the Scottish Stores for two pints of Old Sheepshagger. 'He's right, you know,' said Bryant, setting their beers down on a copper-topped table. 'I'm glad we no longer have an empire. It's better to live in a country that doesn't want to be a world power. Get this down you before the others arrive. Raymondo can break open the petty cash.'

Meera put her head around the door. 'You going to finish your round, sir?'

Bryant tutted. 'You'd rob an old man out of his pension.'

'You haven't got a pension. Wait, that's Abi, the sound engineer.' She darted between the tables and seized Abi by the sleeve of her jacket. 'You told me you saw Jericho and Rose together. You knew they were one and the same person.'

Abi smiled. 'Jerry's a mate of mine.'

'So you know where he is.'

Abi collected her drink from the bar. 'Of course I do, but I'm not about to tell you.'

'Let her go,' said John May. 'We can't prove anything. The case is closed.'

'Not for the family of Samuel Fellowes,' said Bryant, sipping his beer. 'We'll never know whether he provoked an attack. It's better the consul's son remains hidden for now. Cheers.'

BRYANT & MAY MEET DRACULA

Charlie Kemp knew the country wasn't getting many tourist visits at this time of the year because everyone else in the arrivals hall was standing on the 'Nationals' side of the passport line, coming home after working in England. He had headed in the opposite direction, returning to Romania because of Dracula.

There were people who would tell you that Charlie was one of the world's most knowledgeable experts on popular Victorian novels. Charlie knew that you had to be an expert before you could become a great forger.

Alexandra Constantin was also an expert, but she was on the level. Charlie had followed her here to Romania once before, but this time the arrangement was purely business. She had agreed to provide him with access to a very special library, and in return – well, he wasn't sure what she expected to get back. To be honest, he hadn't expected her to agree to anything. The last time he'd seen her she had threatened to call the police on him. But Charlie knew how to turn on the charm, and he was in deep enough debt to take a chance. So he had come here to steal the undead count away from his homeland.

In the world of Victorian pulp fiction the vampire's popularity was second only to that of Sherlock Holmes, but it hadn't always been the case. Stoker had died broke. Although *Dracula* was enthrallingly lurid it was also epistolary and fragmented in form, and had been published to decidedly mixed reviews. Everyone remembered the films and nobody thought much about the book, which suited Charlie just fine. He was seeking to find and forge a very special edition.

He knew that the original Stoker manuscript had been heavily amended and signed by the author. At that point the novel had still borne the title *The Undead*, and contained several marked differences. In Stoker's first version, after Harker and Morris kill Dracula the count's castle is destroyed in a volcanic eruption. The idea wasn't so far-fetched; Transylvania was an earthquake region, although Stoker never went there and only saw Bran Castle, the model for the count's home, in a photograph.

A 529-page manuscript that formed the basis of its first printed incarnation had vanished for nearly a century. In 1980 it reappeared as if from nowhere and was put up for auction by Christie's in New York. When it failed to reach its reserve price it was withdrawn. Nobody knew what happened to it after that. The story of the world's rare objects is a hidden history of wealth and deception.

Alexandra Constantin was a Lithuanian currently living in Transylvania, and Charlie had come here because news had reached his ears through a third party that she might know of the Blue Edition's whereabouts. He thought about her spiky crimson hair and the red fur coat she kept wrapped around her, the Gitanes she drew from the packet with her lips, the cool, assessing look she gave him, the way she never said goodbye when she left a room but turned to leave without a word, the way she watched him from the taxi as it pulled away.

Charlie Kemp was more of a lover than a book lover, but he knew there was a lot of money to be made from the right purchase. Bram Stoker was just another pulp hack who got lucky and died a pauper, accidentally leaving a thousand critical essays by academics like Alexandra in his wake.

He picked up a hire car at Cluj-Napoca Airport and headed off towards Sighişoara to meet Alexandra. If she did know where to find the item he sought, he hoped she would be able to guide him through any access restrictions, but it was important not to alert her to his real purpose.

Transylvania occupied the central part of Romania and was bordered by dark, spear-like mountain ranges. The car he'd hired was a primrose-yellow piece of junk called a Dacia Logan. The Dacia was seemingly the only car available anywhere. It took hills like an old man with bad lungs climbing a staircase.

Charlie passed through villages that hadn't changed in a thousand years, accessed through avenues of tall trees in the tops of which sat bushes of leeching mistletoe like cranes' nests. It was tempting to use the vampiric analogy, because everyone was getting something from someone else; tucked away from the beauty spots were the smoke-belching factories owned by rich corporations reliant on cheap labour.

As the Dacia struggled on Charlie was overtaken by men in black felt hats driving teams of carthorses, hauling logs. It looked as if the whole country ran on burning wood. Every town he passed was walled and had a grave-yard built right beside its houses, as if to remind families that they would always be surrounded by the dead. Stoker may have only worked from what he'd read, but he'd got the atmosphere of the place right.

Sighişoara looked shut. Its main attraction was a complete medieval village with covered wooden walkways. Around that was a town with one hipster coffee bar called the Arts Café, lots of bookshops, a couple of Russian Orthodox churches, some post-war Communist buildings finished in cheap crumbling concrete and some stunning *fin de siècle* neo-baroque houses painted in odd colours: rust red, custard yellow, lime green. Wet sleet slanted across the empty streets. There were a handful of shops selling tourist crap, the weirdest item being the pleading chicken, a china figurine of a bird with its wings pressed together in prayer, begging for its life. Eastern European humour, he decided.

'You do know if it did exist it would be regarded as a national treasure, right?' said Alexandra, smiling with secret knowledge. She raised a glass to her dinner companion. Between them stood a terrifying steeple of pink sausages and pork parts, surrounded by hard-to-identify vegetables in gravy. Luckily, it was more delicious than it looked.

'Everyone said the manuscript was lost,' Charlie reminded her.

'But the "official" manuscript has some glaring gaps, which is possibly why it never reached its reserve at the Christie's auction. It just wasn't that collectable. Stoker was never a great writer, you know that. His prose is purple and really not very interesting.'

'Everybody said the same thing about the Pre-Raphaelites, but look how their stock jumped.' Charlie stabbed another sausage on to his plate. 'And *Dracula* will become more valued in time. You know what makes the difference? Movies. There have been nearly three hundred films made from that one book so far, almost as many as from all of the Sherlock Holmes stories.'

Alexandra pushed back her plate and took out a pack of cigarettes, then remembered that the country's no-smoking policy had come into force. 'You have to face the fact that *Dracula* doesn't have the same cachet.'

The last thing Charlie wanted was Alexandra figuring out what he was up to. He wondered how much she knew about the real value of the book. She was an academic; she cared about language and history, not resale value. He needed her help, but she had to make the offer unwittingly.

'It was the wrong time for the sale of the manuscript,' she said, spearing white asparagus. 'That's why it was withdrawn. Its value is higher now.'

'I still believe the Blue Edition is out there. I'd just like to see it once. Then I'll never have to dream about it again.' For a moment, Charlie even convinced himself. 'What else do you know about it?'

'In May 1897 Constable published the first edition, bound in yellow cloth.' Alexandra held an unlit cigarette between her fingers. 'It wasn't a success. The export edition was also to be in English but printed differently, with more narrowly spaced paragraphs and a blue leather cover. Stoker approved this second limited run even though the advance was almost nothing. He sent off the manuscript and waited for the paperwork to arrive. It never came.'

'So what happened?'

'The theory is that the printer complained. The edition he'd been sent was not the one he'd read. It was longer – a liability for the export version – and had a different ending. I think Stoker sent them his first version of the manuscript not even bothering to keep the master, and this became the Blue Edition. He'd told them they could edit it for length if they wanted. He just wanted the money.'

'You want to smoke that, don't you?' said Charlie, leading her out to the freezing veranda. 'What makes you so sure it's here?'

'I know they ran off at least one uncut copy because there was a photograph of the book in a sale catalogue printed in 1905 in Braşov, Transylvania, and it totalled 556 pages. It had to be from the longer manuscript. The book was described as having eight woodcuts and a dark-blue cover. It was bought by the priest of a town called Viscri. On the receipt he had written his reason for the purchase: to form the centre of a display showing how Transylvania's fame had reached the world outside. The priest didn't die until 1979 – just before the "official" manuscript failed to meet its reserve. No other Blue Edition ever surfaced, making it virtually priceless.

'I have one other interesting piece of information.'

'Please, tell me.'

'I have to be able to trust you, Charlie.'

'Rare books are my life, Alex, you know that. I just want to see it.'

'I have provenance.' She blew smoke out into the pink dusk-light. 'The library at Viscri was appropriated by the government to help make the interior of Bran Castle look more authentic.'

'So you think it's there . . . ?'

'The Blue Edition could be gathering dust on a shelf

somewhere at Bran Castle, a genuine rarity dressing up a shelf of fakes. There's irony for you.'

The next morning they breakfasted early and went to Bran Castle.

Around its base were dozens of wooden huts selling Dracula fridge magnets, key rings, woollen hats, fur waist-coats and snow globes containing castles that swirled with bats when you shook them. Mamas in shell suits were buy-ing vampire teddy bears while feral dogs cruised the takeaway stands, hoping to catch pieces of sausage. Cas-tles always had peasant huts around their foundations.

Alexandra and Charlie headed up to the ticket booth.

Arthur Bryant attempted to crunch the car into gear, but was swaddled in so much padded clothing that he had trouble moving. With his woollen scarf tied around his head he appeared to have been hand-knitted.

As the detectives headed into the black hills below the Carpathian Mountains the weather changed and visibility dropped. The sleet turned to great powdery flakes of snow the size of paper scraps, and soon began to settle. The next few hours were spent stuck behind filth-encrusted trucks lumbering along single-lane highways, barely getting out of third gear while the locals overtook at hair-raising speeds.

'Let me give you a little historical background,' said Bryant, trying to open a packet of extra-strong pepper-mints without letting go of the wheel.

John May had allowed his partner to take charge of the hideous yellow Dacia, figuring that Transylvania might be the one place where Bryant's unorthodox driving skills would go unnoticed. 'As the radio's not working you may as well,' he said.

Bryant warmed to his subject. 'In 1920 Bran Castle became a royal residence and the favourite home of Queen Marie. It was inherited by her daughter, who ran a hospital there in World War Two. The Communists booted out the royal family in 1948, but in 2005 the Romanian government said they'd acted illegally, so the castle was given back. Since then—'

'I have a hangover, Arthur,' said May. 'I drank too much *pălincă* last night. Fruit brandy – never again. Please try to keep it simple for me. A lot simpler, as in no dates.'

'Anyway,' Bryant continued, entirely unfazed by his partner's disinterest. He attempted to overtake a horse and realized the car wasn't up to it. 'It was opened to the public as a private museum but now it's up for private sale, so nobody knows whether it will be preserved or closed down for good. This may be my only chance to see inside it. That's why I wanted to come here. And you said you needed a break.'

'I was thinking of a weekend at a spa in Dorset,' May groaned.

'This is a lot cheaper.' Bryant swerved around a goat. 'Transylvania in February isn't high on too many wishlists.' He tried to see through the windscreen but one wiper had stopped working.

It was still snowing lightly as they passed another walled village that had barely altered in a millennium. Only a couple of cars parked by a church set them in the present. Everything else looked like a medieval woodcut. He was getting tired of staring at tarmac and truck wheels. 'This weather's awful. I can't see, and you know I can't see anyway. Let's get some lunch.'

'Around here?' asked May incredulously.

Bryant pulled into a street that looked derelict. At the

end they found a café with rather too many raffia lamps, but at least the food was heartwarming. They ate goulash served in an entire loaf, and pork ribs sluiced down with Ciuc beer.

A wrinkled babushka who looked like a crazy old woman from a Frankenstein movie came over to the table and tried to press a foot-high icon on Bryant. The portrait of the crucified Christ had been badly printed on to plastic and glued to a piece of chipboard. When Bryant explained that he didn't want to buy it, she swore at him for a couple of minutes before wandering off to sit on the other side of the café, where she ordered a pizza the size of a drain cover and sat glowering at him as she folded pieces into her mouth.

'Cursed by an old gypsy,' said May. 'All we need now is to be chased by wolves.'

Stuffed, they headed back to the car, which was already half buried by fresh snow.

The journey to the castle couldn't have been more atmospheric if they'd chosen to make it by stagecoach. Cutting through the Carpathian Mountains in a snowstorm was an exhausting experience. May offered to take over as his partner's driving was making him queasy, but Bryant was determined not to let the hairpin bends and sheer drops dampen his spirits or, indeed, reduce his speed.

'We're nearly at Castle Dracula,' said Bryant, squinting up through the windscreen. 'DA-da-da,' he sang off-key. 'DA-da-da, you get it? DRAC-u-la.'

'I have no idea what you're talking about,' said May wearily. The springs of the passenger seat were already starting to dig into his spine again.

'James Bernard wrote the music to the Hammer film *Dracula* and keyed the notes around the syllables in his name. Look out there, it's just like a horror film.'

The arrival at the castle itself was inevitably a bit of a let-down; the area proved more suburban than anything in the surrounding region of Braşov. At his first sight of the building Bryant thought: *Is that it?* It was certainly a lot smaller than he'd imagined, and those photographs showing its pointed circular turrets against a background of steep cliffs must have been taken from a very narrow perspective, because it was surrounded by ugly modern houses and what appeared to be a funfair with a boating lake.

Yet as they drew closer he began to appreciate its melancholic grandeur. It was stark and unadorned, imperious and somehow alone.

'We'd better be staying in a decent hotel,' warned May.

Bryant had checked them into a three-star lodge called the Hotel Extravagance. It had a yellow plastic fascia and a life-sized model of a fat pink chef in a chequered apron holding up a severed pig's head. The receptionist was a smiling, pretty girl of about twenty who cheerfully admitted that she had been on duty for over twenty-four hours. It was the standard length of a shift in these parts, she said.

'Can you send the porter for our bags?' May asked, accepting his key.

'We have no porter,' she replied, stifling a yawn.

'Then which way to the lift?'

'We have no lift. You are only on the fourth floor. My mother could manage your bags.'

May was horrified. 'I would never let her carry them.'

'No, I meant she could manage them so you should be able to.'

'Oh, I see.'

The detectives headed for the stairs.

'All right, what are we really here for?' May asked as he hefted both bags.

'I don't know to what you are referring,' said Bryant, looking shifty.

'Yes you do, you're up to something. We didn't come to Transylvania just to wander around a castle.'

'I'm afraid I've got you here rather under false pretences,' Bryant admitted. 'A fellow called Kemp, an antiquarian book dealer based in Mayfair and Paris. Most of the editions he sells are extremely rare and stolen to order, and when he can't fill an order he sells a very good fake. It's a big-time racket, and the Organisation Internationale de Police Criminelle have been after him for several years.'

'What has this got to do with us?'

'They got in touch with the City of London Police, who sent his file through to the unit, but Raymond Land told me not to act on it.'

'Why?'

'Kemp has to be caught in the act, and you don't mess with the Romanian police. But he's our villain. Unfortunately we've got no one on the ground here, and I'd always wanted to visit . . .'

'You crafty old sod. So we're here without back-up. Why do I let you involve me in these things?' May stopped before a door and tried the key. 'This one's yours,' he said. 'What has Kemp done this time?'

'It's what he *might* be about to do. The OIPC intercepted a series of emails suggesting he's come here to pull off some kind of heist. We know he has arranged a meeting at Bran Castle. Casual visitors aren't aware that there's a private library on the premises. It contains works that have been in the castle's collection for centuries and is mostly used by historians. I think he's going to steal a book for a private client.'

'Something rare in the castle's collection?'

'No,' said Bryant, hefting his case on to the bed. 'Rare is a Shakespeare first folio. This is unique. The only full version in the world.'

The next morning, the detectives parked in a sloping field full of strutting turkeys and made their way to the castle entrance. The stone staircase was so steep that Bryant had to keep stopping to catch his breath. May had to push him up the last six steps.

Tall studded doors opened into a courtyard, but the interior of Bran lacked grandeur, and none of the mismatched fixtures were original. The bookshelves were nearly all empty. The walls had been painted white, which destroyed the atmosphere – still, it wasn't a film set, Bryant realized, just the inspiration for a novel. Rereading the book on the journey, he still found the prose flat and earnest, but the sense of dread accumulating in the tale excited him. There were some details he had forgotten, like Jonathan Harker realizing the castle had no staff when he spied Dracula making the beds. He couldn't imagine Christopher Lee agreeing to do that.

Standing in the central courtyard, they could see that the castle was criss-crossed with narrow, open-sided corridors, winding staircases, spires, turrets and a deep well that conjured up memories of old Hammer films. There were hardly any other visitors.

'Now what?' asked May, slapping his gloves together.

Outside the tower an ancient woman with a face like a dried apple handed Charlie Kemp and Alexandra Constantin a set of keys on a huge iron ring.

'Oh, the locals are helpful when you run out of gas, kind even,' Alexandra told him as the guard let them through.

'In the time I've been here I've got to know a handful of them very well. They don't open up to strangers. There's too much terrible history here. It's hard to comprehend what many of them have been through.'

'You're going to tell me they hang out garlic and cruci-fixes at night,' Charlie joked, then wished he hadn't as they passed a seven-foot-high painted Jesus with staring eyes. The narrow corridor had a domed roof and led around the edge of the castle.

'There are no vampires,' said Alexandra with a straight face, 'but the local people believe in Vlad Dracul. He casts a long shadow. That's why you still find paintings in bars and cafés that show him gorily impaling his vic-tims. It's *his* memory they honour. The book is just a useful means to an end, a way to hook tourists into visiting now that the economy airlines are coming in. This is a deeply religious country, so they're very ambivalent about the whole thing. It's a pity the area's solely associated with the vampire trade.'

Charlie wasn't interested in the country's problems. He examined the spines of a few tattered history books on the shelves. 'So if this is the tourist junk, where's the rest of the library? What happened to it?'

'What happened to anything here under the Commun-ists?' Alexandra gave a shrug. 'It disappeared along with everything and everyone else that genocidal maniac Ceauşescu came into contact with. The one thing he couldn't take from these people was their belief system.'

Charlie could think of one thing he could take from them.

A curving chalk-white wall opened on to a tall room with windows overlooking the valley, rocks tapering down to red clay rooftops.

'There's some more stuff up here in the tower,' said Alexandra, unlocking the door. 'I gave a guard a fistful of *lei* to let us in for half an hour.'

He couldn't stop himself from asking the question uppermost in his mind. 'Why are you doing this, Alexandra?'

She gave him one of her assessing looks. 'I always fall for the bad ones. Maybe I want to believe there's still some good in you.'

They climbed the plank staircase to the top of the chapel tower, past dusty looms and farm implements. In a single bookcase at the end of the top floor Charlie glimpsed a handful of leather- and cloth-bound volumes. He headed for the book cupboard and opened the glass case.

'I don't think you should do that,' Alexandra said.

'I'm just having a little look,' he told her. The volumes inside were old but of no interest. Most concerned crop planting and animal husbandry. All were printed in Romanian.

Alexandra seemed to make up her mind about something. 'Look out of the window,' she said. 'See what the babushka is doing.'

Old Apple-Face had retired to the outside wall and was sitting on a kitchen chair in the lightly falling snow, wearing just a thin grey shawl around her shoulders, doing nothing and apparently feeling no cold.

'OK, come with me.' They crossed the tower floor to a rough wooden chest of drawers. 'I know it's not your idea of a library, but it is here. They keep the most valuable items in things like this.'

Charlie studied the chest. It was fastened with a fat rusty lock.

'Is there any way we can get inside?' Alexandra was

timid and culturally over-respectful, but Charlie had no such compunction. 'You want to get lost for a few minutes?'

'You can't just break in! This is what I was afraid would happen. You promised, Charlie.'

'Go downstairs. I'm not going to steal anything, I swear.'

'It's a federal offence to remove anything from the building. You'll go home tomorrow and I still have to live here.'

'I'm just going to take a look, OK? I swear I won't touch a thing.'

'You really are a piece of work, Kemp,' she said, lighting a fresh cigarette. 'You come from a country that has never been sucked dry by a parasitic invader. This is something you can't have. I know these people; they're not thrilled about having a tourist industry built around a book by a British author who never even visited their country.'

'I give you my word I won't do anything,' he said, looking into her eyes. 'It's just closure for me. To say that I saw it. I'll be down in a minute, I promise.'

After she had reluctantly left, he dug out his Swiss Army knife and worked on the lock. It slid open with embarrassing ease.

Inside the drawers were a number of gaudy icons, all fake, priests' robes embroidered with red silk, brocaded white christening dresses, hand-stitched blankets and, at the bottom, a handful of books. He removed the stack, checking out of the window.

Alexandra was stumping about in the courtyard, smoking hard, trying not to look suspicious.

He looked down at the volume in his hands. The blue leather cover jumped out. It was entirely blank, with one gold word embossed on the spine. *Dracula*.

The book had never been read – you could always tell a

virgin copy by the way the pages seemed unwilling to leave one another, the tiny ticking sound the spine made as it was stretched for the first time, the reluctance of the covers to move further apart. It was unsullied, the first and last one, the only one.

Stupidly, he'd forgotten to bring his cotton gloves. He didn't want to release sweat-marks on to the pages, but he had to open it and check. The book had crimson edges and the dye came off on his thumbs, but the white interior showed no discoloration and the smell of the print was still overwhelming.

The publication date matched. The ending was brief but new to his eyes, describing the utter destruction of the castle. It seemed desultory and flatly written, as if it had been tacked on because the author had no other way of finishing the story. He could see why Stoker had subsequently removed it. He wanted to sit down and read right through but had to content himself with riffling through the pages, just to prove that he was not hallucinating.

He fumbled in his rucksack for the forgery he'd had made. He'd known the size and shape of the edition, but that was all. No one had ever mentioned that the real version was a different shade of blue and had painted edges, but no one here would know or care. Back home, the literary world would sit up and take notice when they saw what he had.

Replacing the lock and closing it, he made his way back downstairs. The babushka was still on her chair, basking in the lightly falling snow as if it was a summer's day.

He looked around but there was no sign of Alexandra. He waited but she didn't return. He started to get cold. Beyond the entrance, the turkeys were eyeing him with suspicion. There was no one around. It was beginning to snow more heavily. He set down the backpack and looked at the low hills.

Someone brushed past him.

The snow was in his eyes. He had the sense of a figure, tall and black – and then – and then—

He reeled back. What he saw was not possible. He stared at the scene, half-obliterated by falling snow, and gasped.

He backed into an archway and tried to catch his breath. He had no idea how long he stood there. Moments, minutes, half an hour.

The hand that fell on to his shoulder made him jump.

'You're under arrest, Mr Kemp,' said John May. Behind him was an older, smaller man wrapped in scarves. Accompanying him were two *Inspectori de Poliţie,* the Romanian police.

'I didn't do anything,' Charlie said anxiously, looking around for the backpack. It was already in the hands of one of the inspectors. The other policeman stepped forward. 'You've been under surveillance,' he explained. 'You're being arrested in connection with the murder of Alexandra Constantin.'

'It wasn't me,' he said, panicked. 'It was Dracula.'

The great grey concrete police station at Braşov had not been designed to reassure anyone placed under arrest that all would be well. It was, however, efficient and well ordered, and had, May noted, faster Wi-Fi access than he was used to in King's Cross.

The detectives were received with civility and accorded a meeting with the chief inspector, Ştefan Timmar. The inspector was a small, sharp-featured man who remained motionless in repose but seemed filled with contained energy.

'I take it that's your Wolseley outside?' Bryant said amiably. 'A fine English car. The rest of us seem to be driving Dacias.'

'We make sure we have the best of what is available,' Timmar said, looking from one to the other. 'It is indeed a fine old English motor. Are you retired?'

'No, we're still in active service,' Bryant explained.

'This is good. Life is prolonged by hard work. I must thank you for aiding us in this matter. But you do understand that Mr Kemp is now under European jurisdiction?'

'Of course,' said May, 'and that will be respected. However, we would like to interview the suspect.'

'I'm sure that can be arranged. You can sit in while we take his statement.'

'And we'd like to see the body,' said Bryant.

'That is a little more problematic,' said Timmar. 'There are fewer of us here than we would wish. We have no coroner's office in Braşov – we mostly deal with tourists losing their wallets in nightclubs – so the body will have to be taken to a mortuary in the valley where we have professional staff on site. Obviously it must remain sealed until then to prevent contamination.'

That's never bothered us in London, Bryant thought with some embarrassment. It would be mortifying to think that the Romanian police were more thorough.

'It's Saturday, so we will have to wait for someone to come up on Monday,' Timmar said, 'but you are welcome to accompany them then.'

It was out of the question. The detectives needed to be back in London at the start of the working week.

The three of them visited the cold-storage facility in the basement, where they were able to view the body through

214

sealed plastic. They were handed copies of the initial report.

'She died from a single wound at the right side of the throat,' said Timmar. 'We have no murder weapon. Her blood was found on Kemp's coat. There are no other footprints going out of the castle gate, and that is the only exit.'

'So – no other suspects,' said Bryant.

'None.'

They sat in on Kemp's interrogation. When he heard the British voices once more, he turned anxiously on his stool. 'Can you get me out of here?' he begged the detectives. 'I didn't do anything.'

'I'm afraid that as the arrest was made on Romanian territory you must remain here,' May explained. 'We can have a lawyer appointed by the consulate. Is there anything more you can tell us?'

'They'll find my fingerprints on her,' Kemp warned. 'We spent the night together. They'll find her scarf in my bag. She dropped it at the hotel. I was going to return it. They'll find something else in the bag too . . .'

Bryant was acutely aware that they could be overheard and that his time with Kemp was running out. 'You're a career thief, Charlie, but they're going to charge you with murder. Isn't there anything else?'

'Look, there's some other stuff that's going to come out,' he said uncomfortably. 'We'd been lovers. I lied to her about how I made my living, and when she found out the truth she left me. I couldn't get her out of my mind and came back for her. She filed a complaint against me.'

'You mean you *stalked* her?' May exclaimed.

'I know it was stupid. I was obsessed with her. Then when I found out about the book—'

The chief inspector raised his hand imperceptibly, and one of the officers cautioned Kemp to say nothing more.

The detectives remained for the opening of Kemp's backpack, which contained a few clothes, the dead woman's scarf and a volume of *Dracula* bound in blue leather, the title embossed in gold on its spine.

Three hours later, Bryant and May returned to Bran Castle, leaving the inspectors with their prisoner. The statement had been filed and the consul summoned, but they had seen enough to know that Charlie Kemp wasn't about to be released on bail. They had listened to his story, and had found it hard to swallow.

'Alexandra was a heavy smoker,' he had told the police. 'When I came out I thought maybe she had gone off to find cigarettes. I was about to make my way through the outer wall to where we had parked when something black swept in front of me.'

'What do you mean, something black?' asked Timmar. 'Please be more specific in your description.'

'A tall figure, a man in a long cloak and black hat. I think I walked forward, trying to see. As I reached the corner of the castle, I saw him hunched over someone lying in the snow. I recognized Alexandra. She always wore that red fur coat. I knew she was dead. I felt sick. When I looked back the man had gone.'

'A wound in her throat made by a black-caped figure,' May said as they re-entered Bran Castle. 'A little over the top, don't you think? Anyway, I thought vampires only came out at night.'

'You heard him yourself,' Bryant replied. 'Whether he knows it or not, Kemp is obsessed with Stoker. He must have made up the story, but why? There were no other footprints leading back outside the castle. Don't tell me his cape wiped them from the snow. But Kemp came to steal a book. He had no motive for killing his girlfriend.'

They made their way back to the tower gate. The light was lowering, the sky filled with eerie bands of greenish-yellow.

'He needed her to get him in, so why would he kill her?' May's breath condensed in the falling temperature. 'And to suggest that a real-life Dracula is stalking the castle is pre-posterous. This might have been the home of Vlad Dracul once but there's no coffin in the basement, just a gift shop.'

In return for leaving the police inspectors alone with a British citizen awaiting representation, Bryant had per-suaded them to let him have the keys to the tower. He had promised to return them in half an hour. It had been made quite clear that this was to be the end of their involvement in the matter. They had been civilly treated as guests, but the hospitality had a limit.

'Alexandra Constantin was coming to the end of her time here, wasn't she?' asked Bryant, pulling down his scarf. 'Kemp's passport showed him making a visit here about a year ago. That must have been when he met her. She conducted research at the castle. That was why Kemp had targeted her. He knew she could get him to the book so that he could substitute the forgery.'

'So why make up that absurd story about her being attacked by Dracula?' asked May. 'He must have realized he wouldn't be believed.'

'Unless that was what he really saw.'

'Please, Arthur, let's not go there,' May begged. 'I'm sure you'd love to believe that a real-life vampire is stalk-ing the ramparts of his old castle. You have a terrible habit of muddling fact and fiction.'

'Then we have to find a way of proving Kemp's story.' Bryant pointed over to the gate. 'Let's find out if anyone else saw this creature, starting with Old Mother Riley over there.'

At the mention of the murder the old lady at the ticket barrier grew extremely animated, waving her arms at the sky.

A young guard standing on the other side of the gateway stepped in to translate. 'She says she saw it all. The vampire grabbed the poor lady's throat and bit her, sucking out her blood. Then he turned into a bat and flew off into the clouds.' He tapped the side of his head. 'I think she is a little crazy. She is telling everyone. The story is going all around the place.'

'What about you?' Bryant asked. 'Did you see anything?'

'Yes, sure,' came the reply. 'I saw a man. He was tall and thin, and wearing a black cloak.'

'Did he come past you?'

'No, he was already inside.'

'Did you see him attack the woman?'

'No. I guess I thought he was a priest. You know, the same sort of clothes. I only saw him for a second or two. There was a tour representative waiting to talk to me. I had to attend to him.'

'Great,' said May, finding a bench in the courtyard and seating himself. 'Dracula has two eye witnesses.'

'Or maybe they just saw a priest.' Bryant stood beside him. 'You'll get Chalfonts sitting there in the snow. It's freezing. I want to see that book before they close for the night.'

They made their way back up to the tower repository. A red plastic cordon had been taped around the chest containing the Stoker edition. Bryant was about to pull open the drawers but May stopped him.

'Don't add your own fingerprints, for heaven's sake. We have no jurisdiction here. Timmar was just being polite.'

'But I need to see the book, John. I'm not leaving until I do. It's the only clue we have.'

May sighed. There would be no moving him until he had his way. Bryant was wrapping the end of his scarf around his hand.

'No, you'd better let me do it,' May said, slipping out of a shoe, taking off one of his socks and wrapping it around his hand. Reaching in, he shifted the stack of books to reveal the copy of *Dracula*.

Bryant knelt and studied it for a full five minutes. 'I knew it,' he exclaimed finally. 'Kemp didn't switch books. This one has red edges. The pages on Kemp's copy are plain. It was still in his backpack.'

'Wait, maybe his forgery is the one with red edges.'

'No. You must have noticed that his thumbs were stained red. He's a book lover. He couldn't resist reaching in and opening it. How do you open a book like that?' He mimed pulling the pages apart with his thumbs. 'And it scattered red dust from the dye in the drawer. Look.'

Bryant tugged on his partner's arm for a hand-up. 'There's something else. I'm missing something.' His eyes narrowed as he looked around the room. 'I've seen it around here somewhere. Come on, John, think.'

He turned to the portraits that decorated the room, two bad oil paintings of Vlad Dracul bloodily impaling soldiers, and several Edwardian representations of Count Dracula from the novel. The display finished with photographs of Vlad the Impaler's birthplace in Sighişoara, a tourist trap complete with red nylon curtains, modern-looking candles, and a hardboard coffin with a cheap suit of clothes and a trilby laid out in it.

'It doesn't make any difference,' said May. 'Kemp lied about what he saw.'

'No, he didn't.' Bryant went to the window. 'We've been had.'

'What are you talking about?'

'Look around you.' Bryant pointed to the walls. 'Kemp said he saw a man in a black cloak and a hat, so he wasn't lying. Stoker's Dracula and all of the pictures based on his book show the count hatless. That's how he's always been depicted in English drawings and films. It's only here in Transylvania that he's shown wearing a hat. That ridiculous stage-set in Sighişoara, these paintings and sketches. They dressed someone up. There were no footsteps in the snow leading outside because nobody went outside. It was one of the policemen, and he went back into the castle. They struck a deal. Everybody wins, don't you see? The police get kudos for catching an international thief, the book stays where it belongs and the tourists have a nicely salacious addition to the legend.'

'But the body—'

'We saw *a* body. Remember what Raymond told us? Nobody messes with the police here.'

The light had faded so that the horizon of fir trees appeared like a spiked black wall. Outside, just beyond the castle staircase, a black Wolseley waited with its engine idling. In the passenger seat of the car sat a crimson-haired woman in a red fur coat. She cast a long, cool look up at the castle, dropped her cigarette and rolled up the window.

'She planned the whole thing,' said Bryant. 'Why would she want to be officially declared dead?'

220

'Around here there must be a great many reasons for choosing to disappear,' said May.

Chief Inspector Timmar nodded curtly to May as if in acknowledgement of his words, then climbed behind the steering wheel. Alexandra appraised them, then closed her eyes and rested her head against the back of the seat as the gleaming black Wolseley took off into the gathering night.

BRYANT & MAY AND
THE FORTY FOOTSTEPS

During the Second World War, Winston Churchill employed a man named Colonel Colin Gubbins to set up a number of secret auxiliary units.

These specially trained divisions consisted of around four thousand uniformed guerrillas who worked far beyond the usual constraints imposed on wartime personnel. Their members were known as Scallywags, and during active service their life expectancy was just twelve days.

Britain was uniquely placed to set up experimental, multi-level resistance units because it had seen the nations of Europe collapse in quick succession, and had a head start when it came to planning a counterattack.

The average age of the scientists, inventors, engineers, tacticians and boffins who made up Britain's Scallywag force was twenty. They were sworn to secrecy and disguised as members of the Home Guard. Often those around them thought they were cowards, not realizing that they were fighting a secret war.

After the hostilities, a number of special operations units continued working in peacetime. Some were military, some scientific, some were involved in espionage and surveillance, and many employed freethinkers using untried methods. One branch was the Peculiar Crimes Unit.

But that was long ago. And two young men who had been chosen to think in new ways about the policing of the capital had worked together ever since. Their techniques were eccentric and, to the casual observer, contradictory. Singly they became lost in thickets of information, but together they cut paths to the truth.

Of course, that was long before the truth became lies, news became fake and politicians became children. The art of policing changed dramatically. It was now about numbers and targets and customer care, except at the PCU, where life continued largely untroubled by modernity. Occasionally the detectives were handed cases because nobody else could understand them, and on some very quiet days they uncovered crimes that nobody even knew existed. Today was one of those days.

It started because Alma Sorrowbridge, Arthur Bryant's landlady, complained about his books.

'I don't mind you reading but they're everywhere,' she said as she set a slice of her treacle, lemon and sultana ginger cake before him. 'There's a compendium of medieval socks on my cooker hood.'

'Now that's a very interesting book,' said Bryant, digging his fork into the hefty slice without a thank you. 'Some of their socks were divided at the toes so they could be worn under thonged sandals, which suggests that the English never had any dress sense.'

The kitchen was as fresh and neat as a café on its first

day of opening. The plants had been recently watered, a new gingham tablecloth had been laid, coffee had been brewed, bread baked and home-made jams set out. The pair bickered like an old married couple. It was Arthur's favourite time of the morning.

'All right, what about this?' Alma said, holding up an enormous volume entitled *A Complete History of Bloomsbury*. 'It was in the toilet.'

'That's probably a good place to read it,' said Bryant, munching.

'No, it was *in* the toilet. It had fallen down from that dodgy shelf you put up above the cistern. It could have killed somebody. Books are dangerous. George Bernard Shaw broke my father's nose. His teacher threw the collected works at him, caught him square in the middle of his face. That's how dangerous books are.'

Bryant set his fork aside. 'Fine,' he said. 'As you won't let me eat in peace, is there anything else you'd like to get off your chest?'

'Yes,' said Alma, picking greenfly off her love-lies-bleeding. 'Poisons. I gave you those spice bottles to keep your samples in.'

'And I used them as instructed.'

'Then why are they back in my spice rack?'

'I left them on the counter. You must have muddled them up.'

'Well, that's nice. I've got my church ladies coming later, and now I don't know if I'm going to feed them or kill them.'

'None of the samples are lethal but a few are amphetamine-based,' Bryant pointed out. 'Your ladies will just get through their hymns a bit quicker. Any other complaints?'

'No,' said Alma. 'Go on, finish that and get off to work. I'll leave your mittens on the teapot until you're ready to go. Is Mr May picking you up?'

Bryant was tempted to lick his plate but resisted. 'No, I'm strolling into the West End this morning, Mrs S. My comedy partner is at the dentist and we've no cases on.'

'Then you should cut across the garden squares and get yourself some fresh air.' She poured herself a cup of coffee. 'I've complained to the council about the planting. Their summer bedding is a disgrace and the grass in the college quadrangle is wearing out.'

'You know the gardens play havoc with my hay fever around this time of year,' he complained. 'My nose has been blocked for a week.'

'Fresh air, Mr Bryant,' she repeated. 'You need to breathe more. It'll make you a nicer person.'

You know when summer has finally arrived in London because if you go up a few floors and open a window you can hear people everywhere. Foliage forms great green barriers between the streets, and beneath the trees, in the back gardens, outside the pubs and on the pavements there rises a steady, dense murmur of conversation, punctuated with the odd shriek of laughter.

London was blooming. Bryant found himself surrounded by the buildings of University College. A series of new squares and quadrangles had been constructed over the old gardens. Once there had been open fields here. Now students from around the world sat in groups waiting for lectures to begin. The detective took a good look at the green in Torrington Square and concluded that while the planting didn't measure up, the square itself was well kept. He paid special attention to the slender rectangle of lawn.

At first he thought it had been worn bald by children, but there had been recent heavy rain, and the ground was still soft and damp enough to sprout grass overnight. The bare patches were neatly spaced at regular intervals. They ran north-east to south-west in pairs, with the largest bald patch, about the size of a man's shoe, at the start in the uppermost corner. After seven paces they started to fade out, and by the time Bryant reached the lower edge of the lawn they had disappeared completely. He knelt and examined them more closely. They were very clearly footprints.

'Oh, so you've found them.'

Bryant looked up and saw the ursine academic Ray Kirkpatrick towering above him, hands on hips, studying his old friend with amusement. With his foresty beard, ponytail and studded leather jacket he looked more like a heavy-metal biker than an English professor. Hauling the detective to his feet, he led him back to the start of the footprints. 'They go that way,' he explained, 'from the top to the bottom. I said to myself, I wouldn't be surprised if Arthur turns up for a look. It's odd seeing them back again.'

'What do you mean, again?' Bryant asked, tipping back his hat.

'You mean you don't know about them? Have you got a few minutes to spare? There's a book I'd like to show you.'

'I've nothing urgent on at the moment,' Bryant admitted. 'I can be led astray.'

They wandered over to the British Library, where Kirkpatrick was attempting to prove the provenance of a medieval manuscript that had been found during the City of London's Crossrail excavations. Up at his first-floor desk, he tunnelled beneath a hill of documents and emerged with a yellowed pamphlet. 'I was reading this last night.'

He carefully unfolded the booklet and showed it to Bryant. 'The legend of the Field of Forty Footsteps. The earliest reference we have is from 1692, when the lands around the British Museum were still open meadow. It was always a dodgy area, ladies of ill repute, cutpurses and so on. At the time of the Duke of Monmouth's rebellion, which was, let's see, in 1685, there were supposedly two brothers in love with the same titled lady. She couldn't choose between them so they fought a duel at Southampton Fields while she watched. They were both fatally wounded. After that it was said that the grass never grew where their bodies fell or where their feet had trod. The Poet Laureate Bob Southey was told about the footsteps by his friend John Walsh, whose mother had seen the steps ploughed up, only to mysteriously reappear.'

Kirkpatrick ran his finger down the page, looking for the relevant section. 'Here we are. "We could find no steps within half a mile of Montague House." That's the building which existed before the British Museum.' He went on:

'We were almost out of hope, when an honest man who was at work directed us to the next ground adjoining to a pond. There we found what we sought, about three-quarters of a mile north of Montague House, and about five hundred yards east of Tottenham Court Road. They are of the size of a large human foot, about three inches deep. We counted only seventy-six, but we were not exact in counting.'

He closed the booklet. 'Now, Southey's directions don't match other descriptions, so we think he was guessing about the location. Some put the prints beside a Baptist chapel on Keppel Street, where Senate House now stands. The librarian of Lincoln's Inn first showed Walsh the steps twenty-eight years earlier, and he remembered them being there at least thirty years, and the man who first showed them to *him* about thirty more. The story of the duel caught the public imagination. Right through the nineteenth century playwrights produced dramas about the phantom footsteps. We're pretty sure now that they were just north of Senate House and in front of Birkbeck College, on the remains of the old Torrington Square. The piazza was recently rebuilt, and suddenly the footsteps have reappeared.'

Bryant was unconvinced. 'As much as I adore old London legends, this one seems pretty hard to swallow. Why would they come back now?'

'I'm sure psychogeographers would be happy to offer all kinds of explanations about the past pushing up through the soil,' said Kirkpatrick as he put the pamphlet away. 'I think it's a load of old bollocks, but the odd part of this particular legend is its longevity. Three centuries is a long time to keep up a hoax, don't you think?'

On his way home that night, Bryant considered the point. Three possibilities loomed before him. First, perhaps it was just chance that the grass had worn away in a similar pattern. Second, students who had read about the legend could have decided to recreate it. Or third, somebody knew and was using the story for reasons of their own.

He could not resist returning for one more look at the footprints. The grass around the edges of the prints appeared to have been burned. Kirkpatrick had said that the footsteps went from top to bottom, and when Bryant put the grass under his magnifying glass he found that the professor was right. The leaves were crushed at the heel and dragged at the toe, indicating a clear direction. There were just fifteen individual footprints altogether, not forty pairs, and some of them were only partial.

Bryant hauled himself upright and followed the footprints back. On either side of him were rows of post-war college buildings, but the nearest block appeared to be lived in. He stopped a young Lebanese woman weighed down with folders that looked about to slide out of her arms.

'Excuse me, what's in that building?'

'They're using it as temporary student accommodation until the new dorms are finished,' the student explained before hurrying off.

He entered the reception area and showed his PCU card to the girl at the desk.

'Are you here about Alysha?' she asked.

'Why should I be?' Bryant countered, removing his hat. 'Did something happen?'

'Sorry, I thought you knew,' said the girl. 'The police were here before. Alysha died here last Thursday evening. Nobody's told us what happened.'

'Alysha Hussein, twenty-one,' said Bryant, dropping into his desk chair and sliding a page across to his colleague.

John May raised it and squinted. 'It's very small type.'

'If you weren't so vain you'd wear glasses and be able to read things properly. She was found unconscious in her room overlooking the square at eleven forty-five p.m. last Thursday. At first the admitting doctor at UCH thought she'd suffered heart arrhythmia. Your heart rate is usually between sixty and a hundred beats per minute but it can become irregular.'

'I've read about that somewhere,' said May. 'Doesn't it particularly affect people in their early twenties? Students have been known to die in their sleep.'

'Exactly. They're supposed to be more at risk because they suffer from stress, and that's what this was put down to.'

'So why has it come to your attention?'

'Because her father kicked up a fuss and got a second opinion. And this time they decided it was something she ate.'

'Students eat a lot of rubbish,' May remarked. 'I lived on tins of tomato soup and packets of processed cheese at college. I imagine today's students are more conscious of what they eat. What did she consume on Thursday evening?'

'She was seen sharing a takeaway with a friend, sitting on a concrete bench outside her flat.'

'Have you spoken to the friend?'

'Nobody knows who it was. The girl who saw them together recalls he was male and young, around the same age as her, possibly of Middle Eastern extraction, that's all. But here's the funny thing. They were eating the same meal from a silver foil container.'

'So he would have got sick too.'

'I called the college infirmary but they've had no cases of food poisoning reported. We don't know if he became ill because we can't find him.'

'Can we even get involved?' May asked. 'Is this our case?'

'It falls under our remit,' Bryant replied. 'I'm going to ask for an analysis of her stomach contents.'

An hour later, the breakdown of ingested foodstuffs came in from the pathologist. 'An excessive amount of dichlorophenoxyacetic acid,' said May, tapping his laptop screen. 'Not enough to kill her on its own, but there are several other non-specified trace chemicals in her system. So if we find who she was with . . .'

'. . . and he's not sick, we could be looking at murder,' said Bryant, raising an eyebrow.

The door handle suddenly rattled. 'Why is this thing locked?' called Raymond Land.

'Do you have your membership card?' Bryant called back.

'No, I came out in a rush and left it at home.'

'Then you can't come in.' He shot a cheeky look at his partner.

'Oh, this is ridiculous,' their superior complained. 'Unlock it at once.'

'We're admitting you this time,' said Bryant, opening the door, 'because we're keen to show you that the management listens to its members.'

'I'm management, not you,' said Land testily. 'I've told you before, you cannot turn government-owned rooms into private clubs. What's this about you making requests to UCH about a case? You need to run it by me first.'

'We didn't want to trouble you with it,' said Bryant. 'It may be nothing.'

'If it cuts into your time I have to charge it back. Why didn't it come to us in the first place?'

'Because according to this the coroner hasn't posted anything conclusive yet,' said May. 'She's trying to avoid an open verdict. Perhaps we can help her.'

Behind them, the door unlocked and Janice Longbright came in.

'How did *you* get in?' asked Land, amazed.

'I don't need my membership card,' she replied. 'I've got a VIP pass.'

'Well, obviously there's a two-tier membership system in place,' Bryant explained. 'I didn't mention the case because we don't know what we're dealing with yet. Janice, did you get anything?'

Longbright dropped some notes on the detectives' conjoined desks. 'Everyone says Alysha Hussein was a good student and a hard worker, majoring in urban sociology. Non-drinker, non-smoker, no one she was especially close to, not much of a mixer. Very quiet. Plenty of people saw her around but not many spoke to her. Apparently her father examined her dorm room after the emergency services had been through it, but he found nothing unusual.'

'So based on a single witness report it looks most likely to have been food contamination,' said May.

'She met someone she liked enough to share his meal,' said Bryant.

That evening at seven, May, Bryant and Longbright set off for the old Torrington Square site together. The pleasant weather had been knocked aside by a thunderous sky that chose to empty itself just as they moved beyond the shelter of the plane trees. The college's quadrangles and open passageways were now deserted, and had a melancholic, forlorn air. When they reached the corner of the square they found it harder to find the footprints in the rain.

'The legend has them reappearing throughout history,' Bryant said, pointing down at the bald patches.

'You do realize this is completely bonkers?' said May. 'If

we want to find out what happened to her we should talk more to her friends.'

'And we will,' Bryant replied. 'I have a feeling about this. Someone has heard of the legend and is using it to bring us in.'

'No, Arthur, even you didn't know about it and had to be told by that mad head-banging professor.'

'I don't understand either,' said Janice. 'How did you get from the footprints on the lawn to a dead student?'

'I followed them back.' Bryant pointed up at the student's window behind them.

'So what happens if you follow them forward?' asked May.

The trio looked through the falling rain towards the grey building in the lower right-hand corner of the square.

There were seven males and fourteen females renting rooms in the block at the opposite corner. Four of the male students were Caucasian and two others were away, leaving a single economics student, Raj Kamesh.

May's knock was answered by an exhausted-looking stick insect with bed hair and a distinct odour of weed hanging about him. His room looked like it had been turned on to its ceiling and suddenly righted. After the preliminary introductions had been made the group invited itself in. May crossed to the window and noted that Kamesh had a clear view of Hussein's flat. He could see into the kitchen and bedroom.

Bryant was about to start questioning the student when Longbright stayed his hand and stepped in. 'It's just a formality,' she explained gently. 'We think a friend of yours may be in trouble. How long have you known Alysha Hussein?'

Kamesh's eyes widened, making him even more insect-like. 'Alysha?'

Longbright knew he was buying time to think of an acceptable answer, so she kept talking. 'She's virtually your neighbour. You grabbed a bite to eat with her last Thursday, remember? You were seen on that bench over there. What were you eating?'

'What? Ah – I don't—'

May held his breath. It was obvious that Kamesh knew her. The question now was whether he would admit it.

'The people who saw you guys thought it was noodles – was it noodles? We think there may have been a hygiene issue with the food preparation – did you get gastric problems afterwards? She did . . .'

'Yeah, I had a bad stomach.' Kamesh pulled his hair straight. 'I was up all night.'

May breathed out, relieved. 'Have you seen her since?' he asked.

'No, I've been trying to catch up on my coursework.'

'How well do you know her?'

'I just see her around sometimes and we get something to eat.'

'Where did you go for the food?' asked Bryant.

'There's a pop-up on the quad called Curry in a Hurry.'

'So it was a curry you ate last Thursday. One last thing.' May stopped in the doorway. 'What did you take?'

'I'm sorry?' Kamesh looked even more confused.

'For your stomach, when you got sick. What did you take for it?'

'Oh. Nothing, it wasn't serious. What is this about, anyway?'

'Let's hope it's nothing.' Bryant's smile did not inspire confidence.

The detectives took Colin Bimsley with them, as he had something of a reputation as a human waste-disposal unit. The next day at 11.30 a.m. the curry stall appeared as part of the Bloomsbury Farmers' Market at the north end of Torrington Square. The pop-up was covered in red and yellow bunting, and had rows of gaudy condiment bottles lined up along its counter.

'You eat more curries than anyone I know,' said Bryant. 'You can tell us if it's any good.'

'Are you going to judge that by whether it kills me?' Colin asked. 'I love a good Ruby Murray but I don't want to die over one.' He turned to the proprietor. 'Can I get a pork vindaloo with extra *habaneros*?'

'Make it really hot,' said Bryant, digging for change.

The girl behind the counter pointed to the condiments. 'The ones at the end are the hottest.' She handed him a bottle of water. 'You'll thank me for making you buy this.'

'Oh well, in for a penny.' Colin selected two of the most lethal-looking spices in the row, then added a third.

They took him to the bench and sat him down, waiting. 'Don't all look at me,' he said, unwrapping his spork and peeling the cardboard lid from his curry container.

While May waited for Colin to eat, he looked around and spotted a green plastic gardeners' hut in the corner, wedged between two hedges. 'Where was the witness when she saw them?' he asked Janice.

She pointed to the edge of the quadrangle. 'Somewhere over there, coming out of the main hall.'

'Quite a distance.'

'She insists she saw them clearly.'

Bimsley was tucking in. After five minutes he wiped his forehead and blew his nose. At ten he started sweating profusely.

'What do you think?' asked May.

'There are noodles and slices of mango in here, which is just wrong.'

'Apart from that.'

'I think it'll take six weeks for my taste buds to grow back.' Bimsley fanned his mouth. 'I shouldn't have added any more chillies.'

'Condiments,' Bryant repeated, his eyes narrowed. 'Hm.'

'I hate it when you make your eyes shrink like that,' said May. 'Like you know something the rest of us haven't figured out.'

'I think I do.' He rose from the bench. 'Colin, thank you for your help. I'd love to stay and listen to you eat longer, but I have work to attend to.' He drifted off, thrashing at some litter with his walking stick.

'You heard the old man – work,' said May, rising. 'We need to talk to anyone who knows Kamesh. I know he studies economics, not English history, and there's no earthly reason why he should know about these stupid footsteps, but I'm starting to have my doubts about him.'

'Why's that?' asked Colin, attempting to fold the foil container in half without squirting curry down his jacket.

'He says he was up all night, then says he took nothing for his stomach because it wasn't serious. It felt like a lie. I don't think he got sick.'

'Are you always this suspicious?' Colin asked.

'Of course,' said May. 'I'm a cop.'

*

Over that afternoon they found half a dozen students who were prepared to offer an opinion on Raj Kamesh:

'He's very ambitious. He's running this big-deal start-up at night. I don't know when he ever sleeps. There's a girl who likes him. How much? Oh, a *lot*.'

'He told me he doesn't have time for a relationship right now. He needs to get on with building his career. He's got no social skills and isn't interested in other people.'

'The girl was sending him little notes all the time and driving him nuts. No, I don't think anyone spoke to her much, she was kind of shy. He said he would deal with it.'

'Were they together? Not to my knowledge. He's not much fun to be around, but she liked him for some reason. All Raj ever does is work.'

'Well, I think he showed an interest at first, then he realized she was going to be too needy. He's behind on his coursework because he spends too much time building his online company. He has nothing left for anyone else.'

And finally:

'I think things were coming to a head. She was always hanging around the hall waiting for him. He told a friend of mine he was going to get rid of her.'

'What do you reckon, John?' Bryant asked, creaking back in his desk chair. 'Do we have enough to make a case?'

'What, he couldn't get rid of her so he killed her? Don't you think there are easier ways to deal with that situation?'

'Kamesh is ambitious and prioritizes his career above everything else, and she was annoying him. He could have purchased rat poison and sprinkled it on her side of the curry.'

May tried to imagine the scenario and shook his head.

'No, no. The thing about curry is that it's gloopy, and Colin said it had noodles in it, which means it would have been impossible to separate it into two neat halves. He would have poisoned himself as well. Why am I even thinking like this? It's your fault, you always assume people murder their way out of situations, and you know why? You love murders.'

'No I don't.' Bryant looked quite horrified at the thought. 'There is no circumstance on earth that allows one person to take the life of another. Although I'll admit a certain fascination with devious minds.'

'Tell you what, let's have a little wager, you and I.' May took out his fountain pen and found a sheet of paper. 'I think I know what happened, and I have a way to prove it.'

'That's funny,' said Bryant, his eyes narrowing even more. 'So do I.'

'Then let's both write it down and see who's right.'

They sealed their pages into envelopes and handed them to each other. 'Who's going to go first?' asked Bryant.

'Toss a coin,' said May. 'Let's use mine; I don't trust yours.' He took out a 50p piece and flipped it. 'Call.'

'Tails.'

'Tails it is.'

'Right, I go first. Let's head back to the curry stall.'

The farmers' market was in full swing once more. As they approached the stalls they could see that a long lunchtime queue had formed for Curry in a Hurry.

'Colin suffered no ill effects, then,' said May. 'He even took Meera out for another one last night.'

'Perhaps he didn't try these in the right combination,' Bryant said, pointing at the colourful condiment pots.

He held one up before the counter girl. 'Where do you get these?'

'We mix and grind them ourselves,' she said.

'Ever had anyone get sick after using them?'

'Certainly not. All of our hygiene certificates from the Food Standards Agency are up to date.'

'Nevertheless,' said Bryant as they walked away, 'I think Kamesh had heard about the legend, tore the ground up himself, then invited Hussein to take a look. She's studying urban sociology; maybe it was a subject that interested her. He met her some weeks earlier, then changed his mind about her. Perhaps Miss Hussein started calling too often and disrupting his plans. He decides to ignore her but she comes looking for him. Soon after this he realizes he'll be unable to get rid of her. He concocts a plan, telling her he has something unusual to show her. He buys her a curry, brings a condiment bottle of his own just like the ones on the counter of the stall, and empties it on her side of the meal while she's studying the footsteps. That way, he can be sure she eats it. Then he goes home and everything goes back to normal. The perfect murder.'

'And that's it, is it?' asked May, fishing his partner's envelope from his coat. 'You dismiss my gloopy curry problem without a second thought.'

'You think I'm wrong?'

'I know you are.'

'Then what is your solution?'

May smiled. 'Mine – and you'll like this – involves a paradox that is mundane, yet extraordinary. The boy is a murderer, but the girl wasn't murdered.'

'My dear fellow, what are you talking about?'

'Follow me.'

It buoyed May to be in control for once. There was a spring in his step as he walked across the grass to the top corner of the quadrangle and the small supply hut belonging to the college's gardener.

'You're partly right, of course. Alysha Hussein's attentions were unwanted. She was always there, just across the square or hanging around the common rooms, waiting for him. He couldn't concentrate on his coursework or his extracurricular project. He met up with her to have a talk, and to tell her once and for all to leave him alone.'

'And in this scenario of yours' – here Bryant waved his fingers in the air to indicate the flimsiness of his partner's theory – 'how does the lady take it?'

'She's devastated,' May replied. 'He's invited her to share a meal with him and this is what she gets instead. She's already nervous and hypertense, and overheated from the curry. Now Kamesh's cruel dismissal pushes her heart rate further and she goes into the first of a series of arrhythmic arrests. She can't breathe, let alone speak. She reaches out to him, desperate for his help. Does he realize that all he has to do is walk away from her as quickly as possible and let nature take its course, or does he just think she's being over-dramatic? Either way, he crosses the lawn and doesn't look back until he's returned to his room. You have to admit it's a more plausible explanation than yours.'

'Wait.' Bryant held up a questioning finger. 'What about the forty footsteps?'

'Open my envelope,' said May.

Bryant did as he was told. On the page inside was an instruction. He opened the lid of the gardener's box and looked inside.

'You told me your landlady complained about the poor planting,' said May. 'The gardener was trying to fix it.'

In the green pod was a gigantic yellow container of weedkiller.

'At first I thought he had poisoned her with it,' May admitted, tapping out a rare cigarette. 'But when I did some checking I discovered that few British weedkillers have lethal chemicals in them any more. They could make you sick because they contain dichlorophenoxyacetic acid, but they're not likely to kill you.'

'Then what does this have to do with—?' Bryant started to ask.

'Pick up the canister,' May instructed.

When Bryant did so he found that its base had split, so that there was hardly any liquid left inside it.

'There's a crack in the pod as well.' May pointed his cigarette at its base. 'The weedkiller has been leaking out all this time. We didn't notice it when it was raining, but on dry days it made the path wet. When Kamesh stood up to leave he walked in a puddle of it and trod it across the lawn. That's why there are only a few bare patches – it wore off after a few steps.'

'You mean he accidentally duplicated the original steps that were there on and off for three hundred years?'

May examined the end of his cigarette. He had forgotten how much he enjoyed an occasional smoke. 'Not exactly. I did some further checking with your pal Kirkpatrick. Southey was off by more than just a few feet. The latest evidence locates the duelling site to a spot next to the Royal Academy of Dramatic Art, underneath a coffee shop.'

'If you're correct, I promise I won't be a bad loser,' said Bryant, 'but you have to answer two questions for me. First, what makes you think you're right?'

May pulled a handkerchief from his pocket and passed

it to his partner. 'Your hay fever,' he said. 'You can't smell anything at the moment, can you? It reeks of creosote around here. The odour is added to the weedkiller to stop pets from drinking it. And the second question?'

'How are you going to prove it?'

'Check his trainers,' May replied. 'What does the winner get?'

'Two chicken jalfrezis, please,' said Bryant at the counter of Curry in a Hurry.

JANICE LONGBRIGHT AND THE BEST OF FRIENDS

I. WHAT HAPPENED BEFORE

Gail Barker first met Lily Marshall in the golden, molten days of a Paris autumn, when the air was hot and dead and the leaves were losing their richness.

Lily was taking a selfie next to Monet's *Water Lilies* in the Musée de l'Orangerie in the Jardin des Tuileries. When she caught Gail looking at her she said, 'What? It goes right around the entire room, I can't be blocking your view.' They were the very last people in the place and the guards wanted them out, but Lily was taking her time.

Gail apologized for staring, and finally said, 'I'm sorry, it's just not going to come out like that.' Lily was dangling a Pentax in front of her and dipping at an absurd angle to try and get part of that vast mauve-blue painting in the background.

'Then could you take it?' Lily snapped impatiently. She was eighteen; Gail was seventeen. This was before proper

243

selfies with phones, and Lily was using the timer on her camera, except she always thought it wasn't going to go off and dropped her insouciant pose just as the shutter clicked. Gail untangled the camera from her and carefully took the picture.

Gail was still at school and had come to Paris by herself in the summer holidays. She had travelled by coach and paid for the trip through her Saturday job. Lily's grades were not good enough to get her into the university of her choice, so she had accepted a job at Home & Hearth, the homewares company where she would later be made a director.

After the gallery closed its doors they crossed the Seine to a bar near Notre-Dame called La Brasserie de l'Île Saint-Louis, a *service continu* joint where the waiters would leave you alone all night so long as you kept something in your glass.

Youth, Paris, love and the moon. Well, Gail wasn't in love but perhaps, she decided, she had something better: a friend, the first her mother had not chosen for her. Lily was mature beyond a year's difference. She wore so much make-up that it was hard to tell what she really looked like: foundation, concealer, bronzer, setting powder, two types of contour, highlighter, lip colour and half a dozen shades of eye shadow. She hardly ever went anywhere without this powdered mask. She explained that she'd had acne when she was younger and it had left her cheeks and neck with discoloured patches right down to the collar of her T-shirt, so the warpaint boosted her confidence.

Lily had shiny black bobbed hair which she kept dyed because she said she was natural British mouse. Her eyes were set wide apart and she wore crimson lipstick that looked fabulous at night but slutty in the morning. Gail suspected that without these tricks Lily was probably rather ordinary-looking, practically invisible. Lily was affected, Gail supposed, because she was away from her controlling parents and in love with Paris and could be whoever she liked. But just as the water lilies only appeared whole from a distance, so Lily remained frustratingly oblique at close range.

'Besides,' she told Gail, filling her wine glass, 'Monet painted four hundred and fifty pictures of his garden in every season and every light, and that's how you should see people, always changing.'

The sun had set and the street lamps had come on. Waiters slipped between the tables in their white shirts, black waistcoats and white aprons. 'I'm ordering us *entrecôtes grillées*. They're thin boneless steaks – you do eat meat, don't you? – but you must order it as you would like it to be cooked, otherwise they'll flash it under the grill for two seconds and serve it dripping blood. And we'll have to have fries because Parisians don't seem to understand the concept of vegetables. Order what you like, my father's paying. I've got him enrolled in a system I call Parenting Through Guilt.'

Gail was entranced. She had never met anyone like Lily. She seemed entirely comfortable in her surroundings and her own skin, even though her every movement reeked of artifice. She was from the wealthiest part of Surrey but didn't have the conviction of absolute rightness you so often found in girls from the Home Counties. She was always willing to be proven wrong. Gail was as contradictory in her own way, practical but imaginative. She was a Londoner from a less-well-off family, and it turned out that Lily was moving nearby.

'My parents wanted me to go to university,' Lily continued, 'but I told them I wanted to find a company where I could learn from the ground up. I'm taking an interior-design course to see if I'll like it.'

'But what if you find you don't have the aptitude?' Gail asked.

Lily stopped laughing when she saw how serious Gail looked. 'Oh, you're a worrier, I can tell. The one thing we both have on our side right now is youth, and it's an advantage that will never come again. We can do whatever we please because we have none of the expenses that come with age and responsibility. Ask yourself honestly: what do you have to lose?'

Gail often thought back to that night: the lights, soft and yellow in the trees like glowing fruit, the slender waiters darting across the cobbles with trays, the darkness of the river beyond, and Lily so young and full of electricity. Nothing could frighten her, and Gail knew that if she stayed close by, nothing could frighten her either.

'You don't like it.' Gail turned her head, worried. 'It's the cut, isn't it? I was told it's very fashionable.'

'Now you sound like Mia Farrow in *Rosemary's Baby*,' Lily said, tipping her head to the other side. 'Blonde makes you look washed out. Are you feeling all right? You're not pregnant or anything? I hope not, because that's your third Martini and the baby will come out all stunted.'

'You're dreadful.' Gail pretended to be shocked.

Lily waved the idea aside. 'Oh, I can't be doing with that *toujours la politesse* malarkey.'

The pair still chucked bits of French around in honour of the way they'd met all those years ago. And they were still best friends who told each other everything. Lily always said if you can't tell your best friend everything, then you're not best friends. Of course, this was before she told Gail she was looking older. Gail said, 'Well, I'm not *quite* ready to start presenting baking programmes.' Lily was always far too honest to be considered polite, but you could trust her with your life. If you felt sick at a party she'd barge everyone out of the way to get you to the bathroom.

They argued from time to time, of course. Usually it was over something Lily had thoughtlessly said or done. Volatile storm clouds would suddenly appear and flash about them. Afterwards Gail would write out her anger in letters she never sent, and the sky was clear once more.

When Gail was dating the Brazilian DJ who could stand on his hands in the shower and suddenly announced that he wanted to abandon his hedonistic lifestyle and fertilize her eggs, Lily was the one who told him Gail wasn't ready to settle down. But a best friend does more than save you from a life of salsa, handstands and babies. Lily looked after Gail when her father died and the stress of caring for her mother had brought on shingles; then Gail tried to take care of Lily, which was harder because she was so independent that everyone first thought she was a lesbian.

'Seriously, you do feel fine? Because you're looking your age when you should be aiming for, oh, five to seven years younger. Mind you, I'm thirty-eight, I'll always be slightly ahead of you. I've seen what's around the next corner. Men who talk about damp courses and Pink Floyd albums.'

'You still look like your old photos.' Gail meant it, even though she was wounded by the thoughtless remark. She had always been thin-skinned, lacking in confidence.

'You're being polite again. You're lucky, you have supple

skin; mine is so dry I can practically hear it drinking when I whack moisturizer on it.'

As it was Lily's birthday they were having a drink on a rooftop in Shoreditch that had, ridiculously in London, a swimming pool. Like all London bars it was overcrowded to the point of unpleasantness, and had none of the exclusivity one might expect from a private members' club. But they were both earning good money these days and could afford their overpriced cocktails; Gail was running an online fashion company, and Lily was now the only female director of Afternoon Delight, the homewares store where she had begun her design career, now rebranded. She had been propelled into the upper echelons of the company, but the last three years had been punishing.

Lily's camera fetish had truly blossomed in the age of the selfie, and she now photographed everything around her, from meals to friends to flower arrangements. At first she said it was company research but Gail knew she loved Instagramming it all and counting her followers. This meant that having a drink with her was now like watching a network TV show with all the commercials in it. Every time they started to discuss something serious, Lily broke off to rearrange the table and photograph it. She often put herself in the shot using one of her preplanned facial poses, and was discreetly tilting her phone at the crowd standing next to them when she suddenly stopped.

'My God, look to your left, four o'clock. Sophie What's-her-name – Stewart – almost unrecognizable. Don't stare.'

'Where?' Gail asked. Her eyesight was terrible but she hated contacts and kept a rather old-fashioned pair of glasses in her bag.

'She's right in front of you, in the Orla Kiely-ish thing with the big poppies all over it.'

Gail tried to remember who Sophie Stewart was. Something about a double first in English literature and humanities, and a critically lauded book on British social history. She now extracted sound bites from politicians on breakfast television, making a fortune as the nation's favourite working mother, although her press agent struggled to keep it that way, given that her twin penchants for alcohol and unsuitable younger men sometimes coincided disastrously. Gail wondered if Ms Stewart had been held back by her somewhat maternal looks, which caused men to underestimate her abilities. The unpalatable truth, she suspected, was that the nation liked to see her as mumsy, and her disenchantment with the role was the reason for her bouts of bad behaviour.

While Gail poked about in her bag she tried to stare surreptitiously. She could see the woman Lily was theatrically attempting to indicate, but this couldn't be Sophie Stewart, surely? Around fifteen years younger, with narrow hips and long red hair? 'There's a faint resemblance,' she admitted, 'but it has to be her daughter.'

'She doesn't have a daughter. That's her, I swear. She's been telling everyone she's been on sabbatical. She's had work done.'

'That's more than just work.' Gail located her spectacles and took another look. 'She's completely different.'

Sophie Stewart 2.0 had cheekbones and a jawline. Even her neck looked longer. She had gone from a mother goose to a swan, but without the stretched artificiality that so often accompanied surgery. The effect was so startling that Sophie had chosen to rein it in a little by wearing black-framed glasses, which just made her look even more alluring, like a Technicolor movie star from the 1960s.

'If I could look like that . . .' Lily began. 'What is it they say about men? As they age they either become toads or lizards. Women vanish.'

Gail wondered if this introspection had been triggered by the arrival of another birthday. 'It's not just about looks, Lily. She's well connected. She's smart. But if she can reinvent herself like that she can do anything. You should go up to her and ask her how she did it.'

Lily gave her friend a crooked smile. 'You dare me?'

'Ask her for her secret.'

She pushed back her chair. 'All right. Watch this.'

Gail watched in something close to awe as Lily bounced through the crowd at the bar, apologized to the man Sophie was talking to and brazenly introduced herself. She was one of those people in whom complete strangers took delight. She was gone for twenty minutes, during which time Gail could only sit fiddling with her phone, trying to look like she hadn't been dumped. When Lily finally came back Gail found herself craning forward, desperate for answers.

'So what did she say?'

'Oh – I promised her I won't tell anyone else,' Lily said.

'But you'll tell me, right?'

'Not where she can see. Later.'

But Gail forgot to ask and Lily did not offer to tell her.

The first time they were insulted, or at least conscious of someone being rude about them, Lily and Gail were having a few glasses of cava in celebration of Lily's promotion. They were on their second bottle in a Notting Hill wine bar when Lily accidentally dropped her door keys down the side of the very high bench seat from which they were dangling their legs. It was dark in the corner of the pub, so she got to her feet and tried to move the bench aside.

'They've gone behind the panel.' She pointed to the hardboard sheet that lined the bottom of the wall. 'I can't reach them. You'll have to stand up and give me a hand.' She bent back the panel and held her phone torch over the gap. 'I can see them. They've gone behind some wiring. Hold this end.'

Gail held on to the corner of the panel and Lily reached behind, but the panel came away in Gail's hands and Lily pulled up a dusty cluster of cables instead of her keys and the music went off and the lights went out, and the barman shouted, 'Ladies, don't touch anything, let me do it,' and came over and did something that got the lights and the music working again, and handed Lily back the keys. Under his breath he said something about housewives not being able to hold their alcohol.

'What did you just say?' Lily angrily snapped back.

The barman was Australian, about twenty-one, lean and attractive. He studied her with amusement and said, 'You pulled the bloody wiring out of the junction box.'

'We're not housewives,' Lily said. 'We could drink you under the table.'

'You've already had two bottles, love.' He nodded knowingly at his mate behind the bar. 'Maybe you should eat something.'

'Really? Eat this.' Lily reached down and pulled the cables clean out of the wall, killing everything. Power, lights, all off. And then she was off out of the door, heading down the street with Gail following in horrified admonishment.

*

The next time they met up Lily sat opposite her in Balthazar shredding a napkin into teardrop-sized pieces, and Gail knew there were going to be problems aired before either of them could settle down.

'I've broken up with Bruno,' said Lily. 'He's supposed to be finishing his documentary but he just sits around playing video games and smoking dope. Anyway, who's going to watch another angry diatribe about factory farming? I caught him stealing from me. I noticed my purse magically emptying out whenever it was left in his flat and confronted him. End result, he decided I was too old for him.'

'He was very cute,' Gail said, desperately searching for something positive to say.

'So is my shower curtain, and that has a practical function. I should have listened to you. I want to be equal partners with a grown-up, not mother to a man-child.'

'Me too,' Gail agreed. 'At least you had someone. I've given up looking.'

'Oh, did I tell you? My boss just announced that he's looking for a new team member to head the European store roll-out.' She always did this when she was stressed, skipping subjects or picking up on something they had been talking about when they were last together.

Gail thought it over. 'He'll have to offer you the job first, won't he?'

'He doesn't *have* to do anything. He'll bring someone in on a trial basis, and then decide who gets the role. I speak business French and Italian so I should land it, but . . .' She let the thought trail away. 'So I bought a bikini to make myself feel better, but I know I look ridiculous in it because there's this fold-thing above my navel.'

As Gail listened to her friend's disjointed chatter she got the strangest feeling, as if she should be fearful for her, as if something terrible could happen and there wouldn't be anything she could do to stop it.

'What's really going on?' she asked. 'You're holding something back. You're usually the most indiscreet person I know.' It was true; they would go for a drink and Lily would gather acolytes simply by being open with them. When they were in their twenties Gail and Lily would go out on a Saturday night and Lily would end up dragging around a South American musician, a pair of gay Egyptian comedy performers, a Spanish graffiti artist, or some tortured writer with a chip on his shoulder. She collected exotics because she was smart and bored.

Lily remained silent for a long time, and finally mumbled something that Gail didn't catch.

'Say again?'

'I said I cannot keep this up.'

'What do you mean?'

'All *this* – running around. I'm not young any more.'

'Are you going to overreact to every birthday you have? Because it won't get easier. You're not even forty yet.'

Lily studied herself in her phone screen. 'You know the biggest lie they tell you? That you can have it all. Nobody can have it all. Something always has to be sacrificed.'

'What are you prepared to sacrifice?' asked Gail.

'I want to have children. I want to keep my job. I want a cigarette.'

'You gave up smoking five years ago.' Gail awkwardly changed the subject. 'How's your mother doing?'

After Lily's mother retired from being a GP she grew difficult, and their relationship had become ever more strained. Three years earlier she had been diagnosed with Alzheimer's.

'When I think back, it's obvious now that she'd been

suffering memory loss,' Lily said, 'but we both pretended it wasn't happening. Now I'm the only one who can help her, but she'll barely let me near her. She's going to die telling the nurses I ruined her life.'

'That's not going to happen to you.' Gail tried to sound reassuring.

Lily was hiding behind even more make-up than usual, as if frightened of letting anyone see who she really was. 'I think there comes a point when you start to see the shape of your life,' she said. 'I have to stop pretending to myself. Bruno's gone, I'll take care of my mother until she no longer knows who I am, I'll try to get a better job and fail. I won't be the girl by the water lilies any more, I'll be the woman at the window, the one who takes her time at the shops, the one who thinks of her television as a friend.'

'I can't take all this melodrama tonight,' Gail warned impatiently. 'You don't believe any of this either. Stop feeling so sorry for yourself.'

'I may have ovarian cancer. I had a pain in my stomach; I felt full up all the time. They found two lumps, one small, one larger. I'll know in a day or so.' Lily blurted it out, and Gail was astonished that she would share anything else, *everything* else, before this far more important piece of news.

She did not know what to say, and fell back on meaningless consolations.

Lily brightened a little later, and even ended the evening by coercing the waiter to be in their laughing photographs.

When Lily's phone went straight to voicemail, Gail realized that she had been taken in for the operation. The urgency of the treatment presaged what was to come; although the surgery was successful, she would never be

JANICE LONGBRIGHT AND THE BEST OF FRIENDS

able to have children. Gail stayed with her through the healing process. Lily's useless boyfriend returned and surprised everyone by briefly pulling his weight, but as soon as she felt better he found something more pressing to do that involved smoking industrial quantities of weed and blowing up soldiers on another planet. A few days later he disappeared to a music festival with a Scandinavian waitress.

Gail moved to four and a half rooms situated on the ground floor of a large terraced house in Dalston that had been subdivided into too many apartments. When she discovered that the previous owner had gone mad and died in the place she decided to have the interior ripped out and repainted, with pale wood floors and white walls. Just before the work began she invited Lily over, knowing that she would be full of ideas for the kitchen.

'You've got enough room to put in a central counter with a hob and a breakfast bar.'

'You really think there's space for that?'

'I've seen smaller, trust me. A white Corian sink over there, fridge-freezer in the corner. I can run a CAD and have you fixed up in no time.'

'And how much is all that going to cost?' Gail wondered.

'I can get you a great discount. I'll put you down as a family member.'

'Won't you get into trouble?'

'No. I mean you're practically family and everyone does it. Let's take a look at the living room.'

Gail had some savings and the place was a good investment, plus she had a friend who was ready to help. Lily took the notes back to her office, and a few days later Gail got a call from her designers.

Lily saved her a small fortune. Gail was thrilled with the end result. She handled some of the painting herself and even got a rescue cat called Roger, then settled down for her first week living in isolated splendour. It was a week of spring rains and rolling thunderstorms. On Wednesday evening Lily arrived unannounced, soaked through.

'Well, he did it,' she said, accepting a towel from Gail and drying her hair. 'David appointed a twenty-two-year-old girl to handle the European openings without even bothering to give her a trial. I've been handed the Midlands, which I've been looking after for the past year anyway. My career is pretty much finished in that company.'

Gail immediately headed for the fridge to open a bottle of white wine. 'You've had the same boss for eight years, haven't you? I thought you got on well. Can't you fight it?'

'It's a done deal. The new girl is smart, posh and pretty, she's got more followers than me, and our big buyers are nearly all male. So much for all that stuff about female empowerment and anti-ageism the company spouts at corporate events.'

'Like you didn't know that already,' Gail said, filling her glass. 'What are you going to do?'

'Remember that TV presenter? She told me what she did.' Lily made sure her jeans were dry before tucking herself on to Gail's new cream sofa.

'You mean the one who changed her appearance?'

'It's an entire holistic makeover. Not a single treatment, a whole new way of looking at your life. Not everyone is suitable. It's very exclusive and very expensive, but worth every penny.'

'So it's a health farm?'

'No, no.' Lily laughed and shook her head. 'You go away

for a month to a clinic just outside Vienna, and come back a whole new person.'

'Oh.'

' "Oh"? What's that supposed to mean?'

'Oh, *plastic surgery*.'

'You saw her, did she look like she'd been under the knife?'

'No, but the lights were quite low.'

'I had a good look, believe me. There wasn't a mark or a stitch anywhere. Obviously there's *some* surgery involved, but that's only part of the process. They physically and mentally change you.'

'How exactly?' Gail found it impossible to hide her scepticism. 'I don't like the idea of being "changed" by people who don't even know you. Do they have a website?'

Lily leaned forward excitedly. 'Introduction is strictly through others who have undergone the process. You have to write a *letter* to them. I mean, who writes letters any more?'

'Don't tell me you're thinking of doing it.'

'I've already received a reply.' She opened her bag and handed over a blue vellum envelope. 'Read that.'

Gail put on her glasses. ' "You are invited to attend an introductory session at Younger Woman." Younger Woman? Sounds a bit on the nose.'

Lily took back the page. 'I have to sign all this stuff before I even get to the stuff I have to sign.'

'You mean they're going to check out your bank balance before they shove you full of fillers and chemical cocktails, then come up with a list of incredibly expensive aftercare services for you. Lily, this is crazy. You don't need this. So you got passed over for your promotion, big deal.'

'And I'll keep getting passed over. I have to start looking

for a new job. I don't have a partner. I'm not going to have children. I have money in the bank. Give me one good reason why I shouldn't do it.'

'At least ask some more detailed questions.'

'I put it out to my Twitter followers and they all think it's a great idea. I like these cushions.'

Gail sat back with a sigh. 'You're a flibbertigibbet, you know that?' She picked up one of the cushions and waved it before Lily. '*This* can be fixed if it loses a few threads. *You* can't.'

'I don't understand you,' said Lily. 'You put yourself in the hands of a gynaecologist or a dentist or an optician without thinking twice because they're skilled experts—'

'Exactly. You don't know if these people are experts.'

'Don't worry, I'll check them out thoroughly before I commit to anything. It could give me back my confidence.'

'Nothing I say is going to make any difference, is it?'

'Gail, I always listen to you but you're a pessimist. I'm going to attend the interview. It's in a place called Zwentendorf. I'll be a new me.'

'You'll still be the same crabby old you inside.'

Lily threw one cushion at Gail, then all of them.

Seven weeks later, a coffin-shaped cage of shiny grey material was removed from beneath a train at London Bridge Station by two members of an ambulance team. Inside it were the smashed remains of Lily Marshall's body.

The CCTV showed Gail Barker deliberately pushing her in front of the 21.50 to Luton. In her first interview at the Peculiar Crimes Unit, she turned to Janice Longbright and said, 'On my life, I swear to God I did not kill her. She was my best friend.'

II. WHAT HAPPENED AFTER

'I know Gail Barker,' said Janice Longbright. 'I should be the one who interviews her.'

'How well do you know her?' asked John May, looking through the wired window of the interview room. The woman on the red plastic chair inside was pale, blonde and overweight. As she silently cried into her hands, her shoulders shook. 'She looks in a bad way.'

'She went to my school.'

'Some time after you, I imagine,' said May. Longbright told herself he didn't mean it that way.

'We met through a mutual friend and had a few drinks together. John, you know how you get an instinct for these things. She's kind-hearted.'

May shrugged. 'She pushed her best friend under a train. Whatever she admits in mitigation won't make any difference against the technical evidence. We have the footage from four different cameras. There was no one else around. She ran at the other woman with a look of hatred on her face.'

'At least let me find out why,' said Longbright. 'There could be circumstances we don't know about. I'll record the whole thing.'

'OK,' May said, 'but I can't imagine there's anything she can tell you that will make the slightest bit of difference to her case. It's right there on film.'

Janice gathered her notes and went into the interview room.

'You can take as long as you want,' she told Gail. 'I'll be jumping in with questions, but don't let me put you off. If it gets too much and you want to stop, that's fine, but remember anything you say may be used in evidence against you.' She set a mug of tea before Gail and sat calmly waiting.

Gail wiped her face with the tatters of a tissue and collected her thoughts. 'It began with Patricia,' she said.

'Who is Patricia?'

'Lily's mother. I got a letter from her. She doesn't use computers. She has Alzheimer's. She'd never written to me before. She said she was being held prisoner in her own home.'

'By whom?'

'By Lily. I have it here.' She pulled the letter from her bag and handed it to Longbright.

'Tell me a bit about Lily.'

'She was ambitious. She was funny and fearless. She'd been my best friend since we met as teenagers. Her life suddenly changed. You know, when I got off the train on my way to see her mother, I saw this group of girls who all looked and sounded alike. Same teeth and noses, figures, blonde hair and designer clothes. They made me think of Lily. The new Lily, I mean.'

'Can you explain?' Longbright looked at what she had written down. 'No, tell it your own way, in the order you want.'

'Patricia lives in a mansion block in Highgate. When I arrived she was sitting in shadow with the lights out. The first thing she said was, "I'm afraid of her." '

'Afraid of who? Her daughter?'

'Yes. When I put on the light I saw that her face was badly bruised. She wouldn't say more because Lily was due home right about then. I noticed that all of the family photographs had been removed from the mantelpiece. Patricia told me Lily took them down and wouldn't let her put them back up. She wasn't being allowed to leave the house. I hadn't seen Lily since the operation.'

'What operation?'

'She went away for a month to a clinic in Austria. They rejuvenate you. I guess it's a mix of surgery and lifestyle changes. You're meant to look and feel like a different person afterwards.'

'So Lily Marshall underwent surgery?'

'Yes. I wasn't allowed any contact. They made her give up all social media, because the procedure is patented and lots of celebrities go there. I guess they don't want lawsuits. I tried to find them online and it's like they don't exist. Afterwards Lily was sent away to recuperate, so I didn't see her until that night at her mother's flat. When she came in I just stared at her in astonishment.'

'Why?'

'Because I'd never seen her before in my life.'

'You mean because she'd had so much work?'

'No, I mean she was someone else.'

Longbright tried to suppress a look of disbelief and failed.

'Look, I know everything about Lily and this wasn't her. I mean, she looked a lot like her and in some ways she was *exactly* like her, the movements mainly, but other things were all wrong. She was surprised that I'd turned up unannounced. I explained that I'd tried calling, and had come because her mother wrote for help. "Oh," she said, "that explains everything." She took me into the kitchen and told me that Patricia's Alzheimer's had worsened. She was having accidents all the time and made up outrageous stories to cover for them. She couldn't go out or stay alone in the house for long. She said she'd had to impose rules on her for her own safety. She'd removed the photographs because they upset her too much. But I knew she was an imposter and lying to me.'

Longbright decided it would be best not to contradict the suspect at this point. 'So where was the real Lily?' she asked. 'Why didn't you come to us?'

'What would I have said? I thought it would be better to stay for a couple of days and look after her mother while I tried to work out what had happened. I wanted to think it through logically. The first thing to do was get someone else to admit that she'd been replaced.'

'You say she looked physically different,' said Longbright. 'How much different?'

'I guess she had the same bone structure and height, but everything else ... eyes, nose, voice, nothing was how I remembered.'

'It had been quite a while since you last saw her, yes?'

'Yes, but you do more than just recall the way a person looks. You know them from the inside. I tried talking to her. Lily told me she'd burned her old clothes and letters because the clinic encouraged her to make a completely fresh start. I tried to trip her up by talking about the past. A holiday we shared in Mallorca in our early twenties. When Lily made a mistake she just said I'd remembered it wrong. I asked her about how we met, taking photos of Monet's *Water Lilies*, and the time she blacked out a wine bar, but she wriggled out of every question I threw at her. There were other details that convinced me she was an imposter. I think she changed her phone because it had a facial recognition system. I went through her iPad looking for old photographs but there weren't any.'

'Did you ask her mother?'

'Patricia said she had some old physical photographs but she couldn't remember where she'd put them. I wondered if I could force Lily to have a DNA test. I went to see her brother Charlie. He told me she'd suddenly become unfriendly towards him.'

'But he didn't think she looked different?'

'He's a junkie, he doesn't know what he thinks about anything. Lily had stopped drinking and become a vegetarian. She was dumping her oldest friends to make new ones. I began to think it was me. Lily had been paranoid about losing her edge so she'd had some work done, so what? Then I had an idea. I decided to throw her a surprise party and invite some old friends. Most of them turned me down but I went ahead anyway. Lily handled it brilliantly. She'd told them about her surgery, so they expected her to look different. They were willing to accept an improved version of her without asking questions. Only her mother refused to believe her. "That creature is not my daughter," she told me. She said after Lily came back from her treatment she threw out all her old shoes.'

'Why would she do that?'

'Because they didn't fit her any more.'

'People's feet don't suddenly change size.'

'That's what I thought. And just when I couldn't be more suspicious, Patricia died.'

'How did she die?'

'She was found lying at the foot of the communal staircase in her building the night after the party. She was pronounced dead in the ambulance. The doctor blamed the fall on her frail, confused condition. But Patricia had told me she never felt safe on the staircase so why would she suddenly use it now, and at such a late hour?'

'Did you talk to the latest boyfriend, Will? If anyone noticed the change in your friend it would be him.'

'Of course I did. He came to the party. He said she *had*

changed and he was delighted – their sex life was suddenly amazing. He told me I should mind my own business. Then I did a dumb thing. I accused Will and Lily of working together to try and fool everyone.'

'Oh, I see,' said Longbright, checking her notes on Gail Barker's history. 'It wasn't the first time you'd accused someone of—'

'I made a mistake a few years ago and have regretted it ever since,' Gail explained. 'This was different.'

'How did they respond to the accusation?'

'Will told me I should leave them alone for everyone's sake. That was when I realized they all preferred her this way, as an upgraded version of the old difficult Lily. *I* was the odd one out, not her. I didn't buy it.'

'But if she was happy and everyone else was happy, why didn't you just leave it there?' Longbright asked, already sensing the answer.

'Because I was sure she had killed my friend and taken her place, and pushed her mother down the stairs to shut her up.' Gail dropped her head into her hands. 'I know how that sounds. Crazy.'

'So what did you do?'

'I figured the clinic was the only place where the switch could have happened, so I tried calling.'

'What did they say?'

'I couldn't get hold of anyone. I couldn't even find the right number. But I had another theory.'

'Which was what?'

'I think Lily died of complications during surgery and the clinic was somehow cleared. Lily sometimes – well, she sometimes used recreationals on weekends. If the autopsy found cocaine in her system maybe the clinic wasn't liable. The new Lily didn't want to speak to me, so I ambushed her on the way home at London Bridge Station. That was where I got her to admit who she really was.'

'And who did she say she was?' asked Longbright.

'Someone who'd been following Lily on Instagram and Twitter and Facebook and LinkedIn for years, someone who just wanted to be her.'

'Wait, you mean a total stranger took her place? How would that work?'

Gail shook her head. 'I'm not sure. I think she followed her activities on a daily basis, maybe for years. There was all sorts of footage posted. I think maybe she found out that Lily had died in surgery and just turned up in her place. Lily's mother didn't believe it, but everyone knew that Patricia wasn't well. Her brother Charlie was so wasted that he couldn't even leave his flat. He was once robbed while he was sitting in the living room watching TV. I thought about it. Lily had dumped her old friends. She was between jobs. She stepped out of her old life. Will kept his mouth shut because he preferred the new version. It seemed like everyone was happy except me.'

'So, yesterday evening on the platform. What did she say to you?'

'She said she nearly messed up at the birthday party because she lost a coloured contact lens down the sink. She said, "You don't know me because I'm nobody, just some-one who admired your friend. I knew everything about her. There's nothing you can do because no one will ever believe you." That was when I lost my temper.'

'You pushed her.'

'Yes. I didn't mean her to fall under the train, I didn't even realize it was coming in, I just saw this – liar standing before me.'

'It's a hell of a story,' said Longbright, shaking her head in wonder.

'I need you to prove it,' said Gail.

'There are a number of practical things we can do,' Longbright said. She and John May were standing on the unit's flat roof, virtually the only place in the building where they would not be interrupted. 'Fingerprints, teeth, skin markings . . .'

'Marshall was electrocuted as well as crushed. There's nothing much left of her head or hands,' said May. 'DNA would only be useful if she'd been typed. Did you find the clinic?'

'There's nothing under "Younger Woman". Her death would have been registered. I'm waiting for a callback on that. I tried getting hold of this TV presenter Gail talked about, but she's not in the country.'

'I'm sure you can put something together eventually but there's no time,' said May. 'We'll be charging her just before eleven p.m. Do you think her story is remotely plausible? That someone could just step in and take over a life like that?'

'I want to believe her but I don't see how it's possible,' said Longbright. 'Some women do start to look alike after thirty. Hair dye, capped teeth, straightened noses, Botox. Surface impersonation is easy, but fooling a lover or relative would be impossible unless they were in some way impaired—'

'Like the mother and the brother.'

'—or were willing to go along with the subterfuge.'

'A stalker can find out every last tiny detail about you, and Marshall's life was all laid out online.' May thought for a moment. 'There are plenty of priors in that area.

Remember that guy who was accepted back into his family after going missing, and nobody questioned the fact that he had different-coloured eyes and a French accent?'

'Frédéric Bourdin,' said Longbright, 'known as "the Chameleon". He had over five hundred different identities. Dan's trying to access Marshall's old online posts, but he says getting information out of Silicon Valley will take time and cost a fortune.'

'It's ridiculous,' May complained. 'There must be some way of proving or disproving . . .'

'I'm going with the most obvious solution,' said Longbright finally.

'Which is?'

'Gail Barker was always jealous of her friend, then one day Marshall went in for an expensive surgical upgrade and started dumping her old social circle – including Barker – to improve her own career chances. Nobody wants to think they didn't make the grade. Gail couldn't handle it so she confronted her and pushed her under the train, then made up a cock-and-bull story for us. Maybe she created this fantasy and genuinely believes it. It's the only way she can handle the rejection.'

'At least she's in custody,' said May. 'Arthur and I don't have any time to spare you. We're up to our necks in the Hampstead Heath murder. You'll have to do it alone.'

As Longbright headed back downstairs she began to have doubts about closing the case. *An identity should be an easy thing to prove*, she thought. *What would Mr Bryant do?*

The answer came to her in a moment. He would not spend any longer in the interview room. He would start looking for an answer from the other end of the case.

She called Patricia Marshall's doctor. He confirmed that

she had fallen down the stairs, and supported the verdict of accidental death. Banbury also tried to find a number for the clinic but had no luck. Gail Barker was taken downstairs to the PCU's only holding cell. The clock was ticking.

Finally, Longbright grabbed her coat and headed out, pulling up Gail Barker's address on her phone.

There were so many gaps in the story that investigation was almost impossible, but Longbright did not have time on her side. On the train to Dalston she made notes.

If Marshall really died, where is body?

Wouldn't some member of family have flown out to Austria?

Did clinic hush up death?

Who attended birthday party?

Did no one honestly notice change in her?

By the time the train reached its destination, Longbright was even more convinced that Barker was lying, either unintentionally or deliberately. Everything was against her story. If there was more time, she would be able to pull it apart systematically. She had to hope that something in the flat would point her to the truth.

Any area with coffee bars and graffiti could call itself the new hipster quarter, but as Dalston was just a stone's throw from London's financial centre, gentrification here was well under way. Longbright found Gail Barker's flat in a street already in the throes of redevelopment.

Letting herself in, Longbright switched on the lights and looked around. Clean, tidy rooms, fresh flowers, a perfectly kept desk, a recipe book pinned open on the kitchen counter. The more she thought about it, the more she began to despair. This wasn't how evidence searches worked; you looked for proof of guilt: bloodstained clothing, weapons, drugs. What she sought could never be found so quickly. Proof of mental aberration, delusion, obsession. She honestly had no idea what to do next, so she followed standard methodology.

Wardrobe, desk drawers, kitchen and bathroom bins. Gail's desk was covered in penguins of different sizes. Pinned on the wall behind her were a dozen penguin postcards and several calendars featuring the birds diving, sliding and generally falling over one another. *If you make the mistake of confiding in a friend that you admire birds of any breed*, Longbright thought, *you'll be given them every Christmas and birthday for the rest of your life.*

Looking at the backs of the postcards, she realized they were all from Lily. Little messages. 'Bet you haven't got this one!' 'Here's another emperor!' 'Cute chicks!' There were no recent ones.

Longbright remembered her own schooldays, spending lunchtimes in the library looking at photos of old movie stars instead of talking to her classmates. She'd had a best friend, Polly, who would do anything for her. Longbright had treated her thoughtlessly, knowing she would always be there. Polly had married someone boring so she'd let the friendship slide. She wished she hadn't now.

She found a laptop in the desk and took it. There was no time to start trawling emails and website history; Dan had software that could do the work in a fraction of the time. Beneath it were drawers of letters and old photographs: Lily by the Monet painting, Lily and Gail at parties in clubs and on holiday together. Of course, Gail had photographs even if her friend did not. What Longbright needed now were shots taken at the surprise party, so that she could make comparisons, but there were none in the drawer. She checked her phone: 9.55 p.m. She had just over an hour to find proof of Barker's innocence, but what did it look like?

Perhaps it wasn't a definitive item but something less tangible, something that would show she was unstable, a risk. Barker had caused trouble once before, wrongly reporting a colleague for harassment, but it was hardly proof of an ongoing mental condition.

She called the unit and got Gail on the phone.

'I'm at your flat,' she said. 'Is there anything here that can confirm your story?'

Gail took so long to reply that for a moment Longbright thought she'd rung off. 'I sneaked some photos of her. I never got around to uploading them.'

'So they're still on your phone? Do you have cloud storage?'

'No – and I lost the phone a week ago. I'm on a Pay As You Go.'

'Gail, if you can't think of anything that will clear you, you'll be formally charged with murder in less than an hour. Did Lily always send you penguins?'

'Yes, everywhere she went. If she travelled on business she still found time to post one. She stopped when she was replaced. The new girl wouldn't have known about them because, well, postcards, they're so old-fashioned.'

And analogue, Longbright thought. *She had no way of*

*knowing they'd been sent. It means that this other person,
if she existed, was monitoring online feeds but not physical
activity. She watched from a distance. From another city,
maybe even another country.*

'Is there anything else that Lily's "replacement" might
not have known about?' she asked.

'Not that I can think of.'

'OK, I'll keep working on it.' She rang off.

In frustration she pulled out every drawer from every
cupboard and turned them over on the floor. There was no
time to examine everything in the piles she made, so she
flicked through items and threw them to one side.

The letter was one of several that had been kept in a
shoebox under the bed. Reading it, she made a grab for her
phone.

'John, you can't charge her for the murder of Lily
Marshall.'

'You found something?'

'No big revelation, I'm afraid, not the kind that Mr Bryant prefers. But I think it's enough to warrant further
investigation. I'll be there in a few minutes.'

Gail was sitting on the corner of her cell bed, staring miserably at the floor. Longbright sat before her on a stool.
'You addressed this to Lily,' she said, flattening out the
page. 'When did you write it?'

'I wrote letters all the time,' said Gail slowly.

Longbright read part of it aloud. ' "I'm sorry we argued.
I know you were just being honest and that you don't mean
what you say. You said I was jealous of you, but I'm not.
I'm the only one who knows what you go through, fight-
ing to keep your job, looking great, pretending to be happy.
I bet a lot of your followers want to be you, because they

don't know what it's really like. Your life looks cool to everyone else, but you and I know it's fake because best friends know everything." Do you remember writing that?'

'Yes. It was about a year ago.' Gail raised her head for the first time, lifting her hair from her eyes. She had been crying again.

'You didn't post it.'

'I never post them. We'd had a row. I didn't want to make things worse for her. There are lots more letters.'

'You didn't want to be her, did you? But you knew that others would.'

'I read the comments people left for her. Some of them were really scary. Lily never looked at them. She was too busy putting every detail of her life online. She wanted to show everyone how great her life was. I knew it was dangerous.'

'Well, there's an old expression,' said Longbright. 'When your life exceeds your dreams, keep your mouth shut. You know what I think? You fell for a scam. Lily Marshall didn't go off to a private clinic for surgery. She didn't have any work done. I think the imposter killed Lily and took her place. Then, in the guise of Lily, she lied to you about everything. That's why there's no evidence. It was the ultimate theft of identity, not just online but in reality. Lily was lucky to have you as a best friend. You looked out for her. Do you have any idea who the other person might have been?'

'Not really,' said Gail sadly. 'But there was a name that kept cropping up on her blog.'

Longbright took her hand. 'Listen to me, Gail. You're going to be charged, but hopefully not with the murder of your friend. The letter makes me believe you, but the court will need something stronger. Help us to find out who she was, and we'll find a way to bring you closure.'

*

The charge was deferred and changed. When Longbright and Banbury tracked the author of the comments on Lily Marshall's blog they were led to a German computer programmer seven years younger than Marshall. Irina Hartmann had made an intensive study of her target's online presence. Further examination of the CCTV footage from London Bridge Station showed that Hartmann had slipped as she backed away from Gail Barker.

Hartmann had a history of online stalking and threatening behaviour. Detailed notes about her planned transformation into Lily were found in her apartment, along with arrangements for a meeting. All she had needed for the impersonation was make-up, hair dye and a little weight loss.

Lily Marshall's remains were found in a pond near Hartmann's house in Bremen. She had been drugged and drowned. The exact circumstances of her murder were never fully uncovered, but it was clear that Lily had been lured there around the time that Hartmann said she went to the clinic.

Lily's death had been caused by her quest for a more youthful life. But the dream she'd chased had been a mirage, an optimistic construction of photos and captions. Only the handwritten, heartfelt words of her sister had proved real.

Gail Barker initially received a suspended sentence, which was dropped on appeal.

Every year, on the anniversary of her best friend's death, Gail sends Janice Longbright a card of Monet's *Water Lilies*.

BRYANT & MAY UP THE TOWER

Arthur Bryant remembered that it was in the autumn of 1967, during the thunderstorm that came after the first Summer of Love. That woozy celebration of spiritual freedom had crossed from Haight-Ashbury, San Francisco, to reach London's tallest building, the Post Office Tower, in Fitzrovia.

The silver spindle was like nothing ever seen in the capital before. A shining needle segmented with gravity-defying discs, it had quickly come to represent the future. The tower had been opened two years earlier by the Prime Minister, Harold Wilson, and was now hosting parties in its revolving high-rise restaurant.

Tonight the famous guests peeped out from beneath their umbrellas to have their photographs taken, illuminated by camera flashes and lightning. The storm breaking overhead suggested to some that it would be unwise to venture up a giant conduction rod.

'Tall, isn't it?' commented John May, standing on the steps with his head tipped back.

'It's not the height that bothers me, it's the extreme slenderness of the thing,' said Arthur Bryant. 'Apparently you have to switch lifts halfway up because the structure flexes in the wind. And what do you find when you get up there? A restaurant run by Butlin's.'

'And the whole of London spread at your feet.'

'Perhaps not tonight. The cloud base looks awfully low. Come on, let's go up.'

'Wait.' May grabbed his partner's shoulders and examined him. 'Is that a clip-on bow tie?'

'Look, matey, if Alma hadn't found this shirt in a charity shop I might have tipped up in a string vest. What's the bash, anyway?'

'The Independent Television Hallowe'en Ball,' said May. 'The Met thought it would be a good idea to have someone working undercover and we drew the short straw.'

'Are we to expect trouble, then?' asked Bryant.

'There's a lot of money here.'

Prior to the murder of John Lennon, security at celebrity events – and, in fact, at the door of any public building – was notoriously lax. London was still free of security guards, bag searches, knife arches and ID checks. The anarchists' bomb that detonated in the restaurant four years later would bring an end to the city's open-door policy, closing the tower for good. Tonight, though, the most famous faces in London had fought for a ticket.

'I thought you'd like a night out,' said May. 'Free nosh, lots of stars – look, Tom Jones, Cilla Black, Mick Jagger, Twiggy and, over there, Michael Caine.'

'And an awful lot of Draculas, mummies and werewolves,' said Bryant. 'I notice the bigger stars aren't in fancy dress.'

'They were allowed to remain as themselves, because of

the press value,' said May. 'There's no point in Twiggy turning up as the Creature of the Black Lagoon.'

'There are a few of those, too,' Bryant pointed out. 'I'm getting wet. Let's go in.'

Ah, the heady, hedonistic sixties. A time when John May took to hideous kipper ties and unfeasible sideburns, and Arthur Bryant remained exactly as he always was, a short, portly chap in a gabardine raincoat and Oxford toecaps.

'Over there in the pink abaya and veil, that's Qamar ud-Din, the Arabic singer,' said May. 'She's wearing a yellow diamond ring called the Monarch of the Sands, valued at two million pounds.'

The chanteuse was as tall and graceful as a candlestick, draped in pink and blue, veiled for modesty and accompanied by a large bald man who might have been holding a scimitar, so obviously did he wear his profession. Bryant noted the pair and gave a grunt.

Cliff Richard passed them in an orange kaftan, waving and smiling to the photographer from the *Daily Mirror*. 'He never gets any older, does he?' said Bryant. 'He'll still be going strong in the year 2000.'

'You know what they say about him, don't you?' said May confidentially.

'Of course I don't. What do they say?'

'That he's a Christian.'

'Good heavens. Well, some of my best friends are Christians. Perhaps I should try it. Being an atheist isn't keeping me any younger.'

Now they encountered the main problem with the Post Office Tower: the lifts were tiny. A line quickly formed that went across the foyer and down the stairs. They used their police credentials to queue-jump but it was obvious to Bryant that the building was completely unsuitable for public opening.

The restaurant itself was surprisingly small and unremarkable. It had been blandly decorated and furnished in pale wood, allowing attention to fall on its one sensational feature: the circular view it offered of the city at night.

The restaurant completed a full rotation every twenty-two minutes, and only the central disc housing the waiters' station and kitchen access remained still. While footballers' girlfriends danced with bishops and a band resplendent in paisley shirts and beads played psychedelic nonsense, the detectives circled the floor.

In the time-honoured tradition, class and position decided who had a table reservation and who was left to balance canapés with a wine glass. The standing guests gathered at the windows to watch the storm descend upon the capital. Qamar ud-Din remained seated at a table, watchfully sipping an orange juice. Simon Dee, the highest-paid personality on the BBC, was being photographed with fashion legend Mary Quant, he in a purple roll-neck, elephant-cord hipster jeans and a woven leather belt, she in a black minidress laced with silver chains. Their exchange of warm smiles almost made them look as if they liked each other.

Suddenly the lights went out and the twinkling cityscape appeared. There were a few small screams as people thought lightning had hit the tower's antennae.

'It's all right, ladies and gentlemen,' an authoritative voice told them, 'the storm seems to have taken out our power. Normal service will be resumed as soon as possible.' The waiters began to set candles out on the tables. Without the band playing, voices could be heard.

'Well *really*, the most frightfully poor show.'

'Typical British engineering. Probably the fault of the unions.'

'—delicious little dolly bird over in the corner.'

'Humphrey, darling, there are no corners.'

Only two or three minutes had passed before the lights came back on. One would think the Blitz had just taken place by the way everyone was laughing and joking with each other. *It only takes a power failure for the barriers to come down*, Bryant thought, standing at the inside edge of the room, studying the guests. He started when he noticed the songstress, Qamar ud-Din. She seemed to be drunk. Except, of course, she couldn't be.

He headed over to the table where she sat with her head lolling forward. 'Miss Qamar, are you all right?'

It took both him and John May to rouse her. Holding an arm each, they walked her around the room. 'Where is the bodyguard?' asked May. 'He's meant to stay with her at all times.'

Of course, when he glanced down at the hand that bore the fabled Monarch of the Sands, the ring was gone.

They searched the room, but the bodyguard had vanished into thin air and the singer remembered nothing of what had occurred. 'I sat here with my drink,' she explained. 'I talked to a dull little television producer with bad breath; I sent him away to bring me some food and just then the lights went out. I think I had a little nap. The power came back on and you arrived. There's nothing else to tell.'

'You didn't feel the ring being taken off?' asked Bryant.

'No, and that doesn't make sense because I have worn it since I was sixteen, and it cannot easily be removed. I would have most definitely felt the loss of it.' She searched their faces with imploring kohl-dark eyes. 'Please, you must find the ring. My life will be in danger if it is gone.'

'Why?' asked Bryant. 'Is there a legend attached to it?'

'No, Mr Bryant, just an insurance policy. But it was entrusted to me by the crown prince as a representative of his nation. To lose such a valuable item would bring down the most terrible dishonour.'

'Don't worry, we'll get it back for you,' said Bryant with confidence. 'My partner here will take statements from the guests while I search for the ring.'

'The prince has had innocent men and women put to death in his country,' one of the partygoers told May. 'His repressive regime is coming to an end. Perhaps a greater power is making him pay for his crimes.'

'Wow, man, bad karma,' said a young man in granny glasses and a psychedelic tunic. 'It's like a supernatural force is working, possibly with, er, the government.'

'What are you smoking?' asked Bryant.

'I think we can eliminate Bruce Forsyth,' said May.

The short version was, nobody saw anything.

Bryant stood against the glass and looked back at the crowd, their reflections superimposed over the night landscape. They were bright glowing ghosts, drifting from table to table like bees drawn to pollen.

I'm an idiot, he thought, turning and pushing back through the guests in the direction of the restaurant's central base. Here, between two absurdly narrow waiters' stations, stood the steel dumb waiter to the kitchen on the floor below.

Bryant beckoned to his partner, pointing at the emergency staircase. Together they descended a floor. The chefs froze in surprise as they entered. 'Has a heavyset bald man with a face like a constipated mastiff come in here?' asked Bryant.

'He jumped out of the dumb waiter and ran off,' said the

head chef. 'He was about to get my soup ladle around the back of his head, but he'd gone before I could stop him.'

'So we've lost him,' said May.

'Not at all, old bean. I knew if there was trouble it would be caused by the person closest to Miss Qamar ud-Din, so I pointed him out to the *Daily Mirror* photographer and said if he leaves early, detain him. It was in his interests to do so as there's a story in it for him.'

They took the stairs because it was faster than commandeering the lift. In the foyer they found the photographer taking shots of a police constable sitting on the bodyguard, who was swearing colourfully and blasphemously in several languages.

'Have you searched him?' asked May.

'Thought we'd leave that for you,' said the photographer. 'When I got near him he bit me.'

'I asked him to behave until you got here, Mr Bryant,' said the PC, 'but he called me a – well, he suggested that my mother was no stranger to the embrace of a camel.'

'I'm sure you've been called worse,' said Bryant. 'Let's see what's in his pockets.'

The Monarch of the Sands was a sunlit desert encased in crystal. The flaw that made the diamond glow saffron made it a magical symbol of the prince's country.

'I don't understand,' said May. 'I saw you standing there just after the lights came back on. You already knew she'd had the diamond stolen without even seeing that it was missing from her finger.'

'Well, I *did* have an idea it was about to happen,' Bryant admitted. 'When I listened to the party chatter I overheard Miss Qamar tell someone she'd been given a new bodyguard. And I couldn't help noticing he looked remarkably like "Nosher" Stibbs from Canning Town.'

'But that's not why you reacted like that.'

'No, it was for a much simpler reason. When the lights went out – not the storm's fault, I suspect, but someone the bodyguard bribed – Miss Qamar was sitting at one of the VIP tables. When the power returned, she was in a different seat.'

'So what had happened?'

'I think we'll find that the bodyguard slipped something into her orange juice a few minutes earlier. As soon as it was dark and the outside view provided the only lighting in the room, "Nosher" removed her from the room and took her to the central waiters' station, where he managed to get the ring off, possibly with the help of an accomplice. Then he returned her to her chair. But he slipped up in the dark. The restaurant revolves 360 degrees every twenty-two minutes, which means that in the time he had been removing the ring from her finger, her chair had shifted about forty-five degrees. He returned with her from the waiters' station and sat her down in the wrong place, outside of the VIP section. The moment I saw her there, I knew what had happened.'

'Let's go and return the ring,' said May. 'We could have a bit of fun and tell her the culprit was Michael Caine.'

BRYANT & MAY AND THE
BREADCRUMB TRAIL

'Arthur – don't do that.'

'What?' Bryant looked up at his partner in surprised innocence.

'Take your knife out of the toaster. Or at least unplug it first.'

Bryant waggled the table knife between his thumb and forefinger. 'You know, when I was a lad we used to get a two-prong plug into a three-prong socket by wedging the third hole open with a pencil stub. Everyone's so safety-conscious now.'

'So you're prepared to risk electrocution for a slice of toast. Amazing.' May rattled his copy of the *Guardian* and vanished behind it once more.

The detectives were seated opposite each other in their private room (private insofar as it had a lockable door) on the first floor of the Peculiar Crimes Unit, King's Cross. Outside, the steady rainfall made the sound of a bonfire. Bare-headed office workers in soaked summer shirts darted between vans and taxis; the rain has to be heavy to make a real Londoner raise an umbrella.

Bryant had the toaster balanced on a pile of encyclopaedias, alongside a 1960s Pifco Teasmade that invariably shot boiling water over their paperwork.

'We should get a modern coffee machine with those little capsules,' said May. 'You can choose the strength of your coffee.'

'I don't want to choose the strength of my coffee, I want a cup of tea. Leaves, not bags. Whole milk. No sugar.'

'You're stuck in the past,' sighed May, returning to his paper.

'I'm not, I'm just too busy catching up to deal with the present. I'll get to the present eventually.' He dug his knife back into the toaster.

'You mean you'll get to it at some time in the future.'

'Yes, when I've finished with the past. I want to know everything before I die, and I'm running out of time.' His knife slipped and catapulted breadcrumbs across the office. 'It's an awful paradox. The more I learn the less I truly understand. Have you looked in our box of unsolved cases lately? The Chamber of Horrors Maniac. The Deptford Demon. The Odeon Strangler. The Limehouse Ratboy. We'll never be able to close them. The verdicts were all "murder by person or persons unknown". I'm only hanging on to the files out of sentimentality.'

There was a bang and the lights went out. Unconcerned, Bryant withdrew his knife from the smoking toaster and lit a candle in a saucer.

'D'you know, at night I recall everything about London that I thought I'd lost. I remember the dockyards at Deptford Creek and the walk from Blue Anchor Road to the China Hall, and waiting for my father outside the Dog &

Bell – he met Rudyard Kipling, did you know? Long story – and my mother went to prison and I investigated the bombing of the Post Office Tower.'

May lost his place in the conversation. 'Wait, your mother—?'

'It's all stored away up here.' Bryant tapped his temple. 'My head's like an attic full of ephemera, old record albums, paperbacks you can't bear to throw out and those moulds dentists use to make of your teeth.'

May sighed and pulled his chair closer to his desk. 'OK,' he said, 'do you want to talk about it?'

Bryant's refulgent blue eyes widened. 'What?'

'Well, there's obviously something on your mind that's making you introspective, so out with it.'

'I think the world has moved into a new technological phase, and it hasn't taken me with it.'

'I could have told you that years ago.'

'All these apps and drones and smart-doodads – they don't make life simpler or easier. What's the point of buying things online that don't fit when you can go to the shops? I don't understand what anyone gets at the end of it all.'

'Have you tried asking Dan?'

'Yes, he spoke to me in great detail. When I woke up he'd gone.'

'Look,' said May, 'this is you.' He cleared a space on their conjoined desks and placed a pencil on it. 'You see something online that you want to buy, and you contact the seller.' He placed a rubber band next to the pencil. 'This seller takes your money and passes your information along to another company, who pays the seller.' Here he set down his fountain pen. 'The company uses your details to find you another product, advertising it on the site you first looked at, and sells you something new. Everyone pays everyone else.'

'I'm not happy being a pencil,' Bryant complained. 'I'd be happier as a fountain pen. The pen makes more money.'

'Yes, but you get the product.'

'That was a straight transaction. I'm not in profit, plus I lost my information. Even the rubber band's better off than me.'

'Perhaps you should stay away from transaction technology,' said May.

'How can I when it's everywhere?' Bryant's wrinkled face loomed over the flickering candle. 'I read in the paper that a private school asked its pupils to make Christmas cards, and the pupils outsourced them to a Chinese service they found online. I'd happily go back to living without the internet. And electricity, for that matter.'

The lights came back on. Bryant winced theatrically, a portly vampire hit by dawn's rays.

'Thank God for that,' said May just as Janice Longbright stepped into the room.

'I thought you'd already gone,' said Janice.

'Where?'

'There's a case in. Didn't anyone tell you? A murder in Soho. Sounds pretty nasty. They've got someone in custody.'

Bryant rose, pushed his trilby over his ears and knotted his scarf. 'Then why do they need us?'

'The young lady says it was all the fault of her phone.'

'How come we only get the nutters?' May asked.

'Because urban madness is our trade.' Bryant handed Longbright the blackened toaster. 'Throw this out, would you? Something's gone wrong with it.'

*

'That is the most disgusting bloody thing I've ever seen, and I've seen what Colin eats,' said Meera Mangeshkar, peering into the waste bin. They were standing in one of Chinatown's shadowy back alleys, at the rear of Gerrard Street.

Dan Banbury stood back against the alley wall, breathing deeply and trying to prevent himself from throwing up. John May stayed with the accused while his partner took a positively unhealthy interest in the bin. It was a brown plastic trough with a broken lid, filled with the remains of a hundred Chinese dinners, and a body. Sticking out from the noodles, beansprouts, special fried rice, chicken feet and fish heads were a pair of jean-clad legs ending in snakeskin cowboy boots. It was an unpleasantly humid evening and the smell was almost tangible.

'It looks like he drowned in someone's sweet and sour sauce,' said Bryant, fascinated. Banbury made another throwing-up noise.

'What happened?' May asked the suspect. 'Wait a minute, who are you and who's the bloke in the bin?'

In her floral summer top and white jeans the girl looked normal enough. She seemed a little annoyed and impatient, but was not confused or disturbed in any way. 'My name is Naomi Sams,' she replied, holding up her smartphone. 'I don't know who he is, and if it wasn't for this stupid thing I wouldn't even be here.'

'Right, we have to get him out,' said Meera, uncapping a pot of Tiger Balm and dabbing some under Banbury's nose. 'Dan, grab a leg.'

'Really? Is this in my job description now?' The crime scene manager looked over at the body half submerged in meal remains.

'It does you good to get away from the keyboard occasionally,' said Meera. Together they leaned over the lip of the bin and each pulled an ankle. It took longer than they expected to pull him out, thanks to the suction effect of so much warm wet food. The body emerged with the sound of a wellington boot being pulled from mud.

Sitting him up in the bin proved to be a bad idea as he started to sink again, so they laboriously lifted him out and propped him against the alley wall. 'OK,' said Banbury, wiping pieces of pork from his sleeves, 'we're looking at a white male, late thirties, light build, suffocated.'

'You're already sure of that?' asked Bryant.

'It seems highly likely, Mr B.,' said Banbury. 'There's a prawn up his nose.' The corpse's head was covered in bright orange slime. Even his eyeballs were treacly with sauce. There were noodles hanging out of his mouth and slices of lemon stuck to his neck.

'Do you want to talk us through what happened here or back at the station?' May asked the suspect.

'What, I get a choice?' Miss Sams looked surprised. 'You're not normal police, are you?'

'We're from the Peculiar Crimes Unit and this doesn't look like a normal crime,' he replied.

'OK.' She took a deep breath, but glanced over at the corpse and hesitated.

'Can you get that fellow out of here, Dan?' May asked.

'He's stuck to the wall,' said Meera.

'Just get rid of him.'

'I've got this stupid app on my phone,' said Sams, showing May her mobile screen. 'It's called Breadcrumb. The idea is that—'

'Is this relevant?'

'I'm not an idiot. You asked me what I was doing here.'

'Sorry.'

She tapped her screen and a series of orange dots

appeared on a black map. 'It keeps track of where you are so you can always find your way back. It doesn't show you the surrounding streets, just your route. Breadcrumbs, get it? But it's buggy. I was trying to find the tube station and it sent me down here. As soon as I realized it was a dead end I stopped and tried to get it working properly again. I looked up and realized that this guy was standing in the doorway at the end watching me. He had a knife in one hand, a big kitchen knife, the sort of thing you use for cutting through bones, and he made this gesture like – oh, I don't know, like I was the last straw and he'd had enough of everything. Then he ran at me. The knife was still in his hand. I just sort of – froze, I suppose. It all happened so fast.'

'Was the knife raised?' asked May. 'Was he threatening you?'

Sams gave him a look. 'What do you think? Just as he reached me he slipped.'

May looked down and saw that the alley pavement was black with oil. A single skid-mark led to the bin.

'I gave him a shove while he was off-balance and he fell in head first. He tried to get out but sort of floundered around, sinking in deeper the more he wriggled, and there were bubbles of sauce coming out and he stopped moving.'

'You didn't try to help him.'

'He came at me with a bloody knife!'

'So if we empty that bin out we'll find a knife,' said May.

'I am so not doing that,' Meera warned.

DS Mangeshkar unearthed the kitchen knife after ten minutes of poking about with a piece of bamboo she had found in the restaurant.

'It'll be interesting to see if we can get prints off the handle,' said May as he and Bryant walked to the end of the alleyway.

They reached the back door of the Lucky Dragon Chinese restaurant, an insalubrious Cantonese joint with yellow flock wallpaper, waterfall calendars and red paper lanterns. Banbury called out a warning: 'If you go in there you'll be compromising a potential crime scene.'

'Don't care, going in,' Bryant called back. May found a light switch. The restaurant's storeroom was filled with drums of oil and poly-boxes of vacuum-packed duck breasts. 'Cooked on the premises, my arse,' said Bryant. He stood in the doorway and looked back into the alley. 'Do you think her story makes any kind of sense?'

'It does now,' said May. When Bryant turned, he saw that there was another pair of legs sticking out from between the boxes. The concrete floor was sticky with blood.

'I think she caught her attacker in the middle of something,' said Bryant.

Back at the PCU, the detectives gathered everyone in the operations room and set up whiteboards. Information was coming in thick and fast, but at this stage the problem lay in assigning importance to each detail.

'I can smell sweet and sour fish,' said Raymond Land. 'Can you not eat lunch in this room? Where are we?'

'Two dead, one suspect,' said John May. He explained the circumstances to the unit chief.

'You think she saw him attacking this other bloke and he went for her, is that it? Get rid of the witness?'

'We don't know yet,' May admitted. 'He may not have realized he was still holding the knife. She says she saw him as a threat and shoved him.'

Dan Banbury arrived and set down his kit. 'I've got an update if you're ready?'

May sat down and gave him the floor.

'Everything at the site fits with Miss Sams's description of what happened. I've got footprints of the two males going inside, one coming out again, one set for Sams entering the alley.'

'Have you got IDs on the men for us?'

Banbury ran his hand over his tufted fair hair. 'The chap who asphyxiated in the bin is Archie Marlow, a small-time "entrepreneur" very familiar with the staff at Southwark Crown Court. Marlow died from inhaling a mixture of liquids and solids. There was a spring roll stuck in his throat. The chap on the floor of the storage room is Nikos Petrides, known to his pals as "Little Nicky", equally dodgy. He died from a single stab wound to the heart. Floor prints are all consistent with Marlow launching an unexpected attack on Petrides.'

'Any idea how they knew each other?' asked May.

Dan checked his notes. 'Little Nicky is also, guess what, an entrepreneur. They both toyed around with IT start-ups, failed to raised VC—'

'Explain,' said Bryant.

'Sorry, Mr B., venture capital. Most start-up entrepreneurs are losers who still think the internet is a meritocracy. After running up debts they have a habit of turning up in other corners of the non-employed universe hawking stuff to mugs. No obvious connection between the two just yet, but I'd suggest we're looking at a falling-out among thieves. Open and shut. Except.' He unfolded a note and pinned it to the board. 'Little Nicky had 250,000 pounds in his current account, put there by an offshore company in the last week. Before that the account averaged a figure of less than three hundred. If you're wondering about Archie Marlow's money, there isn't any. He died broke.'

'So a young lady studying her phone app takes a wrong turn into an alleyway just as Mr Marlow finishes off Mr Petrides,' said Bryant, scrawling across the whiteboard in handwriting no one could decipher. 'Marlow spots her at the worst possible moment and goes off on one. Someone in the restaurant must know what Petrides was doing there.'

'We're on it,' Banbury said. 'Nothing so far.'

'What about phone records?' asked Longbright. 'Petrides and Marlow might have spoken to one another.'

'It seems there was a flurry of calls two weeks ago, on Thursday evening at, let me see, eleven twenty-four p.m. They continued for the next four days. We've no transcripts.'

'Two weeks ago,' Bryant repeated. 'Wasn't that the day . . . ?'

'Yes,' said Banbury.

'Could this be something for the Special Ops bods?'

'It's our case, Mr B., our problem.'

Bryant passed a hand across his face. This was the last thing they needed. Two weeks earlier, at the end of the evening's rush hour, a van had mounted the pavement in Piccadilly and had gone through the window of a fashionable, busy and very expensive champagne bar and restaurant called Servicio that was frequented by international politicians. Four people had died, with a further two still in intensive care. The driver of the van had been captured alive. He proved to be an incoherent British national from Manchester with a history of mental problems.

'Can you get anything on Petrides' political persuasion?' asked May.

'I already have it. St George's Cross flags in the windows of his flat.' Banbury handed out screenshots.

'Are you telling me that these two no-hopers are somehow connected to a massacre?' asked Bryant. 'I don't believe it. Look at them.' He jabbed a finger at the shots Banbury had added to the board. 'Archie the jobless wonder and Little Nicky, Dr Frankenstein's assistant. They'd be turned away from a McDonald's. And how could there be any connection with the money that turned up in Petrides' account?'

'I may have a way to find that out,' said May, handing Bryant his trilby. 'Come with me.'

'We're going around the corner to York Way, to a place you walk past every day. I bet you've never even noticed what goes on in there.' May gripped Bryant's arm and marched his partner along the pavement.

'Rubbish. I know every square inch of this revolting neighbourhood.'

'Not this inch, you don't,' replied May.

Although he must have passed the place a thousand times, Bryant had never before taken note of the building. It existed between two restored warehouses, a dark glass wall with heavy curtains obscuring the rooms beyond. May used a swipecard on the door panel.

'This is HubKX,' he said.

'It doesn't have a sign,' said Bryant indignantly.

'It doesn't need one. Everybody who needs to use it knows where it is.'

The door opened and they stepped beyond the black curtains. It took a few moments for Bryant's eyes to adjust. He saw why no further light was needed. A handful of laptop users were sitting close to the ground on green and pink toadstools. It looked like *Alice in Wonderland* for nerds.

'What's going on here?' he whispered, loosening his scarf.

'This is Casper. He'll explain.'

The teenager on the floor had clearly been expecting them. He scooted over to allow May access to his laptop. As Bryant looked more closely he saw that Casper was not a child at all but a man in his mid-thirties, dressed in a grey hoodie several sizes too large.

'Usually we're raising money for Community Land Trusts,' Casper explained. 'We crowdfund restoration work and launch start-ups via share offerings through blockchain banks.'

'I see your lips moving but only nonsense comes out,' said Bryant apologetically. 'You might as well be French.'

'Look at it this way.' Casper walked Bryant over to the coffee bar that stood in a recess at the side of the room. 'Traditionally nobody shares information across different industries, but we can because our disruptive new networks are replacing the old hierarchies.'

'It's like tuning in an old radio,' said Bryant. 'I'm hearing slightly less than thirty per cent of what you say. Keep going.'

'In a hierarchy you report to the floor above and receive information from the floor below, yes? So you've no room to manoeuvre. In a network everyone receives information equally.' Casper gestured to a toadstool. 'Have a seat.'

'Thank you, I'm not a pixie,' said Bryant. 'John, how is this relevant to the investigation?'

'Dan and I keep you away from this sort of thing because we know how you feel about technology. This is what I want to show you.' May folded his legs with easy elegance and dropped before the screen. Casper took his phone and transferred three numbers. Pulling up a map of London, he expanded the image to reveal an animatic of the streets around them, pulsing in real time.

'Can you roll it back to seven forty-five p.m. last night?' May indicated the centre of the screen. 'These are GPS traces on everyone in Soho last night. We can follow just three of them. That's the girl, Sams, turning into the alleyway from Gerrard Street. Casper, can you take it back another ten minutes and give me from then to seven fifty p.m.?'

'So what you're doing is . . .' Bryant raised a finger, then stopped. 'No, it's gone. Technology and I aren't on speaking terms. I can't even take a proper selfie. The other day I accidentally sent a picture of my nostrils to the vicar.'

'These three lines show you the movements of Naomi Sams, Little Nicky and Archie Marlow over the period in question.'

Casper's screen now showed a spidery matrix overlaid across the street map. As the new information scrolled up Bryant peered at it intently. 'I haven't got my trifocals,' he apologized.

'Locations, ages, social groups, dates, times, everything's traceable,' Casper explained.

They watched as the three protagonists moved into place. Two of the orange dots suddenly converged. 'When Naomi Sams turned into the alley, Petrides had already been attacked in the storage room. It looks as if Marlow was standing over him when Sams interrupted them.'

'I've pulled the files Dan requested on Petrides and Marlow,' said Casper. 'I've sent them to your laptop.'

May thanked Casper for his time while Bryant reknotted his scarf, ready for take-off. As they stepped on to the street May opened the documents on his phone. Rain had decided to put in an appearance and was starting to darken the pavements.

'Is this how we're going to conduct all future assignments?' asked Bryant. 'Tap away at our telephones and trust whatever they tell us?'

'Is it any less reliable than talking to someone who swears they were nowhere near the crime scene?' May asked, absently pulling his partner from the path of a bread van.

Bryant watched in surprise as the vehicle passed him. 'The battery must have gone in my hearing aid.'

'I keep telling you, they're electric vehicles. Please try not to die. We need to go back and check through these files.'

'You can do that. I'm going to take a look at the crime scene.' Bryant pulled his coat collar straight and took a tentative step on to the rain-slick pavement.

'Dan's already been over it,' said May, still studying his phone.

'I don't mean *that* crime scene,' said Bryant. 'I mean the one on Piccadilly.'

It's impossible to tell that an act of terrorism ever occurred here, Bryant thought as he examined the plate-glass windows of Servicio, the champagne bar through which a stolen builder's van had been driven. The bar was situated near the circus end of Piccadilly, a crowded area that could not be easily screened off with concrete barriers. Bryant tapped his walking stick on the ornate carved-wood surround of the window, marvelling at the neatness of the rebuilt frame. It was impossible to see where the old and new woods were joined. It was policy now, he knew, to restore the damaged areas as quickly as possible. Only in

Bloomsbury's Tavistock Square, where a bomb had detonated on a double-decker bus, were there still signs of
destruction; the nearest building was pock-marked from
flying debris.

Bryant entered the champagne bar. Along the rear ran a
beaten copper counter. At the front was the restaurant,
resplendent in starched white linen and napery. After he
had explained the purpose of his visit, the manager, Davina
James, offered to show him around. Her pinned-up hair,
black-framed glasses and tightly cut black suit suggested
efficiency and authority.

'Business has been terrible since it happened,' she said,
keeping her voice low. 'People are so stupid – events like this
never occur twice in the same place but they still stay away.
I saw the whole thing. I was standing over by the counter.
The kerbstone outside is quite high and I saw the van bounce
up it. My first thought was that he was just parking badly.
They do try, once in a while – they last about twenty seconds before the police drop on them. Then I realized he
wasn't slowing down.' She stopped, looking out of the window. What she saw was not today's rain-glossed thoroughfare
but the evening traffic from two weeks ago. 'I froze on the
spot. I could see what was going to happen. I couldn't go
forward without risking my own life, and I suppose a sense
of self-preservation was trying to pull me away. I grabbed
the nearest chair and dragged it back. The woman sitting in
it fell on the floor and rolled aside. Everyone was looking at
me, not at the van, so I raised my arm and pointed.

'Just then, its grille hit the glass. The central pane broke
into three enormous pieces. One went over to that first
table like a guillotine and hit the lady sitting there. The
whole vehicle lifted over the window edge and came into
the restaurant. I heard the van's engine revving above the

first screams. The front four tables all went under the wheels. There was a boy of about six sitting just there – he was the one the papers all featured – he simply vanished. The woman who had been hit by the glass dragged the tablecloth off when she fell. As it settled over her it turned red. The van's engine suddenly stopped, I don't know why, and the room fell silent. The driver stayed in the vehicle. He didn't move an inch until the officers dragged him out. He was – well, not smiling exactly, just content, as if he was at peace.'

Bryant did not trust himself to speak. He could see the scene as it unfolded. He had been at the site of the Tavistock Square bombing, had seen the red bus ripped apart as if a giant can opener had cut off the roof.

Reliving the moment had tainted everything. He could not see the restaurant as a place of sociable dining any more, but only heard the crying of the wounded. Thanking her, he took his leave and headed out across the road.

Standing on the wet pavement opposite he found himself by a Costa Coffee shop. Two Japanese tourists were taking selfies and smiled at him. He bought a tea and sat outside at one of the tables, sheltered beneath a striped canopy. The van driver had been in and out of care homes and mental health institutions all his life. He was no terrorist. He had copied something he had seen on television, imitating other atrocities to assuage his own demons.

Bryant sat back and sipped his tea, studying the frontage of the champagne bar. Could the two dead men have met the assassin somewhere before, in a care home or hospital? Did Archie discover that Little Nicky was somehow involved on that terrible day?

He called John May and asked him to speak to Counter Terrorism Command, to see if they would share any withheld information. Then he returned to his tea and looked back at the bar. Tourists were passing it without any idea that just two weeks ago it had been a devastated ruin.

And then, quite suddenly, he knew what had happened.

May and the rest of the team had been over Casper's documents and had drawn a blank. Neither Archie nor Little Nicky had ever had contact with the van driver. Neither had been in any of the same institutions. Yet the first time they had called each other in over a year was two hours after the attack. The call log showed they had once been in contact for a period of six weeks, around thirteen months earlier, but that was it.

Little Nicky had gone to the Lucky Dragon to collect a payment from the manager as part of a protection racket he was attempting to foist on to new restaurants. Archie had followed him there. That was all the information they had.

When Arthur Bryant came in out of breath and opened a laptop, everyone looked at him as if he'd gone mad. Meera Mangeshkar held her breath while she waited to see if he could unlock it. When he did so successfully, Dan Banbury began to worry. If Bryant could do this, he might find the app for the trackers that Banbury had hidden in his coat, hat and briefcase. In his experience it was best to keep the old man as far away from technology as possible.

'Reverse engineering,' Bryant said excitedly. 'It's working backwards to the components, isn't it? That's what I've been doing. I thought I could leave the computer stuff to you lot and concentrate on what I could see. I went to the spot in Piccadilly where the van crashed into the restaurant, and what did I find on the other side of the street? A coffee shop.

Archie Marlow happened to be there two weeks before his death, on the evening of the attack. I spoke to the barista, who remembered him because he complained about his latte not being hot enough. Archie saw it all.'

Archie Marlow was broke. It was raining, and his right sock was wet from the hole in his shoe. His girlfriend had dumped him, his gambling debts were sufficiently big enough for a loan shark to threaten him with a Chelsea Smile* and his landlord was about to kick him out of the rathole he illegally rented.

Archie never stopped looking for an angle. He'd tried everything above, below and far beyond the law. Usually he relied upon a febrile sense of opportunism to find ways of scraping together a few quid, but tonight even this had escaped him. He was thinking about ways of faking his own death when he saw the builder's van suddenly accelerate.

He had never seen Piccadilly looking so drab and emptied out before. It made the white van stand out. His phone was in his hand, and without thinking he started filming. When the van suddenly mounted the kerb and ploughed into the restaurant, shattering its plate-glass frontage, he knew he was holding solid gold. He continued to film, remembering not to pan about or zoom too quickly, until the first police arrived.

All he could think of was Abe Zapruder, and the most examined piece of film in history. Twenty-six seconds shot at Dealey Plaza on 22 November 1963. The plume of crimson at Kennedy's throat. Jackie climbing over the back of the presidential limousine in her pink pillbox hat. Solid gold.

Who was in the restaurant? It looked fancy, expensive,

---

* Razor cuts to the corners of the mouth

the kind of place world leaders visited incognito. If it turned out that the van had been deliberately aimed, his footage could prove almost as valuable as Zapruder's. His hands were sweating so heavily that the phone almost slipped from them. With trembling fingers he stopped filming and played back the footage.

It was all there, the whole thing. Thirty-seven seconds.

Sirens made him look up. There were flak-jacketed officers running and cordons appearing. He needed to get out fast. As he slipped from the coffee shop he started placing calls.

The first news agencies he tried wanted him to stay on the line while they checked out the story. He rang the cable channels first. They wanted to see the footage before opening negotiations. Nobody would commit. Worse, everyone wanted to know his name.

His stomach sank as he realized he was sitting on a goldmine he could not sell. If he went through any official channel they would need to verify his identity, and would quickly find out too much about him. He tried to think of someone he could call, and the only name he came up with was someone he wouldn't trust with a milk carton, let alone a piece of film worth a fortune.

'You can see what happened,' said Bryant. 'It was thirty-seven seconds of footage that could transform his life. He called Little Nicky because their paths had crossed before. Dan, do you still have Naomi Sams's phone?'

Banbury gave it up with reluctance. Bryant squinted at it and stabbed at the key pad. 'It's four – three – zero – seven,' said the crime scene manager impatiently.

'A year earlier Archie Marlow set up a company to develop an app, and in the course of raising money for it

he met Little Nicky, who promised to help him get funding, stole the idea and ripped him off,' said Bryant,
continuing to poke at the phone. 'You know what they say
about chaps like Archie: once a loser, always a loser. Despite their history he trusted Little Nicky a second time
because he had no one else to turn to. Little Nicky agreed
to act as a broker and put his own name down as the
owner of the footage. Then he sold it all over the world
and pocketed the payment. Getting ripped off twice by the
same creep is more than enough reason for murder, don't
you think?'

'And you figured all this out without technology how
exactly?' asked Banbury.

'Tortured grammar but I take your point,' said Bryant.
'It's simple. I sat where he sat, and saw what he saw. Like
the rest of you I'd watched the footage repeated endlessly
on TV. There was no other angle it could have been filmed
from.'

Satisfied with what he saw on the screen of Naomi
Sams's phone, he turned it around so that everyone could
see. 'Breadcrumb. The best way to find your way home.
Registered to a company owned by Nikos Petrides. It's
right there on the screen. What it doesn't say is "Based on
an idea stolen from Archie Marlow". You see what this
means? Archie got caught out by his own invention. Breadcrumb brought to his door the person who would
accidentally cause his death.' He chucked the phone aside.
'Technology's all very well but sometimes you simply need
to see what's before your eyes.'

AUTHOR'S NOTES ON THE CASES

Bryant & May and the Seventh Reindeer

Every Christmas I walk through Covent Garden, and last year it snowed on their giant illuminated reindeer. I watched the performers in James Street and remembered I'd known the true sad story of the fellow inside the Alien suit. That was all I needed for the tale, plus an opera diva, *obviously*.

Bryant & May's Day Off

It's fairly clear that this tale is set in the post-war years before London's riverside resort Tower Beach closed down in 1971. The idea of swimming in the Thames now horrifies us, but I liked the idea of trying to find a criminal on a beach, where everyone looks the same.

Bryant & May and the Postman

I thought it would be fun to show the PCU involved in the nuts and bolts of a case, persistently questioning a suspect until an answer emerges, but this was also a chance to show their shortcomings. My father never quite managed to become a modern man, although he did have a crack at using hair gel. It didn't end well. He looked like a shampooed dog.

Bryant & May and the Devil's Triangle

This is a real corner near my flat and a genuine accident black spot, although not designated as such. I'm interested in the areas that remain ignored because they appear to have nothing to offer. Developers leave them alone, the oddest tales often come from them and they have the weirdest shops (this corner boasted a rubber maid's uniform store for many years).

Bryant & May and the Antichrist

A couple of years ago I moved flats for a while and had to keep memorizing different codes to get in (the property was on a canal with a series of gates). The only way I could remember them was by doing what Bryant does to solve the case. Plus, I like making the reader do a bit of work!

Bryant & May and the Invisible Woman

A combination of factors caused this: a visit to Dalí's astonishing theatre-museum in Figueres and an open night at the Tate Modern, when a woman told me it was the best way to find a date in London. Plus, I'd been wanting to give the PCU women more of the spotlight for a while.

Bryant & May and the Consul's Son

This is very much the centrepiece of the book, a long-gestating mystery that began as little more than a throwaway gag in *Strange Tide*. I was going to resolve it in the next novel but couldn't find a place to fit it in – too long for a sub-plot, not long enough for a novel – so I decided to write it up as a separate case. The locations are all real; one spot is where I headed to record an audio version of a book, an odd little London corner hidden in plain sight.

Bryant & May Meet Dracula

Otto Penzler owns a wonderful store called the Mysterious Bookshop in New York, and after visiting all the locations mentioned I wrote him a Transylvania-set tale called 'Reconciliation Day'. I thought it would be cool to adapt the research for the telling of a different story, one taking Bryant & May out of their comfort zone, and this is the result.

Bryant & May and the Forty Footsteps

I stumbled across the legend of the forty footsteps in several differing accounts in rare volumes of London history, and as it had happened near to me I set out to track it down. This proved harder than expected, as it's mostly underneath the concrete of University College London. I think I located the exact spot, but I can't be sure. As with all London legends it's the idea that grips.

Janice Longbright and the Best of Friends

This started out very differently, as a synopsis for a novel that I never got around to writing. My editor at the time was unenthusiastic and I soon became excited by a different idea, so it was shelved. But writers never throw anything away, and stories can sometimes find their feet with a fresh look. Originally it was going to be entirely set in the Younger Woman clinic.

Bryant & May up the Tower

This started out as a vignette in *The Casebook of Bryant & May*, a graphic novel drawn by the excellent Keith Page, but I'd always felt I could have fun with it in written form. My first job was at a company based at the foot of the tower (then named the Post Office Tower) which always fascinated me. I managed to go up to the restaurant before they closed it. Sixties futurism rocks!

Bryant & May and the Breadcrumb Trail

Ah, a sadly ever-topical London subject, to which I added Arthur Bryant vs technology, a disgusting death and an odd little newspaper item. I was very much on home ground in this tale. As the modern policing world becomes ever more reliant on technology the detectives look increasingly out of touch, but at the root of all detection is the idea that human nature never changes.

MURDER ON MY MIND:
AN AFTERWORD

Golden Age detectives in a modern age? That'll never work, said an editor. I remember thinking, *Fair play, she's probably right.*

I had a very exact idea in mind; when I thought of traditional Golden Age crime fiction, what came into my head were all the clichés: bodies in libraries, country house murders, butlers and maids, gentleman thieves, dowager duchesses losing their pearls, vicars and 'flighty' chorus girls, formal tales that could be enjoyable as brainteasers but which were also bloodless, class-ridden, recidivist and reactionary. I found the cap-doffing deference of servants and coppers to the untrained, entitled interferers who barged in and solved their crimes most off-putting. Today psychology is part of the writer's arsenal, leaving many Golden Age mysteries looking like linear crossword puzzles, logical in plot terms but psychologically nonsensical.

Equally, I didn't want to write a modern police procedural, there being too many fine practitioners of the art already. Besides, too many crime novels revel in degradation and pain, with a particularly unpleasant emphasis on cruelty to helpless women. Crimes involve tragedy and poverty, of course, and police work is rule-bound and repetitive, but I wondered if I might not employ a sense of playful trickery and still score a few relevant points.

Mystery authors are notorious tricksters; the wonderful, underrated crime novelist Pamela Branch used to drive about town in an old taxi with its 'For Hire' light on, and would mail out blood-smeared postcards and boxes of poisoned chocolates purportedly from her characters. Some of us like to hide puzzles, jokes and references inside our books – we can't resist it. Musicians do it all the time. I think of Gerard Hoffnung tricking an audience into standing for the national anthem with a muted drum roll that turned into a completely different tune, and the crime novelist Edmund Crispin (real name Bruce Montgomery) hiding musical jokes in the scores of *Carry On* films. I tuck peculiar running gags into the Bryant & May novels in the hope that it makes somebody laugh in recognition. Mystery writing is not just about the gradual revealing of information, it's also about making connections where there were none before, so I love it when readers make those connections.

There's something about mixing esoterica with low comedy that's very appealing. The most obvious joke is that the names of my detectives were taken from a matchbox. Throughout their adventures Arthur Bryant mentions other cases, a habit I adopted in deference to Arthur Conan Doyle, whose consulting detective named other 'affairs'. Conan Doyle's son Adrian teamed up with John Dickson

Carr and produced another collection out of the missing cases in *The Exploits of Sherlock Holmes*.

For Bryant & May's first collection of lost cases the UK title was *London's Glory*, a phrase deliberately altered from the old black and yellow matchbox labels. Of course, another word for a match is a lucifer; it's a self-igniting one that's coated in phosphorus and sodium chlorate, and they're now banned. Conflagration, history, Englishness and a whiff of sulphur; it seemed a perfect way to describe my detectives.

When you try to keep track of an ever-expanding number of characters, it's helpful to name them after people or things you already know. Several of mine came from my love of barely remembered British comedies. For Janice Longbright I used a friend of mine, plus bits of Diana Dors, Liz Fraser, Sabrina and other pin-up models from the 1950s. There's also a touch of Barbara Windsor's toughness in *Sparrows Can't Sing* and Googie Withers from *It Always Rains on Sunday* – this is the film in which Googie exudes sex appeal buttering an upright loaf and slicing it afterwards while dangling a fag from her lower lip. The film is explicitly mentioned in one of the PCU bulletins that always start off the novels.

Arthur Bryant's friend Maggie Armitage is a real person and even more peculiar in reality, while the name of Dame Maude Hackshaw, a member of her coven, is a homage to an old St Trinian's film, as is the idea of the two Daves never leaving the PCU office.

The Victoria Vanishes is a tribute to Edmund Crispin's *The Moving Toyshop*, one of my favourite Golden Age mysteries. I've also broken the fourth wall a few times in the style of Crispin. The Commando Comics artist Keith Page made some of these homages explicit in his drawings for the Bryant & May graphic novel, *The Casebook of*

Bryant & May, packing his scenes with recognizable character actors from the past.

Why would I have chosen to pay homage to forgotten B movies instead of, say, serious-minded British literature? Because I like the peripheral pleasures of small independent enterprises. I grew up with the last series of home-grown British films that were made without Hollywood interference. They tend to be rather stagey and have too many scenes of middle-aged men in offices, but many have strange moments and quirky characters. In the bizarre mystery *Miss Robin Hood*, about a stolen beer formula, a taxi driver tries to impress girls by learning entire segments of the *Encyclopaedia Britannica*. British people are portrayed as inherently odd and unfathomable, but few books and films explore this national notion, let alone celebrate it. My father adored *The Man in the White Suit* because, as an experimental back-room scientist, he completely identified with Alec Guinness.

I admire outsider writers like Magnus Mills, who explores something rarely encountered in fiction: the inability of human beings to put their idealism into practice. I wanted to do this in a series of crime novels that suggested the ending might turn out differently if the main characters could get their act together.

There are other references to mysteries in the Bryant & May books, most notably to those by Robert Louis Stevenson and R. Austin Freeman. For a long time I couldn't find a way to parody Agatha Christie because of her recognizable style, but Mrs Christie was quirkier than perhaps even she realized. Her obsession with clockwork plots gave her a strange view of life. No room is ever described without its egress minutely detailed. If she saw my study she'd say it was a wooden-floored room with two means of entry, neither of them locked, when the first two things you actually notice are that it's made of glass and overlooks St Paul's Cathedral. Every work of fiction, however lowly, gives away a little of its author's heart. I've been asked a number of times to catalogue all of the jokes and puzzles tucked in the pages, but that would spoil the fun.

Someone I hadn't caught up with for a while said to me, 'So, you're still churning out those Bryant & May books, are you?' as if it was something I had to do occasionally between my more avowedly 'serious' novels. I pointed out that yes, mystery novels were one type of book I wrote, although there were many others. Never one to give up when he was behind, he added, 'Then why do you bother with the crime stuff? They're all the same, aren't they?'

I explained that the mystery novel, which is after all just one branch of the crime genre, can be a Trojan Horse for whatever you want to smuggle inside the gates of the reader's mind. It can be a vehicle for zeitgeist stories and subversive themes, or simply a method for dropping in forgotten historical facts. The genre is a doorway to pretty much any kind of dramatic story.

The crime genre generates tales about secrets, lies and betrayal, of extreme emotion and acts committed under stress, of passion, death and survival, but they can also be unreliable and subject to reinterpretation. Examples include Agatha Christie's *The Murder of Roger Ackroyd*, *Trent's Last Case* by E. C. Bentley, *The Iron Gates* by Margaret Millar and *Snowdrops* by A. D. Miller. Characters can change depending on the angle from which they are viewed. It's said that if you're writing about Charles Manson, you should remember that he doesn't wake up each morning thinking he's crazy. He wakes up each morning thinking *you're* crazy.

Worried that I would start to repeat myself with the Bryant & May series, I've been keen to constantly ring the changes, trying different types of mystery story, regularly altering the line-up of characters and even the style of writing.

Traditionally, authors who write a large number of stories featuring specific detectives survive over ones who write fewer (Dorothy L. Sayers was an exception, writing only 11 Lord Peter Wimsey novels). Sir Arthur Conan Doyle and R. Austin Freeman post similar numbers – Sherlock Holmes starred in 56 stories and 4 novels, while Freeman's terrific Dr Thorndyke appeared in 40 short stories and 22 novels. Agatha Christie used Hercule Poirot in 33 novels, while her contemporary, the far less well-remembered Gladys Mitchell, used her wonderful detective Mrs Bradley in 66 books. Robert van Gulik wrote 25 Judge Dee volumes (although as these contain several cases in the Chinese style do we count them as more?).

However, when it comes to totals Christie wrote an additional 50 short stories featuring Hercule Poirot, so she wins on volume. Critical mass is clearly important as readers develop a loyalty, but it also creates its own problem – critics generally stop reviewing you after the first few outings, and every time you have a fresh title out new readers buy the *first* volume, which is logical but may (as in my case) be very different from the rest of the series. It's tricky finding the balance between offering up familiarity and evolving to provide new surprises.

It's not all about numbers, of course. Colin Dexter did not write a huge number of Inspector Morse novels, but an exemplary TV series kept his character alive with fresh, character-driven stories often created by respected playwrights, and, despite the death of the superlative actor

John Thaw, continued into both the future and the past with spin-off series. The Bryant & May books are slightly unusual in that they're simultaneously pastiches and full of real London history (I never make anything up when it comes to research, which I regard as sacrosanct), but they also contain an ever-expanding cast of characters – what I term 'the Springfield effect' – all of whom I have to keep annotated.

For a long time these factors, and the rather esoteric plotlines, kept the books below the parapet of main-stream awareness, but it may just result in the series being long-lived. There's a terrific writers' maxim: *When you think a story has reached the end, take it further.* It would have been easy to stop after six Bryant & May novels (do you have any idea how much of my life these annoying seniors consume?) but I was intrigued about new possibil-ities, and the more urban life changes the more I have for them to do.

When the first Bryant & May book was written as a stand-alone novel for the publishers Little, Brown, it was turned down. To be fair, they had supported an author who was chronically unable to settle into any style or genre, and who pushed aside all attempts to be pigeon-holed. All I can say in my defence is that I had a demanding day job, and writing novels came a distant second after making sure our staff got their wages on time. When mem-bers of your company start planning their babies around the safety of their jobs, the question of priorities is instantly resolved and writing vanishes.

So, armed with a murder mystery my publishers did not want, I reluctantly left and looked for somebody new. Transworld immediately 'got' Bryant & May, thanks to their editor, Simon Taylor, who saw a future in them that I hadn't considered. He enthusiastically suggested a sequel, and since the first book had started out as a period romp I rewrote it as an origin story. I'd planned to stop at six books, with a story arc buried within the separate plots that involved a man called Peter Jukes (the real-life Jukes is a political journalist) and a Ministry of Defence conspiracy covering up a series of deaths. The arc was based on a number of real incidents occurring at the time of writing which involved the strange suicides of several Indian workers. A now-defunct website asked what it was about scientists working at Porton Down that made them want to commit suicide. One was found in a field, another drowned . . .

When I closed the arc of six tales in *The Victoria Vanishes*, I adopted a wait-and-see approach to the books, which were selling to a small group of dedicated fans but were certainly no threat to the big names in the genre. I started to trim down the history lessons within the books, and began enjoying myself with the subsidiary characters. The first Bryant & May cover had been created by a wonderful artist, Jake Rickwood, who was represented by Meiklejohn Illustration. Coincidentally, I had known Chris Meiklejohn for years, and could have put him in a B&M novel; a darkly handsome man missing a hand, he always wore a sinister black leather glove that fascinated me.

I loved the cover of *Full Dark House*, which seemed to perfectly catch the tone of the books. There's a rare misprinted cover in circulation, on which May is smoking a pipe, not Bryant, but it was withdrawn and replaced with the corrected version (hang on to it if you have a copy).

When I came to write the second book, Mr Rickwood announced that he was retiring, so we had no artist to take the series on. There were several attempts to recreate the first cover, leading to one known as the 'Simpsons' artwork, because Bryant & May had become bright yellow. We finally discovered the brilliant David Frankland, who understood the semiotics required for the books: a hint of those old railway carriage posters, an appealing Englishness, a balance of architecture and humans and a touch of darkness. But he retired too, and now I have the excellent Max Schindler combining old and new elements beautifully.

Over the books, one of the greatest pleasures for me has been confounding readers who said 'you can't surely get any more out of this situation' by proving that I could. What's more, I found that they came more naturally to me than my stand-alone non-crime novels, each of which requires the creation of an entirely separate reality.

By this time I realized I had constructed a weird subgenre of my own, certainly not as comfortable and timeless as so-called 'cosy crime', which was fanciful but weirdly within the realms of possibility. Festival organizers get especially confused and put me on panels with fantasy writers, even though the books contain no fantasy elements. The original concept had been rooted in hard fact, my father having worked in just such a post-war unit. The earliest research I included in the books had come from him. Still, I planned to end the series at Volume 12 because it was where the second arc finished, and I had an idea for a new crime series. When I ran the idea for this new series past agents they all hated it, which was enough to make me want to prove them wrong and make it work.

Once again my plans were rerouted, because writing *Bryant & May and the Invisible Code* provoked a sea-change in me. From that point on the books were fundamentally altered; they trusted the reader and had more confidence. What had changed?

There's an old story: year after year, a boy paints

terrible pictures in art class, until he gets a new teacher and starts coming top every term. His mother asks, 'What do you do to make my son paint such wonderful pictures?' The teacher replies, 'I know when to take them away from him.' This is what my agent Mandy Little did for me. She intervened and instructed me to set aside new characters and concentrate solely on what I'd already started in the novel. It proved to be great advice.

Most of the crime writers I know don't really write about crime at all. They write about people. It's just as well, because real-life crime is sad and sordid, a combination of poverty, stupidity, sexual frustration, hatred and sheer bad fate that has very little to do with the world of fictional crime writing. Most serious crimes are not planned, but happen in a momentary flash or gradually, over time. Even men who deliberately stalk girls are often unable to acknowledge that they set out with a plan. They don't understand themselves, let alone other people. Murderers don't leave corpses arranged according to Masonic rituals or Da Vinci paintings; if they could do that they wouldn't be murderers, they'd be museum curators or company directors.

It's when you visit the collection colloquially known as Scotland Yard's Black Museum and see the sad, cheap little square-cut cloth masks worn by house-robbers that you realize just how little real crime had in common with its fictional equivalent. As you walk through the rooms and study all the usual suspects – Haigh, Crippen, Christie, Ellis, trunk murderers and poisoners, guns and nooses, knives and knuckledusters, spying equipment, drugs, an umbrella gun and the Krays' execution suitcase – it's shocking to realize how mundane, makeshift and small everything appears. Could this ridiculous little knife really have cut a throat? Could this tiny pistol have actually shot someone through the heart? Victorian criminality is desperate and depressing – and perhaps that's the point: crime has none of the grandeur we afford it, not then, not now.

Of course it's more fun to think that murderers might be playing complex, abstract cat-and-mouse games with their investigators instead of battering their poor girlfriends to death before lying pathetically to the police. So crime writing is almost always a construct, no matter how often authors insist that their gritty thrillers are truthful. The true parts – the parts with which we readers identify – come from unchanging human nature.

Mysteries are everywhere. *Hamlet* is one, of course, and so is *Bleak House*. Although Hamlet's actions remain a deeply human mystery to us, he's a messed-up thirty-year-old and it would not be hard to find, in our present society, those who think and behave like him today.

Bryant & May have elements of my father, my grandfather and friends I've known. The investigations are based on the London myths and scandals I grew up with, and still hear all around me, although I worry that much of it is disappearing as the city changes. I do a lot of research in libraries but I also talk to a great many Londoners, so the books become a patchwork of the city's lore and life, each one reflecting the London – and the Londoners – of its time.

ACKNOWLEDGEMENTS

I was caught by surprise when my first collection of missing Bryant & May cases found an enthusiastic readership. I wasn't sure if short-form mysteries would work, but I've always felt that the Sherlock Holmes short stories were better than the novels, so I decided I should at least try. I had such fun writing the first collection, *London's Glory*, that it seemed impossible not to write another volume of cases. My editor Simon Taylor enthusiastically waved them through, sterling agent James Wills agreed that there should be a further set of bizarre cases and sharp-eyed Kate Samano and Richenda Todd kept my timelines untangled. Team B&M makes sure that the decrepit duo live to fight another day!

Twitter: @Peculiar

www.christopherfowler.co.uk

Christopher Fowler is the author of nearly fifty novels and story collections, and the author of seventeen Bryant & May mysteries. His novels include *Roofworld*, *Spanky*, *Psychoville*, *Calabash* and two volumes of memoirs, the award-winning *Paperboy* and *Film Freak*. In 2015 he won the CWA Dagger in the Library for his body of work. His latest novel is *Bryant & May: The Lonely Hour*.